To Wendy & Don

A present from B

Hope you enjoy th

Richard Rees

THE ILLUMINATI
CONSPIRACY

THE ILLUMINATI CONSPIRACY

Richard Rees

Hodder & Stoughton
LONDON SYDNEY AUCKLAND TORONTO

The Wellcome Institute Library, London has kindly granted permission for use of the photograph of Dr. Beatty's longhand report on the death of Lord Nelson which appears on page 251.

British Library Cataloguing in Publication Data
Rees, Richard
  The Illuminati conspiracy.
  I. Title
823'.914[F]   PR6068.E38/
ISBN 0-340-41282-8

To Richenda – see you in the morning.

ACKNOWLEDGMENTS

After completing your first novel there are so many people to thank one hardly knows where to begin. In the fear of missing someone out, here goes. My gratitude to my late wife, Richenda, my son, Huw, and daughter, Elisabeth, for putting up with me. For their practical help: my parents, and two special aunts. For their research assistance: Robert Songhurst, David Langford, and W. C. Rogers of Swansea. For their critical comments: J. Reynolds, K. Pheelan, J. Crown, G. Callen. For her word-processing: Marie Ashfield of Wordcraft. For their joint typing of the first manuscript: Sheila Roscoe and Linda Ball. To Jeffrey Archer, for pointing me in the right direction. To John Bright-Holmes and Jan Seigler for their invaluable editorial advice, to Joan for the use of her cottage, and finally, to Nick Sayers of Hodder & Stoughton for so many things, not least of which was his infinite patience.

PROLOGUE

Dusk was approaching as the rider reached Ermenonville. Pierre-François Réal was a man of no great height, pale with a narrow face, his longish hair turning to white. The coat and breeches he wore were of the darkest cloth as befitted a pioneer of the Revolution, and a lawyer.

The village of Ermenonville, some thirty kilometres to the north of Paris, was surrounded by forest and woodland, its fields watered by the River Lauratte. The château which dominated it was an elegant building with a sculpted façade and wings which extended out to form a courtyard. Surrounded by parkland, the elaborate grounds encompassed lawns, lakes and cascades; bedecked with statues and ornamental marbles, its ostentatious outward appearance told nothing of what could be found inside.

The huge double main doors thudded to a close behind Réal. He was familiar with the room into which the servitor led him, a large vaulted chamber, its walls painted black. The sepulchral effect was accentuated by the flickering shadows created by the sputtery lights of four lanterns, suspended from rounded, stone pillars in the four corners. Between them stood a large oblong table draped with a black cloth on which lay an unsheathed sword. Woven on to the fall of the cloth were two symbols, on the left a triangle, with an inverted cross inside it; on the right side a square enclosing a death's head surmounted by crossbones. Into the floor were inlaid seven concentric white circles with, in the middle, the emblem of a blazing torch.

ix

A door opened and seven men dressed in long black habits filed in, their features hidden by their cowls, and stood motionless before the table. The one in the centre spoke:

Brothers, we are witnesses to the signs of the Illuminati, by which name are the Enlightened Ones known.

The brethren slowly raised their right hands, arms outstretched. The spokesman continued:

To the one Cause, we of the Areopagus, the Illuminati's Supreme and High Council, dedicate ourselves.
The triangle is three. The world is three. Earth, sea and air.
The square is four. The world is four. North, south, east and west.
The triangle and the square together are seven. The world is seven. This is the number of its continents and seas.
The triangle is three. Man is three. Body, mind and free spirit. In this present world all three are kept in subjection by the evil lies of the Church which through a crucified Jew has ever sought to impose its blasphemies. By this the Church shows itself to be at enmity with the true nature of man and must be destroyed.
The square is four. Man's desired freedoms are four. Freedom from want, freedom from fear, freedom from kings, freedom from existing governments. In this present world all four are kept in subjection by the evil oppressions of autocratic regimens and aristocracies. By this they show themselves to be at enmity with the true estate of man and must be removed.
The triangle and the square together are seven. The Illuminati are seven. This is the number of the Areopagus, its Supreme and High Council. Soon man will be seven, four and three added together, as man was ever meant to be. To this cause, the Illuminati is dedicated. To that end this chamber is a constant reminder. Its darkness signifies the darkness which at present covers the whole earth, and thereby the seven continents represented by the circles. The torch in the centre shows that man will not always be kept in subjection to the world's present evils for soon will come the light of the Illuminati to irradiate the darkness. The sword shows that this light cannot be purchased without the spilling of blood and much sacrifice, a sacrifice which is inevitable if man is to be liberated. In the name of the Illuminati.

x

The response was taken up by the six brethren. And by the lawyer, Pierre-François Réal:

In the name of the Illuminati I refute this world into which I was born. Henceforth I live in another dimension which cannot be reached until I have renounced this evil globe which has been cursed by man's deceit.

Their voices echoed hollowly around the dark, cavernous room and rebounded off the walls, lifting high to fade away into the blackness above them:

I honour the sword. It is a quick and essential medium of removing from earth those who oppose the truth and those who try to take it from our hands.

Always I shall reveal to the Illuminati all that I have heard or found out, and I shall seek out and observe things which might otherwise escape me.

Together we stand.

Ourselves Alone.

To the fulfilment of our Cause.

Liberty! . . . Equality! . . . Fraternity!

The seven men sat down. The spokesman lifted his cowled head and addressed Réal:

"You may address the Council. Make your report." His voice was flat and expressionless.

Considering the events which had taken place in Paris over the past few days, and the effect these would have on the Illuminati's plans, Réal was surprised by the man's lack of emotion, but then, the spokesman had not been a witness to it all, as Réal had been; he had not been there in Paris, powerless to help, forced to watch the gruesome death of his friend, Maximilien Marie de Robespierre, and the untimely end of the Illuminati's purging Reign of Terror. The scenes were imprinted on Réal's memory, a horrible nightmare, commencing with Robespierre's arrest, and those of his constant advisors, at the Hôtel de Ville, when one of the counter-revolutionists fired his pistol, the ball smashing Robespierre's lower jaw and hurling him out of his chair. Robespierre's brother, Augustin, tried to escape by jumping out of a window, slipped and broke a leg; Couthon was thrown down the stairs and his forehead split open, Hanriot was hurled out of a window but he got up and began to run, only to be caught by a soldier whose bayonet thrust tore out one of his eyes, which was left to hang by the ligaments down his cheek, a most terrible sight. Philippe Le Bas shot himself, Saint-Just fingered a pistol as though considering the same end, but then threw it away and surrendered.

The injured Robespierre was carried on a plank to the offices of the Committee of Public Safety and dumped on a table in the green-painted anteroom. For an hour he lay there without moving, his eyes closed, the blood pouring from his shattered jaw. Then he opened his eyes and began to wipe the clotted blood from his mouth with a pistol holster of soft white leather. A surgeon was sent for to stop him from bleeding to death. The man placed a key in Robespierre's mouth, pulled out three teeth together with fragments of broken bone, then bandaged the lower part of his face. Through it all Robespierre remained silent, although he must have been in agony, then he pushed himself off the table and went to sit in a chair, his face as white as death, the bandages round his jaw already saturated red with his blood.

His friends were then brought in to join him: his brother Augustin, Saint-Just, Couthon on a stretcher, Hanriot, Dumas, and seventeen other members of the General Council of the Commune, all of them members of the Illuminati. They were arraigned before a specially convened tribunal and condemned to death. At five o'clock in the afternoon they were taken by cart to the guillotine at the Place de la Révolution, along a route thick with people who shouted insults and curses at the prisoners.

It took them two and a half hours to reach the guillotine. As the blade fell on Robespierre the crowds threw themselves into one another's arms, dancing and shouting out with joy, "The tyrant is no more".

The lawyer from Paris related the events, fighting to keep the anger out of his voice; and the fear, because he himself was not yet safe; even as he spoke he knew that throughout Paris and the rest of France Robespierre's more open allies were still being hunted down and guillotined.

"Robespierre proved to be a fool," said the spokesman as Réal concluded his report. "He was his own downfall."

Réal was tempted to say that, knowing Robespierre's background, the error he had committed to give his political opponents the opportunity they had been looking for should have been considered by the Illuminati's Supreme Council, and thus averted. But inherent caution prevailed and Réal remained silent.

"By that one fatal act," the spokesman continued, "Robespierre has set back the Illuminati's plans by at least ten years."

"Set back," Réal agreed, "but not negated."

"Never." The spokesman was emphatic. "The Illuminati's aims will continue. The last Revolution succeeded exactly to plan. In like manner we must now orchestrate a second. If our universal aims are to be achieved France must first be brought back into our control. But, just as before, patience is all-important. It took years to place our brothers in positions of authority throughout France, only to have them betrayed by the folly of one man. Now we must begin to rebuild again and in this second revolution, Citizen Réal, you are chosen to play a greater part than before. Then, once France has been restored to us, England will be our next goal. Our cells in that country are already well established—"

"And the present war between France and England?" Réal interrupted.

"We trust will continue," answered the spokesman. "War cripples a nation. The rich are protected, it is always the common people who suffer, which makes the discontented masses a breeding ground for revolution. It is therefore our hope that this particular war will continue indefinitely, until both countries are weary and completely vulnerable. That will be the moment to strike again."

The spokesman's voice rose in power:

"That day, Citizen Réal, will herald the universal rule of the Illuminati. First France, then England. And once their military and naval forces are combined, who then shall stand against us? Certainly no other country in Europe; nor Russia; nor any other nation on the face of this earth."

PART ONE

Article 29. When the government violates the rights of the people, insurrection is for the people and for every portion of the people, the most sacred of rights and the most indispensable of duties.

Article 35. Men of all countries are brothers and the people of each ought to yield one another mutual aid according to their ability like citizens of the same state.

Robespierre: Declaration of the Rights of Man

CHAPTER 1

Having witnessed the paying-off of his ship's crew and wished a number of them 'godspeed', First-Lieutenant Richard Machen completed his own duties, then attended the Paymaster's Office in Chatham Dockyard where he was formally placed on the Naval Reserve.

He had no desire to leave the Navy, even though a period on shore was welcome after fourteen years on active service, including being at the terrible Battle of the Nile under Lord Nelson. But Napoleon Bonaparte, the young Corsican general who was now First Consul of France, had offered Britain a peace treaty. From what Machen had heard and read – the British government was reputed to have built up a crippling National Debt of over £500 million during the nine years of fighting – it was not surprising that Napoleon's offer had been accepted, despite the reservations about the man's reasons. With hostilities ended, many British ships of the line had been recalled to port, their crews either discharged or transferred to other duties, and the officers, including Machen, placed on the Reserve List and sent home on half pay, but ready to return to duty if war ever broke out again.

For Machen the route from Chatham to his home on the lonely Gower Peninsula in South Wales was via London, Bristol and Swansea. Luckily, there was one vacancy on the stagecoach leaving the Sun Inn at two o'clock that afternoon. Dressed in his faded uniform, Machen took the seat, on the outside gammon board, with the guard.

Only one other person boarded the coach at Chatham that day and he had already reserved a seat on the inside. For two hours now this man had been sitting in a secluded corner of the parlour of the Sun, deep in conversation with a young naval officer, but not from the same ship as Machen. Eagerly looking forward to going home again, Machen paid them scant attention, but even if he had done he would have seen very little of his fellow passenger, a tall, erect man who was wearing a heavy blue greatcoat with an upturned collar that hid much of his face. The one thing Machen noticed, and that in passing, was the green silk umbrella with a hooked yellow handle, which the man carried in his hand like an army officer's cane.

At three minutes to nine that same evening, three minutes ahead of its scheduled time of arrival, the stagecoach from Chatham clattered up Whitehall. With a last, loud blast from the long horn the driver drove straight over Charing Cross and swept, with a hollow, metal-wheeled thunder, under the low arch of the Golden Cross to draw up, with a grand flourish, in the coachyard.

Machen did not wait for the descent ladder to be put into place. Dropping his long-bag to the floor of the yard, he followed it down by stepping on the wheel spokes of the coach. He picked up his bag, slung it across his shoulders and pushed his way through the beggars and street vendors, who, even at that late hour of the evening, clamoured round the coach, importuning their wares and causes with well-rehearsed pleas.

He crossed the yard, and found out from the booking-office clerk that there were no available seats for Bristol until the New Post coach, leaving the Golden Cross on Thursday. He reserved a seat then went in search of the landlady of the Golden Cross and secured a room for the two nights.

Realising he had not eaten for some time and that he would not sleep without a meal inside him, he tipped a pretty chambermaid to take his bag to his room and was rewarded with an inviting smile from the young woman. She brazenly studied the tall, dark-haired naval officer, taking in his solid white-breeched thighs and his lean, weather-tanned face set above a firm determined chin, then turned to climb the stairs, with a pert swish of her hips. Machen had been at sea a long

4

time and was sorely tempted by her obvious invitation; but he was not the man for her kind of loving – a raising of the skirts, a quick five minutes, and then a hand held out for a coin before the landlord called her back to her duties. Besides, his stomach was crying out for food.

He found the door of the snug bar, but as he reached for the handle the door itself was flung violently open from within and a young soldier in the uniform of a guardsman burst out of the room, cannoning into Machen and sending him reeling across the passageway, while he himself fell against the opposite wall.

Before Machen could recover, another man, stocky, florid and a good few years older, walked through the doorway and picking the guardsman up from the floor where he had fallen, calmly, and with no trace of emotion, punched him repeatedly to the head and stomach rendering him almost senseless. Twisting the guardsman's arm up behind his back he half-carried him back into the room and over to a cubicle against the far wall. Groaning and bent double, the soldier fell into the high-back settle and sat, rocking himself slowly to and fro, his arms folded tightly across the pit of his stomach, facing a third man sitting at the table.

Machen turned to follow, reacting instinctively as years of fighting had taught him. Whatever his offence the soldier did not deserve such treatment. Suddenly he felt a restraining hand on his shoulder. He spun around, prepared for more trouble. Facing him was a man of medium height, not much more than thirty years old, dressed in the sombre clothes of a professional person – brown, broad-skirted coat, waistcoat, breeches. "If you accept my advice you will leave well alone," he said in a low voice. The warning was given with the air of imparting a well-guarded confidence and there was the strong smell of brandy on his breath.

"Your advice was not asked for," Machen replied, turning dismissively, but the hand on his shoulder remained, surprisingly firm.

"Nevertheless," the man returned, "I am still offering it. And offering it without charge." He smiled at Machen, broad and friendly. "Those who know me well will tell you I do not normally offer such advice without exacting a high fee."

5

His anger cooling, Machen looked at the man for a moment, then put out his hand. "Thank you. Your advice is well taken. My name is Machen, Richard Machen."

"Mine is David Gregor," he replied, slapping his hand into Machen's and returning the handshake over-enthusiastically. "And now," he smiled again, "if you promise not to create any disturbance, I would be pleased if you would have dinner with me." Giving Machen no time to refuse he took hold of his elbow and led him into the snug. "I could do with company so that I may talk and hear the sound of my own voice."

They walked into the room, which had a roaring fire at the far end. Gregor led Machen to a table some way from where the guardsman and the other two men were sitting. They sat down and were immediately attended to by a dark-clothed waiter. Without consulting Machen, Gregor ordered mutton chops and two large brandies, the latter to be served immediately.

"Now," said Gregor, looking across the table at Machen, his left eye half closing and his manner becoming almost conspiratorial, "let me first admit that our meeting in the passageway a moment ago was not entirely coincidental."

"In what way?" Machen was finding it hard not to laugh; the man was only too obviously under the influence of drink.

"I followed you from the booking office," Gregor explained. "I was purchasing a ticket when you came in. As I will also be travelling to Swansea on Thursday on that same coach I thought to make your acquaintance."

"What business have you in Wales?"

"Another coincidence, this time to your calling," said Gregor, pointing to Machen's uniform, then turning and beckoning impatiently to the waiter for the brandies to be served. "Like yourself my employment is with the Admiralty. I am a solicitor," he made the statement with a pronounced authority intended to impress Machen, "and work for the Admiralty Court, which, as you no doubt know, is the Navy's legal department. I am travelling to Swansea to discuss supply contracts with a compatriot of yours. I have to be there by Saturday because the gentleman has business in Ireland and

6

wishes to set sail as soon as our negotiations have been completed." Gregor paused. "However, that is enough of my affairs. You are going home, I imagine? Have you a wife awaiting your return?"

"No," replied Machen, "I have no one."

"A very fortunate man," said Gregor. "It is now ten years since I signed away my freedom but thankfully I work late hours and this inn, being only a stone's throw across Charing Cross from the Admiralty, serves my purpose well until my marital obligations call me home. The Golden Cross may be a trifle noisy at times, but it is clean and pleasant and the food is good." He turned in anticipation as the waiter approached the table. The man placed the glasses down and Gregor slid one across to Machen.

"And their brandy most palatable. Your good health, Lieutenant."

"And yours, Mr Gregor," Machen responded, no longer able to restrain a broad grin. "May our journey be a pleasant one."

They drank slowly, Gregor questioning Machen about his last ship and his service in the Navy. Afterwards Machen asked, "Who are they, those people in the corner?"

Gregor hesitated for a moment then he leant forward, and touching the tip of his right nostril with his right forefinger, assuming the air of a man about to take someone into a highly regarded confidence, he said solemnly, "They are revolutionaries. Their aim is the overthrow of our government." He then sat back to study the effect of his words on his newly acquired friend.

Machen turned to look at the three men on the other side of the room: the huddled young guardsman; the stocky, florid, middle-aged man; and their companion of about fifty years of age. This last had an erect and military bearing and although he could, at one time, have been handsome, life had taken its toll, for his face was now pinched and drawn, with no trace of gentleness or humour. He wore a heavy blue greatcoat and on the table before him lay a green silk umbrella with a hooked yellow handle.

"Revolutionaries?" he asked Gregor, the tone of his voice

7

evidencing his complete surprise. "But the elder man has just travelled openly in the same coach that brought me from Chatham. Surely you're not serious?"

"Never more so," replied Gregor, his face betraying pleasure at Machen's incredulity, and deciding to become even more expansive. "Colonel Despard's presence in Chatham does not surprise me. It is an area he has chosen for recruiting volunteers, although not one of his normal haunts. Usually he is to be seen around the City itself. The Angel in Cecil Court just around the corner from here is one of the taverns he frequents. It was catching sight of Despard and his cronies walking these streets some weeks ago that prompted me to make enquiries. Call it, if you will, the inborn curiosity of the legal mind."

"The older man is a colonel?"

"His full name is Edward Marcus Despard, of the family seat of Donore, in Queens County, Ireland. Once a serving member of His Majesty's forces, he is" – Gregor was obviously a man who became loquacious with drink – "of Irish and French descent. Once Superintendent of His Majesty's Affairs in Honduras and once" – another significant pause – "once, over twenty years ago, a friend and fellow combatant of a certain Horatio Nelson."

"Admiral Nelson?" Machen asked with surprise.

"The same. Over twenty years ago, Despard and Nelson, who was only twenty-one years old at the time and already a post-captain, fought together in the West Indies. It was the time of the War of American Independence. Some Jack-in-office," said Gregor dismissively, "the Governor of Jamaica, I think, concocted the idea of an expedition up the San Juan River to take over the supremacy of Lake Nicaragua, thereby securing direct access to the Pacific Ocean. Nelson and Despard were both on the expedition. It was an ill-fated campaign; most of the men died and only Nelson and Despard emerged with any credit."

Machen turned and looked again at the erect figure of Despard. "Then what is such a man doing associating with bullies and ordinary soldiers?"

David Gregor picked up his glass and drained the dregs of

the brandy. "He was relieved of his post in the Honduras and was sent home to England, only to be ignored by his superiors for a further position. Disillusioned, five years ago he founded a new radical society which he called the United Britons, one of its aims being to give active support to a French invasion of Britain. Soon after, four men were arrested near Margate on the coast of Kent on suspicion of being French agents. They proved to be members of a similar revolutionary body, the United Irishmen. One of them, a priest named O'Coighly, was carrying papers that advised the French what political action they should take after France had conquered Britain. The priest was tried and executed; but during his interrogation he had mentioned Despard's name. A few weeks later came the outbreak of armed rebellion in Ireland. The Colonel was arrested and sent to Tothill Fields prison in Westminster. Although the Irish Rebellion was crushed while he was there, Despard was transferred to Shrewsbury and kept there without trial. He was released just over twelve months ago. Since then he has convinced himself that Britain is ripe for revolution and sees himself as the rebellion's leader."

Machen reacted, "He must be insane!"

Gregor continued in full flow, his face a picture of studied seriousness: "No, he's not, at least not in the way you mean it. Obsessed, certainly, but he visited Ireland a while back and he returned with two Irish revolutionaries suspected of being involved in the uprisings of '98. They were the Macnamara brothers. Little is known of the younger brother Conor – he seems to be a man of the shadows. But John, the elder – that's him facing Despard – has become the Colonel's right-hand man. Together they haunt the taverns and back streets of London, recruiting for their scheme. It is reputed that they are building up military divisions in Soho, Whitechapel, Southwark, Newington and Lambeth; which is why they are keen to enlist soldiers like your guardsman over there. Despard believes there is much discontent in the British Army. The more soldiers he recruits, the more there are to spread his ideas through the barracks. He has been seen recently at the Tower of London and at Windsor Castle where the First and Third Battalions of the Grenadier Guards are stationed. Also, so I

9

am told, in Chatham, where the Third Battalion was last posted."

Machen leaned across the table and spoke with some emphasis:

"If your investigations have revealed this much, surely you should tell the authorities?"

Gregor replied slowly, the brandies beginning to take effect and forcing him to think through his reply. "The authorities know all I have told you. It is from them that I obtained the information. No, that is not what worries me."

"Then what does?"

"Ah, Mr Machen, first you must understand why the authorities have not thus far acted against Despard. Although he and many of his people are probably violent men individually – which is why I restrained you just now – they have not caused any trouble as yet as an organised body, and little has been demanded of the recruits. They have named themselves the Constitution Society. Each new member has to be sworn in, part of the ritual being to kiss a card on which is written the aims of the society. But they do little else. They simply meet in certain taverns, hold secret meetings in upstairs rooms, drinking, smoking, and talking of what they will do when they take over. They've been doing this for months, but have not gone any further. It seems the main object of the meetings is to provide themselves with company, and thus pass the evenings away. In time the authorities are convinced the interest will die. And when the interest has died, the organisation will die and they will hear no more of Colonel Edward Marcus Despard. At least, that is their theory."

"But something makes you take a different view?" questioned Machen.

The solicitor nodded. "The Golden Cross is not the sort of inn that Despard usually frequents. Normally he is to be found in back-street taverns. But two evenings ago when I saw him leave the coach booking office I felt it incumbent upon me to make enquiries."

"And?"

"He has booked a room at the Golden Cross and two seats on a coach which leaves at six o'clock tomorrow morning. His "destination" – and here Gregor gave one of his pauses – "his destination is Canterbury."

"And from Canterbury?" Machen asked, suspecting the answer.

"It is just a suspicion," Gregor replied, "but Canterbury is only twenty-one miles from the coast. There are many fishing villages he can choose from, especially around Deal. It would be a simple matter to hire a boat—"

"Why not take the stage through to Dover," Machen interrupted, "and take the packet boat openly?"

"Despite the peace the packet has not commenced sailing. Also, anyone asking to be taken to France would still be an object of suspicion in a garrison town like Dover. Despard would not want that. No, if France is indeed the Colonel's destination, then Deal would be his best plan, there are many smuggling gangs operating that part of the south coast. If he has money no questions would be asked." Gregor picked up his table knife, and regardless of damage, he scratched two parallel lines, close together, across part of the table in front of him. "Twenty-one miles of water and he is in France. Three days later in Paris. Never forget that, though he has fought for Britain, Despard is of Irish and French descent. A dangerous cross-breeding. He has already been imprisoned for being a member of a revolutionary society which advocated a French invasion of this country. And though we have just concluded a peace treaty with France, who knows the mind of Napoleon? In my opinion the little corporal is using the treaty to purchase time to regroup his armies. If war should ever break out again between England and France, only think what value people like Despard would be to the enemy, ready to act as agents within the boundaries of our shores. In the meantime, what is our First Lord of the Admiralty, Lord St Vincent, doing to defend the realm? Reducing the fleet and depleting the dockyards, all in the name of administrative reform and economy!"

Gregor looked up, only to see the waiter bearing two dinners, steam rising from the plates.

"But let us put Colonel Despard aside for a while," Gregor murmured, "and attend to the needs of the body."

The two were half way through their meal when Despard

and his companions stood up. They walked out of the snug, the young guardsman, ashen, casting nervous eyes in all directions, and still with John Macnamara's arm clamped firmly across his shoulders.

Gregor watched him go. With a large piece of mutton raised to his mouth he turned to Machen, his face all serious and melancholy. "You know, Mr Machen, I was thinking how capriciously Lady Fate treats us, smiling on one, frowning on another."

"In what way?" asked Machen, deliberately coughing in order to resist an overwhelming desire to smile.

"Nelson and Despard," replied Gregor. "Twenty years ago they were friends, fighting shoulder to shoulder out in Nicaragua. Now one is famous, the victor of mighty battles, friend of the exalted, and hero of all England. And the other . . . the other lives in alleys, his company the flotsam and jetsam of London. The leader of revolutions, but only in his dreams. Still," he added, "I don't suppose their paths will ever cross again."

CHAPTER 2

Machen did not fall to sleep easily that night although the room was comfortable enough.

There were still a good few hours to dawn but he removed only his top clothing before climbing into the four-poster. The mattress was still tepid from the heat of the warming pan. Instead of leaving it lumpy and untouched after the last guest, the pretty chambermaid had turned it over and made it comfortable for him, and changed the sheets, which felt crisp and fresh. Machen blew out the candle and lay there, with both hands behind his head, looking past the two long-posts at the foot of the bed and at the fire still burning in the grate. In the darkness, broken by the flames and sudden flares in the fire, he thought about the last few days.

When they had told him at Chatham that he had been placed on the Naval Reserve, he was left with a sense of utter purposelessness. He had wandered down to the water's edge and looked out at the ships riding at anchor on the Medway. It was a warm day and the sun was reflected through the tall masts and the rigging, silhouetted dark and bold against the clear blue sky.

He was twenty-six years old and unmarried. Since the age of twelve, when he joined the Navy as a midshipman, he had known no other life, save for a period in 1790 when he was fourteen and was invalided home with scurvy from which he was not expected to recover. But under the tender care of his grandmother – who had always looked after him since his mother died giving birth to him, and his merchant captain father had been lost at sea some months earlier – he eventually did recover. But it took a full six months.

Home, then, was a limestone-walled cottage down on the seashore at the foot of Port Eynon Point, a lonely headland on Gower, the remote peninsula in South Wales where his grandfather was bailiff to Sir John Lucas, owner of the manor and estate of Culver Hall. It had been through his patronage that Richard received his midshipman's appointment, on board a ship captained by a family acquaintance of Sir John.

The Gower peninsula – although near to the bustling and growing port of Swansea – was so isolated that the roads were too rutted and uneven for wheeled carts and the few inhabitants had to travel by pack horses or primitive horse-drawn sleds. One warm afternoon, when Richard's grandmother had allowed him out of bed to sit on the stone bench outside the cottage, looking out over the bay and watching the gulls as they swooped and dived over the waters searching for fish, Sir John Lucas rode down from Culver Hall followed by another rider, a young girl, some three or four years Richard's junior. Even to Richard's dispassionate eye, she was admittedly pretty, with a profusion of dark, curling hair past her shoulders. But it was the expression in her eyes which drew him, a sad, bewildered, hurt look which seemed out of keeping in a person so young. She remained seated on her pony, staring down at him without saying a word, while Sir John dismounted and took Richard's grandfather to one side, where they spent some minutes in subdued conversation. The two men then seemed to come to some agreement, Sir John remounted his horse, and followed by Miss Serious – as Richard had christened her in his mind – they rode away, back towards Culver Hall. Meanwhile Richard's grandfather came and sat beside him, to explain that the young lady, Miss Jane – as he called her – was Sir John's niece, his sister's daughter, from London. Her name was Jane Ashford and she had recently lost her father in a tragic coaching accident. She and her mother had taken the loss so hard that Sir John had virtually forced them to spend the summer months with him and his wife, Lady Katrine, at Culver Hall, in the hope that the peace and tranquillity of Gower would, if only in some small measure, help lessen their grief

14

and give them strength to face the years ahead. For Sir John's sister, Jane's mother, the good intentions had begun to succeed, but Jane remained in her shell, hardly speaking a word to anyone.

In desperation Sir John hoped that Richard could help, that the company of someone of her own age, who was himself fatherless, could perhaps break through her barrier of sorrow. Richard's grandfather had agreed, and as from the following day, Richard, the young fourteen-year-old midshipman, who, despite his tender years, had already seen, heard and experienced the reality of men dying, was to be the companion of a girl of ten, who could not come to terms with the unexpected death of her father.

Richard's first inclination was to protest. He could already imagine the banter of his shipmates if word of it was ever to reach their ears, but then he realised the futility of such a reaction. Sir John and his grandfather had agreed and he was therefore obliged; besides he owed Sir John so much for his education and his naval appointment that it was time to repay the debt.

The next morning Richard dutifully presented himself at Culver Hall, a horse was ready saddled for him, and once Jane had been brought from the Hall – reluctantly it appeared judging by the look on her face – the rest of the morning was spent riding the near-by hills, with Jane, a look of grim determination on her round face, ensuring that her pony kept pace with his, yet responding to Richard's attempts at conversation with no more than a 'yes' and a 'no'. The next morning, however, she was already mounted and waiting when he arrived, and during their ride was full of questions about the Gower, the type of birds flying overhead, how far across the Channel was Somerset, what are these flowers called, the trees, the vegetation and so on, that Richard found it hard to provide all the answers. On the third day her curiosity was all about himself and his life in the Navy, and on the fourth they had their first quarrel when Richard told her not to take her pony along a narrow, cliff-side path. She rounded on him – Machen could still remember the flash of her eyes – and continued along the path despite his advice. In that moment

Richard realised, despite his youth, that under Jane's mantle of grief was someone with a very strong, determined will.

The events of that day led to them becoming firm friends, and during the rest of their time together on Gower they were seldom parted. Daily they used to ride the grassy clifflands, carpeted with bracken and banks of yellow gorse and – with Richard now recovered from his illness and growing stronger every day – chasing, but never catching, the wild horses that roamed in bands across the moors. On hot days, in one of the many coves that abounded in the area, cut back in the coastline of high, limestone cliffs, they would remove their top clothing and he would teach Jane to swim. After, they would lie drying in the sun, undisturbed on the beach of fine yellow sand. In the evenings, as the aroma of his grandmother's baking bread filled the cottage, grandfather would make them sit on the settle inside the wide hearth from where they could look up through the wide open chimney and see the stars. They would kindle the rushlights and listen to the stories the old man told of the smuggler gangs that once operated out of Port Eynon, control-ling the Bristol Channel and much of the Irish Sea; and Richard would find it hard not to steal a glance at Jane's face, flushed with the excitement of it all.

But in the autumn of 1790 Jane returned home to London and he to the Navy. Three years later, the revolutionary government of France declared war on Britain. Since then he had not been home. He was at sea at the time of the mutinies of Spithead and Nore in 1797 but, thinking about it afterwards, he knew that, had he been in Portsmouth, and witnessed the bad conditions – inadequate pay, brutal punishments and poor food – he would have sided with the Spithead mutineers. He had no sympathy, however, with the revolutionary aims of the Nore uprising. In 1798 he had served under Nelson against the French at the Battle of the Nile, but the carnage exacted by Nelson so sickened him that for a while he even thought of deserting. That year too his grandfather died, followed in less than twelve months by his grandmother. Now there were no ties between Machen and his birthplace, save for the graves on the hillside overlooking the sea, which held the bodies of his 'Granny' and 'Grancha' and of the mother he had never seen.

But two days ago, as he gazed out at the waters of the Medway, he knew he had to visit his home again. And who knew but that the Gower would provide a diversion? Which reminded him again of Jane Ashford. Where was she now, a grown woman of twenty-two, and good-looking with it, of that he had no doubt. Married? Probably; with a child, perhaps even two. Perish the thought that was creeping into his mind! Rich heiresses, the Jane Ashfords of this world, were not meant for the likes of poor naval officers, eking out an existence on meagre, half-pay.

Machen burrowed his head into the soft pillows. He thought briefly about the wretched guardsman whom, accompanied by Despard and Macnamara, he had seen climb the stairs and enter the room next to his. But as the warmth of the room encompassed him his eyelids grew heavy, and he fell asleep, the glowing fire in the grate replaced by the red sun sinking over the Bay of Aboukir as the English ships sailed in against the French fleet anchored in the bay.

Suddenly the black sky was punctuated by the flash and the thunder of guns and, as the sound and fury grew, the French ships caught fire, lighting up the oily waters. A jagged, gun-lit sea. The shadows of falling spars and broken men passed Machen's eyes as he ordered broadside after broadside into the crippled French ships. Annihilation had been Nelson's order. Annihilation! The battle raged into the night and in his restless sleep Machen saw the screaming men, their clothes on fire, leaping off the ships into the flaming sea, he heard the cries for help . . .

Instantly he was awake. Another sound had interrupted his dreams.

From the gallery outside, which ran around the building and looked down upon the yard, he could hear scuffling and a murmur of voices. For a moment there was silence, then came a sharp cry of pain, quickly stifled.

Machen leapt out of bed and threw open the door leading to the gallery.

In the poor light of the glass lantern he could see the young guardsman lying flat on his back on the gallery floor. Straddling him, his bent knees pinning down both of the soldier's arms, was John Macnamara. In his right hand he held a long, thin-bladed knife, its point against the soldier's throat, breaking the skin; and a trickle of blood oozed from the wound. In his left hand, Macnamara held a card pressed against the soldier's lips, his weight down on to the soldier's chest, forcing him to lie still. He leaned over the guardsman's face.

"My young friend," he whispered, "there was no need for this! All you had to do was to kiss the oath and swear to keep it a secret. Now it's too late!"

The soldier's body bucked violently upwards in a last, desperate effort to throw the Irishman off, but the advantage of weight was with Macnamara. He pressed down and the soldier's attempt collapsed.

"Much too late," he repeated.

Machen strode across the gallery, forced his right arm under Macnamara's armpit, and pulled the man up in one sudden movement, lifting the knife away from the soldier's throat. As the Irishman rolled over, the card still in his hand, Machen kicked him hard, then brought his fist down savagely on the back of his neck. Macnamara sprawled flat on to the floor.

Machen went to help the soldier but the guardsman picked himself up and tore along the gallery and down the stairs to the yard, falling down the last few in his panic.

At the foot of the stairs the erect figure of Colonel Despard stepped out of the gloom, brandishing a green silk umbrella by the stem, aiming to use its yellow ivory handle as a club. As the young man saw him he scrambled to his feet again, turned into the yard and ran diagonally across the cobbled surface towards the archway leading out into Charing Cross. Simultaneously came the warning sound of a post horn as the metallic rumble of the wheels of an incoming coach reverberated in the tunnel of the Golden Cross. The soldier tried to reach the protection of the yard wall but he was too late. As the coach burst into the yard the powerful chest of the lead horse hit him, hurling the soldier forward, and under the hooves of the rest. Panic-stricken they reared into the air, and descended again, lashing out in fear. It was some time before the coachman and the ostlers who ran out of the stables to help could calm them down.

Machen watched in frozen horror, then rushed down the stairs and over to the bleeding, crumpled figure which lay still, in the centre of the yard. As he knelt by the young man's side, the latter's eyes flickered open, his face contorted in pain, and he tried to speak. Machen lowered his head and heard the soldier whisper:

"Changed . . . my mind. Could not . . . do it. Stop them. Stop . . . them. Before . . . too late."

The soldier's eyes opened suddenly, he clasped Machen's shirt and, with a supreme effort of will-power, lifted his body some inches from the floor. "Before . . . too late," he repeated. "Oh, God . . . Save . . . the King." The body suddenly became heavy in Machen's arms and, with a rasping exhalation of breath, the soldier died.

Machen slowly lowered the broken body to the floor, and stood up. He looked around the yard and up at the gallery. Despard and Macnamara had disappeared.

Machen could not see inside the dark recess of the door of the booking office, or the man hiding there. But the man could see Machen, and his eyes followed his every movement.

Minutes earlier, from that same position, he had looked up across the courtyard and in the amber glow of the lantern he had watched the naval officer knock out his brother John. The lieutenant could have prejudiced their plans. If the guardsman had lived and told all that he knew . . .

The man now studied the face of the naval officer. If their paths should ever cross again . . . Conor Macnamara's hand tightened around the hilt of his knife.

Within fifteen minutes normality had returned to the Golden Cross. The death was declared an accident by all the observers, including the anxious coachman. On the instructions of the landlord the body was placed on the dirt floor of a small outbuilding to await collection by the soldier's regiment and the yard was washed clean by copious buckets of water.

The coach drove out of the Golden Cross in a flurry. A few

minutes later, as it slowed down at the end of Parliament Street to turn on to Westminster Bridge, a tall man, erect and carrying a yellow-handled umbrella stepped into the road and flagged the carriage to a stop. Having shown his reserved seat ticket to the coachman Colonel Despard climbed inside the coach and settled into his seat. From the shadow of the bridge wall a second man emerged. Dressed in a dark suit and a black coat with a high, turned-down collar, he entered the coach and sat down opposite Despard. He nodded at the colonel, acknowledging that their long journey had started, then he leaned back, closed his slate blue eyes and relaxed. Despard gave a short grunt. Conor Macnamara's ability to relax in moments of tension had always annoyed him.

The coach threaded its way through the wagons and market-bound cattle herds which, even at that early hour, were already filling the roads leading into the city. With the bridge behind it the vehicle was soon roaring down the New Road on its journey south. It was the six o'clock coach to Canterbury and the coachman, impatient at the two unscheduled interruptions, was anxious to make up time.

CHAPTER 3

Two hours later the coachyard of the Golden Cross was all
noisy activity again as yet another stagecoach arrived. The
dishevelled and weary travellers were helped down to the
accompaniment of the cries of the beggars. Around them
luggage boys bumped and jostled, yelling instructions to one
another as the baggage was thrown down from the top of the
coach.

Richard Machen pushed his way through them, entered the
tunnelled archway that led into Charing Cross, and the localised bustle of the coachyard was replaced by the all-pervading,
constant street roar which came from the sea of wagons and
animals and people that thronged England's capital.

The main hall of the Admiralty building was painted in the
Navy's colours of white, gold and blue. Its walls were festooned
with brass openwork candles, and black oak chairs were ranged
around the floor.

The commissionaire gave Machen instructions how to find
David Gregor's room, up a wide imposing stone staircase. As
Machen climbed he thought – not for the first time – of how
much the inside of the building typified the accepted order of
things in Britain, the colossal difference between those who
had and those who had not.

The ground and middle floors of the Admiralty were divided
into spacious suites and apartments, reserved for the use of the
naval lords and their senior colleagues. The lower staff had to
fit in wherever they could, in draughty attics and damp,
windowless basements, courting pneumonia, eyestrain and

creaking joints, in working conditions that were, at best, little better than primitive. Not that the sea lords noticed, of course, but it almost made one wonder whether men like Despard were not right in their view that society needed changing. It was a fact that, in parts of this so-called enlightened country, one man could sit down at a meal big enough to feed ten, whereas elsewhere ten people might be forced to share a meal which would hardly feed one.

Change was needed, Machen reflected. And it would come. It would have to come. But not in Despard's way.

Gregor's room was a cubby-hole at the end of a long passageway on the top floor. The solicitor sat behind a table piled high with papers and files, his face – wan and pinched from the effects of his previous night's drinking – resting on his hands as he listened to Machen's account of the death of the guardsman earlier that morning in the yard of the Golden Cross.

"I confess," he said slowly, each spoken word seeming to make him flinch with pain, "that what happened seems to justify my concern. I will ensure that the authorities are made aware of the facts. Just give me time to word my report in such a way that you will not be involved?"

"Not involved!" Machen protested. "Hell's bells, the man was killed right before my eyes!"

"True, Mr Machen," Gregor agreed, hesitatingly, "but the way you describe it, Colonel Despard could easily claim it to have been an accident. The soldier actually *ran* into the path of the horses. Although I am certain that but for your own intervention Macnamara may very well have caused him harm, we have no actual proof that Despard himself meant to kill him."

Machen remembered the look on Despard's face as he stepped out of the gloom to intercept the fleeing soldier. It had been enough to convince the guardsman too.

Machen insisted. "But the soldier's last words? 'Save the King'?"

"The patriotic declaration of a dying man?" Gregor offered, looking across at Machen as though appealing to him to agree with his suggestion. "Many times, with his new friends, he had sat, drunk, smoked and debated treason. In the last moments of his life perhaps he sought absolution?"

"Mr Machen!" Gregor cut across as Machen made to reply, taking a deep breath as though nerving himself for what he was about to say. "It would seem that I must beg your understanding in this . . ." he paused ". . . sorry affair, and your trust that I will report the facts of the soldier's death to those who are investigating the current activities of Colonel Despard. But in truth, if you force me to relate your own concern in the matter, then I shall also be forced to confess as to how you came to be interested in the Colonel in the first place. As you must be aware, Mr Machen, I should never have confided in you, but . . ." he essayed a laugh ". . . an unhappy marriage, and the temptation to take one drink too many in order to drown one's sorrows, I trust you will try to understand. If my superiors became aware of my indiscretion I'm afraid I would lose my employment . . ." and Gregor's voice trailed off as he nervously awaited Machen's reaction.

Richard stood to his feet. "Then you must act on it as you think fit, Mr Gregor, just as long as I have your word that the authorities will be informed?"

Gregor's relief was immediate, he pushed back his chair and rushed around the table to place his right hand on Machen's shoulder. "On that you may rest assured, Mr Machen. And as for my suspicion that Despard could be headed for France, why, I had no cause to propose that that was his destination. It could indeed be Canterbury and his purpose an innocent one. And when all is said and done, even if France is his objective what will the journey avail him? Are Napoleon or the French government likely to listen to the mad scheme of a dismissed Irish colonel. I think not. Come, Mr Machen," he pleaded with a smile, "what say we forget the man and look forward instead to our journey to Swansea together on the morrow, and a new beginning to our brief acquaintanceship?"

Uneasily Machen agreed. To be cooped up in a draughty stagecoach with a man as fond of his own voice as was Gregor, did not fill him with any degree of enthusiasm. Ah well, he consoled himself, perhaps the fellow will prove to be a might more tolerable when sober.

*   *   *

Machen crossed the Admiralty's crowded front hall and went out through the main door, in time to see an open chaise pull out of the noisy traffic of Whitehall and enter the courtyard. As he descended the stone steps it turned a slow half-circle across the cobbled surface and drew up alongside him. Machen halted, his eyes instantly drawn to the female of its two occupants, a remarkably pretty young woman, wearing a rich, green velvet dress, its tight bodice accentuating the slimness of that part of her body which was visible above the sides of the chaise, yet at the same time giving evidence of a fullness of bosom that was a delight to behold. To add to her charms she was endowed with a curling profusion of dark, nut-brown hair that fell past her shoulders, framing a pale, oval face.

Machen hesitated. There was something vaguely familiar about her, especially her features, the high cheekbones, the small, straight-bridged nose, a mouth that suggested determination yet with a certain sensuous curve to her lips that hinted at a warm, generous nature, even impulsive perhaps? And lastly her eyes, deep, brown pools beneath soft, curling lashes which returned his gaze, direct and unflinching, yet with a slightly puzzled, almost searching look which seemed to reflect his own uncertainty. Machen's memory stirred . . .

"Sir!" The sharp voice of her companion interrupted his mind-searching. "Must you stand there blocking my descent; and pray withdraw your presence, you are causing offence to my ward by your unwelcome attention!"

There was no mistaking that cold voice! How often in the past had Machen heard it, from the time when, as a raw, frightened, young midshipman, barely twelve years old, he had stepped aboard his first naval ship and was taken to meet his new captain. Slowly Machen turned to face Sir Robert Noble, the man under whose command he had served the earliest two years of his naval career, and would have served more, had the scurvy not sent him home and severed their unhappy relationship. Despite the passing of twelve years Noble had barely changed appearance. His narrow face was, perhaps, more lined than before, and his thin hair slightly greyer, but his body seemed as wiry and taut as from the old days. Even in that brief moment Machen found himself wondering how a man so devoid of humour could ever have been a friend of the blunt but genial Sir John Lucas; but then he remembered that that was not the situation. In securing Richard's midshipmanship his patron had simply prevailed upon a blood relationship that had existed between Noble and Sir John's own brother-in-law, William Ashford, the father of that young girl, Jane, in whose company he had spent those unexpectedly pleasurable months of recuperation on Gower, twelve years ago . . .

In that instant Machen recognised Noble's companion. He glanced up at her to make certain, at the same time puzzled as to why she was at the Admiralty in Sir Robert's carriage. She returned his gaze, direct and yet still uncertain, not yet having made the connection between the boy of fourteen and the man who now stood before her. But Machen was now in no doubt that she was Jane Ashford – the little girl once so serious and sad, but who had quickly turned into a tomboy – now gloriously grown up into a striking young woman, with a beauty that would cause the heads of most men to turn and admire.

"Sir Robert!" Machen turned excitedly to direct his next words to Noble, yet intending them for Jane's ears alone. "Do you not remember me? Richard Machen! I served my first years at sea under your command."

He should have expected it; Noble's response was typical of the man, being no more effusive than of old, his inherent manner, reticent and somewhat brusque, allowed him to show no trace of emotion.

"Yes, Mr Machen, as I recollect you were a passable sailor; but with a somewhat modern mind when it came to discipline, not one for the strict, old-fashioned methods of exercising control expected in officers aspiring to one day command a well ordered ship of war. I trust you are quite well?" The last sentiment was made so grudgingly that before Machen could reply Noble sought to terminate their conversation. "And now, if you would forgive me?" he said and turned to address his companion, only to see Jane Ashford moving sideways along the chaise's richly upholstered seat and positioning herself against the side of the coach. Her eyes were aglow with excitement as she extended her gloved hands impulsively towards Machen. Richard stepped swiftly to the side of the coach and took them in his.

"Richard!" Her voice was low, almost whispered. "And do you remember me? The time you were invalided home, and should have been resting instead of acting as my escort? Oh, but you must have forgotten," she said almost wistfully, "it seems so long ago."

"Forgotten!" Machen found it hard to control his voice; even to his own ears it seemed to be betraying his excitement. "It would be impossible to commit such a crime!" He wanted to continue, to pay a compliment to her beauty, but after years spent divorced from female company he was bereft of the verbal graces required to frame his thoughts. He therefore remained silent, but still holding her hands tight in his.

Sir Robert coughed, interrupting the moment. "Jane, it would appear that you are both well acquainted?" His tone was openly disapproving.

Jane replied without turning her head, continuing to look at Richard with a pleasure to match his own. "We met as children, Uncle Robert, during the months mother and I spent at Culver Hall, after father died. Richard became my saviour, in more ways than one, especially when he risked his life to save mine."

"You exaggerate," said Machen. "There was no risk."

"On the contrary, Richard, there was considerable danger as well you know. Had I but heeded your advice and not taken that path."

"Your pony stumbled."

"Because the path was treacherous," Jane replied, turning to explain to Sir Robert. "I fell . . . down a slope at the bottom of which was a cliff with a huge drop on to the rocks below. Fortunately, I was halted by a providential bush only feet away from the cliff-edge. Without hesitation, Richard climbed down to my rescue, knowing that the slightest slip would cause his own death. He reached me, gave me his hand, and then – goodness knows how – he slowly pulled us both back to safety."

"As I would expect any midshipman of mine to act in similar circumstances." Sir Robert's face remained impassive.

26

"Nevertheless I thank you, Mr Machen, rather belatedly, I regret, as this is the first I have heard of the incident."

"We swore to keep it our secret, Uncle Robert," Jane explained. "Richard did not want me to be in bad favour with Mother and Uncle John."

"I see. Still, you displayed courage, Mr Machen. If Jane's mother were alive today I know she would have added her own gratitude."

Machen tightened his grip on Jane's hand. "Your mother has passed away?" he asked, his voice becoming subdued.

"Of the fever, five months ago," Jane replied, her eyes suddenly clouding over. She responded to Machen's concern by returning his clasp. "Sir Robert is now my guardian."

Machen's awkward sympathies led to a gap in the conversation, which Sir Robert decided to break, now feeling under an obligation to show some interest in Machen.

"Your visit here this morning, Mr Machen: is there any way in which I can assist you? Having retired from active service I am now employed within the Admiralty building."

"No, sir." Machen deliberately elaborated, "My visit was merely to inform a friend the time of my departure to Gower tomorrow."

Jane was quick to respond, "Richard! Will you be home this summer?"

"Yes, Jane, and with little prospect of being recalled to sea now that we are at peace."

"Then has Uncle John not let the cottage?"

"No. When he sent me the news of my grandmother's death, he informed me that the cottage would be left vacant in case I should return."

"How like Uncle John!" Jane smiled fondly, before assuming a firm voice. "Then, my bold young officer, as I shall be spending August at Culver Hall, for the first time on my own without Mother, you shall again be my companion, just as you became years ago when Father died." Her eyes shone as she spoke, then a sudden blush suffused her cheeks as she realised she was betraying her excitement. She withdrew her hands and sat back in the chaise, looking down at her skirt and brushing away at a non-existent crease.

Sir Robert took the opportunity to stand to his feet. "And now, Mr Machen, we must all take our leave, I to my duties, Jane to her milliner's, and I'm sure you have other matters to attend to."

He opened the chaise door and descended the steps, then turned his back, deliberately placing himself between Machen and his ward. Machen took the hint but as he passed between the two white pillars guarding the entrance to the Admiralty, he turned his head for a final glimpse of Jane. His reward was to see her looking over her shoulder away from her guardian. She gave him a final, brief wave of her right hand. Machen responded, then entered Whitehall and headed back for the Golden Cross.

Colonel Despard had been obliterated from his mind.

The stagecoach from London lumbered on towards Canterbury. The coachman alternately chivvied then nursed his horses over the rut-pitted road as the welcoming saloon bar at the end of the journey drew nearer.

Inside the coach the noise of the wheels reverberated in the ears of the passengers, making conversation impossible. In the right corner seat facing the front of the coach, Colonel Despard sat apparently oblivious of his dark-suited companion opposite, his blue greatcoat wrapped tightly around him against the dust which gusted in through the open windows.

In any event, had conversation ever been possible, he would not have engaged in it, for his mind was completely engaged in planning his mission. Simply stated, this was to cross the Channel by whatever means possible, then journey to Paris. Once there he would persuade, or beg, the French government to finance his plans for the overthrow of the English monarchy and Parliament.

The revolution was set for 23 November, the day of the ceremonial Opening of Parliament. The plans included one killing. Somewhere along the route from his Palace to Westminster, it was Colonel Despard's intention to assassinate the King.

*　　*　　*

28

Jane's visit to the milliner having been successfully completed, the coach slowed to a gentle trundle as it crossed Clapham Common on its way home to Glebe House.

It was a fine day, extremely warm for this time of year. Surrounded by the spacious, tree-dotted peace of the Common, so far removed from the city noise, Jane closed her eyes and tried to picture Richard's face. How strange, how exciting to have met him again after so many years, and how he had changed, tall, tanned, and so good-looking; dressed in his well-worn, faded Navy uniform, he was the very opposite of the pale, immaculately dressed young men who usually attended the functions within her social circle. She looked forward to their next meeting in three months' time, with a strange, tingling anticipation. In truth, if she could start the journey tomorrow it would not be too soon!

That was wishful thinking, though. For this year's invitation, as always, was timed to coincide with Uncle John's return, supposedly from visiting his estates in Ireland. But in reality Jane had long since suspected that his sea-journeys were really to France and, in the historical tradition of the Lucas family, almost certainly connected with smuggling.

Jane closed her eyes, remembering last year's visit to Culver Hall, as clearly as the events of yesterday.

Once the preliminaries of greeting her uncle and aunt were over, Jane had run up to her room, closed the door and crossed to the window to take in her favourite view. She opened the window to allow in the air. The breeze was warm and balmy, strong with the smell of the sea, and she leaned past the sill and looked down, always with an excited fear at rediscovering how near this side of Culver Hall was to the edge of the cliffs. Below her the waters rolled in from the wide channel and crashed against the rocks. To her right, the wild Gower coastline, with its high rugged cliffs and innumerable coves, stretched away into the distance towards the open sea.

This view always evoked in her a wildness, a call which reached right down inside her, stirring emotions that were normally curtailed by the rigid conventions of her days, and her spirit responded . . .

The following day, as she rode her horse across the sands, it seemed once again to Jane that she had been meant for this place. A strange excitement took hold of her. She nudged her horse into a canter, and then, when this was not enough, she stretched it into a gallop. Across the sands they flew and into the shallow waters of the bay. Eventually she turned the horse's head and pointed it back towards the headland on which stood Culver Hall. Her mount sped along the waters' edge, churning through the curling riplets and sending showers of spray into the air. She was wearing a blue velvet riding habit with a divided skirt and thus rode as she always did when she was on Gower, sitting astraddle in the manner of a man, leaning forward, feeling herself at one with the horse. The water splashed over her clothes and her face, she tasted the salt water on her lips.

She lifted her gaze, saw they were approaching the rocky stretch of the shore and pulled her horse up.

To her right along the beach, where the sand turned to rock, was the cottage built upon a high-walled quay. She knew it was empty from when Richard's grandparents had died some two years before, but although Jane had called on them every year since Richard's departure, after their death she had never been tempted to venture inside. This time, acting on impulse, she directed her horse towards it. She tethered the animal to an iron ring in the jetty wall and climbed the stone steps. To her surprise the door was unlocked. She went inside.

The familiar room ran the width of the cottage, with a rear window that looked out on to the headland. It was obvious – by the thick layer of sand inside the threshold – that it was some time since the dwelling had been occupied, and just as obvious that until then it had been someone's treasured home. Inside the deep, open, stone fireplace were the two grate baskets, one holding small pieces of chopped wood and some shavings, the other logs. The two polished settles drawn up before the hearth still showed the care which Richard's grandmother had once lavished upon them; as did the large table along the far wall, scrubbed so many times over the years.

The door in the left corner of the room led to the bedrooms. It was the first time she had been in this part of the cottage. The first of the two rooms contained a large double bed and by the stone fireplace were two baskets of logs. On the bedside table was a candle holder and alongside it a large, black family Bible closed tight with an ornate brass clasp, its title inlaid with letters of gold.

She sat on the edge of the bed and opened it. From inside the front cover a folded piece of paper fell to the floor. Jane picked it up, and opened it.

It was a letter, the ink already beginning to fade. Written from on board one of His Majesty's ships, with the place and date being recorded as: "Off the coast of Egypt. August 3rd 1798".

The start of the letter, "Dear Grandfather and Grandmother", meant it was from Richard. Jane read on as he told of the mighty sea battle which had been fought in the Bay of Aboukir just two days before. It described the British victory and the awful price paid in French lives. In conclusion Richard thanked God for his own deliverance and went on to say that the casualties had been so high he would have paid any price not to have been part of it. He then concluded with a verse:

> Oh for a lodge in some vast wilderness,
> Some boundless contiguity of shade,
> Where rumour of oppression and deceit,
> Of unsuccessful or successful war,
> Might never reach me more.

The lines, Jane knew, were taken from a poem by William Cowper. The letter was signed, "from your loving grandson, Richard Machen".

In that moment, in the silence of the cottage, she had suddenly felt terribly close to Richard, her memory of him as a boy giving her a curious understanding of the almost contradictory nature of the grown man who had fought so bravely under Nelson in that terrible encounter between Britain and France, and yet, while others around him were no doubt celebrating victory, had hidden away in some corner of his ship to express in writing his reflections on the terrible consequences of war.

In the days that followed, Jane passed much of her time

idling around the cottage, enjoying the peace and contentment she found within its walls, and lying on the sand dunes, her face to the sun until it was no longer pale, but brown, tanned like a gypsy's . . .

Last year, she had tried to visualise Richard but could not. Now, as the carriage drove into the driveway to Glebe House, Jane opened her eyes. The summer months on Gower lay before her again, but she would not be alone. The boy had returned a man. And this time Richard would not have to return to the war.

CHAPTER 4

It was eleven o'clock on the morning of Wednesday, 5 May 1802, at the Tuileries Palace. Joseph Fouché, France's Minister of Police, stood by the window of the anteroom next to Napoleon's study, looking out contemplatively across the waters of the Seine and the mottled skyline of southern Paris.

Fouché, an ex-Jacobin and once an associate of Robespierre, was dressed in his habitual frock-coat, old, dark and badly cut. He was forty-four years old, thin-faced, with eyes permanently hooded and half-closed, while his short hair was brushed straight forward and clipped into an untidy fringe over his forehead.

Fouché had first studied for the Church, but refused to take vows or to be ordained. Instead, three years after the outbreak of the Revolution, at the age of thirty-four, he threw away his clerical garb, having got himself elected to the National Convention by the citizens of his home town, Nantes. He sat with the Jacobins in the Legislative Assembly, and his supreme political skill had kept him in government ever since – despite the fate of his one-time allies.

From his headquarters in the Hôtel de Juigne the Minister of Police controlled Paris through a complex system of spies and informers drawn from all classes of society and, whenever it suited him, by exercising his powers to make arrests based on nothing more than his personal opinion or whim. Hard factual evidence was not necessary to Fouché's method of policing. If it was advisable for the good of France – or for the good of

33

Joseph Fouché – a man could be put away until the Minister decreed otherwise.

On this day, Wednesday, 5 May 1802, Joseph Fouché was – ostensibly at least – on the side of Napoleon. The latter, though he knew Fouché to be a turncoat, nevertheless acknowledged that his peculiar talents were ideally suited to the maintenance of France's internal security.

The door of the First Consul's study opened and Louis de Bourrienne, Napoleon's private secretary, beckoned Fouché in and then left, closing the door behind him. It was a large square room with high embossed ceilings, airy, but only sparsely furnished. Around a large conference table stood fifteen chairs, their velvet surfaces faded and scuffed. On the right wall, between two long windows – which, like the one in the anteroom, looked over the Seine – was an ornate fireplace and above it hung a large, gilt-framed mirror. From the open doors of a working cabinet papers spewed on to the floor. Set at an angle across the corner, to benefit from the far window, was Napoleon's imposing rosewood desk. In front of the desk were two high-backed, wooden-armed chairs and across its surface were spread papers, charts and innumerable maps.

Behind all this sat 'the little corporal'. Fouché crossed the room and saw, with increasing uneasiness, that in his pudgy, white hand the First Consul of France was holding a short-bladed dagger which he was repeatedly stabbing into a large map spread out before him, oblivious of the damage he was causing to the surface of the desk underneath. As Fouché waited by one of the chairs he noticed how the desk was already scarred with other recently cut notches and grooves, all bearing testimony to a new habit which Napoleon had recently acquired.

Fouché waited. Thirty seconds passed before Bonaparte looked up. With the point of his dagger he waved the Minister of Police to the chair on the left.

"Sit, Monsieur Fouché," he muttered, thin lips hardly moving, his pale brown eyes staring up, fixed, unblinking.

"Thank you, Monsieur le Premier Consul." Fouché pulled back the chair.

Again there was a long silence then, with a sudden

movement, Napoleon once more stabbed the knife down. It embedded itself in the desk and remained there, quivering. Napoleon sat upright, the fingers of his left hand drumming on the arm of his chair.

"Monsieur Fouché!"

The First Consul leaned over and from the floor beside him picked up a sheaf of papers and hurled them on to the desk in front of Fouché. The Minister of Police recognised the daily police reports which, from the beginning of his administration, Napoleon had insisted should be laid on his desk before eight o'clock every morning, together with reports from all the other governmental departments. The raw material for the police reports was provided by area prefects of police and general commissaires. This, digested by the confidential clerks in the bureaux of the four *arrondissements*, was submitted to the central bureau to be combined into a single report by a clerk whom Fouché personally had released from prison and given employment in December 1799. The report was then passed for approval to Desmarest, Head of the Sûreté Générale and Secret Police and, finally, to Fouché himself for his approval. Two copies were then prepared. One copy was placed on Fouché's files. The other, tied with green ribbon and sealed by Fouché, was carried direct to the First Consul by a courier of the State Secretariat.

Napoleon placed his elbows on to the desk and, interlacing his fingers, formed them into a bridge over which only his cold eyes were visible.

"Your daily police reports are beginning to depress me, Fouché. Negative. Everything negative. One gets the impression that the First Consul of France is surrounded by nothing but intrigue and the virtual certainty of open rebellion."

Fouché started to protest, but Napoleon interrupted.

"No, Fouché, you cannot deny it, that is the impression they give, constant reports of unrest from all Departments of the city."

The First Consul looked up at his Minister. "Do the people of France not realise what I have done for them, Fouché, and how much they should be grateful to me? Do they not know the depths to which France had descended before I took over? That the Treasury contained only 77,000 francs and this pitiful sum represented the entire fortune of France. The army was unpaid. Cities and towns were without food. The countryside was infested by brigands from Brittany to Marseilles. But now," with a sudden, abrupt movement Napoleon tilted his chair back and waved his soft, small hand imperiously at the window behind him, "after only two years the change in France is obvious to all who have eyes to see. Civil order has been restored, the provinces are reorganised, and new building schemes have been planned for Paris. And soon trade will recover because of the new markets that will open up through my domination of Europe, and then the people will have full bellies again. And yet they still moan and complain when they should be showing only gratitude." Napoleon paused reflectively. "However . . ."

With a crash Bonaparte brought his chair down again. He pushed a sheaf of papers across the desk. "The reports on my soldiers cause me the greatest concern. Fighting with the public. Forcing their way into shops and taking goods out without payment. Duelling. Drinking. Raping. Looting. If one is to believe these claims, hardly a moment passes without one violent disturbance or another!" He paused again and extracted one of the reports from the sheaf. "Here. See here, for example. Only last week, apparently, members of two of my best regiments, the Twelfth Hussars and the Fifteenth Light Infantry, took over the Bois de Boulogne and made the park into one large fighting arena to contest for the favours of a group of street harlots. And here," Napoleon jabbed at the report, "a unit of the Twentieth Light Infantry threw the customers out of a cabaret on the Rue de Vangirard and drank the place dry. And here too, an inn at Saint-Cloud, totally wrecked by men from the Eighteenth."

The First Consul hurled the report on to the desk.

"Well, Fouché? Well?"

"With respect, General, I think the soldiers are merely displaying high spirits after years of war and fighting. The mood, I am sure, will soon die down. Especially when they see the example I intend to make of those already arrested."

Napoleon pushed back his chair and sprang to his feet. The chair toppled backwards and crashed to the floor but he ignored it.

"Nonsense, Fouché. Nonsense." His voice rose in anger. He picked up another paper and strode around the desk to confront his Minister of Police. His face was flushed. He leaned forward to shout, then he controlled himself:

"For myself, Fouché, I cannot share your high opinion of my army's responsibility. And shall I tell you why? Because the problem stems from the top. The soldiers misbehave because the officers do not discipline them. The officers fail in their duty because the generals are not watching over them. And why? Why is this?" Napoleon's voice had risen to a crescendo and his eyes bulged. "Because the generals are too busy plotting against me, that's why!"

Fouché tried to protest, but Napoleon continued:

"No, Fouché. My instinct is never wrong in matters like this. My loyal and trusted generals: Bernadotte, who owes me so much, Decaen, Lannes, Brune. The whole damned brood of them are conspiring against me. And against the office of the First Consul of France. Is nothing sacred? After all I have done for them. At the moment I have no proof, but I will obtain it. And then . . . !"

Napoleon glared at Fouché. Then, with effort, he restrained his anger, and not for the first time the Minister of Police wondered at the varying moods that the man was able to exhibit and apparently master, all in the space of a few minutes. The First Consul returned to the other side of the desk.

"Monsieur Fouché, I have a task for you. An important task which needs your particular abilities."

He looked carefully at the Minister. "Now that we are at peace with Perfidious Albion I intend to appoint trade consuls and send them to England to represent France. I want you, Fouché, to administer the scheme."

"Trade consuls?" Fouché was confused. "Surely, General, that is a matter for a chamber of trade to administer, not the police?"

Napoleon's lips broke into a thin smile. But the unblinking eyes remained cold and hard.

37

"Normally that would be true, Fouché. But in this case the promotion of reciprocal trade and understanding will not be their main function. It is, shall we say, a little deceit."

"I regret, General, but I don't understand . . ."

"These men, Fouché, will be highly trained officers of artillery and engineers. The task to which they will be appointed comes under your administration. You alone will choose them. There must be no mistake – or you will answer to me." Napoleon paused for a moment, then continued. "When they reach England – with the concentration of course on southern England – they will each proceed to their appointed towns where they will first establish themselves as bona-fide commercial agents of France. Having accomplished this, they will then devote themselves to their true task . . ."

Napoleon pointed at the map at which he had been stabbing when Fouché first entered the study. Fouché saw now that it was a map of England.

"Each agent," he emphasised, "is to map out the strategical points of his area. In the case of inland towns I will want to know the location of every garrison, the strength of the forces stationed there and the roads of communication leading to it, in particular all roads leading to the south coast itself. The agents assigned to the coastal towns should have naval knowledge; their task will be to map the harbours and the harbour entrances, the names of the ships in the various ports, their size and the number of guns each one carries. I will also re-quire . . ." and again Napoleon paused to search amongst the papers strewn across the desk; he found the document ". . . the soundings, the shoals, prevailing winds and the best times, in relation to the tides, for ships to enter and leave each harbour."

Napoleon looked up and handed the document to Fouché. "This is your copy, Fouché. Today is the 5 of May. The files of each officer being considered for selection will be with you by the end of the week. Three weeks for preparation. A month for the agents to establish themselves in England. Two months should be sufficient for them to map out the details. That means the reports can be collated and on my desk by the first week of September at the latest.

"You will appreciate, Fouché, the importance of the task I am giving you, in particular that relating to the plans of the harbours and the naval details. The very success of my scheme depends on our gaining control of the Channel for a week – without interference from the British Navy. If we accomplish this, we succeed. If we do not, we fail. And France cannot, must not, be allowed to fail!"

Fouché found voice once more. "Forgive me, General. A moment ago we were talking about the unrest being shown by our soldiers here, on the very streets of Paris. Now we seem to be talking about sending spies to England. I fail to see the connection."

"The answer is simple, Fouché. Vision."

"Vision, General?"

Napoleon leapt up. "Vision, Fouché, vision, vision, vision!" The voice was irritated again. "You present me with problems, nothing but problems. Unrest. Intrigue. Do I answer you on the same level? No, Fouché, I answer you with *vision*. Let me ask you, what would your answer be to all this unrest?"

"There can only be one answer. Arrests, followed by imprisonment or deportation. In some cases, possibly the guillotine."

"Of course, of course. What more can one expect from a policeman! That is the difference between us, Fouché. I was born to rule, you were born to follow. And why? Because the gods, in their infinite wisdom, granted me *vision*. With such foresight I do not resort to your mundane solutions. I see beyond all this and into the future, and because of this I am able to offer these bored soldiers, these disgruntled generals, a dream which will become a reality if they will but follow me. Riches. Honour. All to be achieved on the battlefields fighting for the glory of France. The wealth of the world is ours for the taking, countries like India and the West Indies and all their riches. Soon, very soon, Fouché, a new French Empire will rise that will one day surpass the glory of ancient Rome itself."

He stopped and a sudden silence descended on the room.

"Well, Monsieur Fouché, have you any questions?"

Bewildered, the Minister replied, "But, General, how is all this to happen? We cannot just take over countries like India

39

and the West Indies! What about England's reaction? Any threat to her world influence and she is bound to retaliate."

Napoleon looked up, surprised, pained. "But Fouché, I thought you understood. There will be no England – because by November, England will belong to France. I have been working out the invasion plans for some weeks now."

"But General, the ink on our new peace treaty is hardly even dry!"

"To hell with the damned peace treaty!" exclaimed Napoleon.

Deep in thought, Fouché walked slowly along the Quai des Tuileries on the right bank of the Seine. He reached the Pont du Carrousel and turned on to it, oblivious to the charm of the waters which flowed beneath. Half way across, he paused. Then, his decision made, he hurried across the bridge and into the Quai Malaquais along the left bank of the river. He walked a few yards down the Quai, then into the courtyard of a building, the windows of which opened on to the river.

This was the Hôtel Juigne, which housed the Ministry of Police, and also Fouché's private apartments of which the great salon was reputed to be "the most beautiful room in Paris, a noble apartment, richly decorated".

To the Ministry came all reports of the suspects taken for interrogation to the dungeon hells of the Temple, Vincennes, the Fort de Joux, the Fort de Ham, the Conciergerie, La Grève and the Place Grenelle. In the dark offices, and even the corridors, lay piles of mysterious dossiers on people from all walks of life, in France itself and the far corners of Europe, a fantastic accumulation of information and notes put together from the wealth of reports disgorged daily to the Sûreté Générale by the multitude of spies which that organisation employed. Here, Fouché, the former Jacobin, who had created this tool of government, was more powerful even than Napoleon.

This morning, as on every morning, Louis Dubois, the man appointed by Fouché as Paris's Prefect of Police, was waiting in the Minister's room. An avaricious server, devoted to his superior, Dubois looked up narrow-eyed as Fouché entered the room, sat down opposite Dubois and began to talk . . .

Two minutes later Fouché had concluded his narrative of all that had taken place in Napoleon's study.

"This invasion must be stopped," he declared, his tone low with menace, "or it will ruin all our plans."

"But could it succeed?"

"I suppose it could," replied Fouché, grudgingly. "The man has spent much thought on his plan. A hundred thousand men or more to be barracked in hidden camps some miles from the coast. Then to be moved up in one day to various embarkation points, and transported across the Channel in specially constructed barges in the dead of night. Then by building up our Navy to be the largest in the world, and with the British Navy at less than half strength because of the peace, if he could gain control of the Channel, the necessary supplies of equipment, guns and horses could be shipped across for days without being challenged . . ."

"Then why . . . ?"

"Because its success cannot be *guaranteed*, my good Dubois. If it could that would be an entirely different proposition. Then even I would support the plan. After all, England is a country full of rich pickings and the thought is doubly attractive when one considers the wealth of its Empire. But unfortunately there can be no such guarantee. And for you and me to think otherwise would be folly."

Fouché paused and fixed his calculating gaze on Dubois. "Just consider what would happen if but two or three British ships of the line chanced across the troop carriers. The barges would be completely defenceless. Within minutes our army could be at the bottom of the sea and our northern defences open to British counter-attack. Within days, instead of our being in charge of London, all of France would be under British military rule, and," Fouché spoke slowly, emphasising his question, "where would that leave the two of us then, eh, Dubois?"

Dubois opened his mouth to speak but changed his mind and instead nervously ruffled his thinning hair.

Fouché's smile was cold. "The thought upsets you, my loyal

friend? And rightly so, because the failure of our First Consul's plans would certainly provide the death knell to our, shall we call them, joint business ventures and prospects of a prosperous old age."

Fouché picked up a red ledger which Dubois had placed on his desk and slowly and thoughtfully turned over its pages. "No, Dubois, we cannot allow this power-mad Corsican to gamble with our future, not now." Fouché read the totals on the last written page of the ledger, looked up, and smiled. "Especially as Mammon is so favouring us with his grace day by day."

He replaced the book carefully, almost tenderly, on the desk. Its pages, written up daily by Dubois in a code which had meaning only for his superior and himself, recorded the private financial arrangements of Joseph Fouché, Minister of Police for France, and Louis Dubois, Prefect of Police for Paris in the year 1802.

In that year, some 75,000 prostitutes were operating on the streets of the capital. The most popular area was the Palais-Royal; there, under the arcades, were the hovels in which these seductive young women offered their services. And it was not only there that these attractions could be found. In the side streets off the boulevards, at the doors of the theatres, in the winding streets of the Butte des Moulins, in the roads near the Carrousel the young ladies lingered everywhere, seeking their fortunes. It was in the Palais-Royal that the best-known gaming houses were to be found, leading into the same arcades as the brothels. In these gaming houses the biggest fortunes were always made by the owners, and the leases of the gaming tables changed hands for huge amounts because of the certain profits to be made. Smuggling also flourished and in certain parts of the city the gangs did little to disguise their trade from the authorities. Indeed, so openly did they conduct their business that one gang had even taken over the cellar of the Convent of the Filles-Sainte-Marie as a storeroom for its goods. The good nuns appeared to be the only people in that part of the city who didn't know about it.

All these people – prostitutes, gamblers, smugglers and the like – owed their licences to trade to the oral agreements which the heads of each vice ring had been able to negotiate with Dubois, acting on behalf of his silent partner and superior. And each agreement was made at a price to be remitted weekly. As a result Joseph Fouché, one-time cleric, one-time Jacobin, who took to himself the larger share of these disbursements, was on his way to becoming a very rich man. And Dubois himself was far from being a poor one.

There was a long silence as Fouché let Dubois ponder the bleak future which the failure of Napoleon's plan might open up to them. Dubois spoke plaintively, "How is it that we first hear of these plans from Napoleon himself? What happened to de Bourrienne and Josephine? Perhaps, if you had been warned, you could have argued him out of this mad scheme?"

"Possibly. But there I think we might be wasting our money. From de Bourrienne I get little but useless information, and as for Josephine . . ." Fouché grimaced, "to her, secrets seem to mean only one thing: the sexual deficiencies of the First Consul. Apparently – and I must say the matter is of small interest to me – a twelve-year-old child could perform better in bed than our masterful dictator."

"But," complained Dubois, "we hardly need to pay her 1,000 francs a day for this kind of information." He hesitated and looked apologetically at Fouché. "Have you thought, though," he asked, pondering aloud, "that the two things could possibly be connected? That despair over his lack of virility makes him want to prove himself and—"

Fouché exploded. "Dubois," he snarled at his assistant, "sometimes you can talk the most arrant nonsense. What the hell has his love life got to do with it? No, the man is an unbalanced egotist, dominated by a lust for power. And unless we act quickly we will all suffer for it."

"But there is no urgency, surely?" Dubois was hesitant after the rebuff. "The invasion, if it takes place, is not until November . . ."

"There is every need for urgency," replied Fouché. "With his sixth sense for knowing when people are conspiring against him he is already suspecting the generals. From that it will not be long before he realises my complicity. Once he suspects me, your own position, Dubois, will be—"

"Then what is to be done?" his assistant interjected, panic in his voice.

"Two things," Fouché muttered, his eyes half-closed with cunning. "First I will see Bernadotte and convince him that everything must be brought forward . . ."

"But . . ."

"Dubois, it's now a matter of self-preservation. And to ensure this we can use the opportunity to rid France of the last remaining Jacobins at the same time. Listen carefully."

THURSDAY, 6 MAY 1802

Paris in 1802 was a city without definite frontiers between rich and poor areas. Rather, its inhabitants of every degree lived close to one another, the division of class being marked by the floor levels at which they lived, a hierarchy which was strictly observed. Tradesmen occupied the shops at ground level, those with money the first floor, the less well-off the second, salaried people the third, work people the fourth and the poor the upper storeys, the levels within each building usually being reached by a single dirty staircase.

In a garret apartment on the heights of Montmartre, Philippe-Michele Buonarroti sat with only his thoughts for company, awaiting the arrival of Louis Dubois.

One hour earlier Buonarroti had received word that Dubois, the assistant of Joseph Fouché, had presented himself – alone and without escort – at the Café des Bains Chinois on the Rue Marivaux and asked the proprietor of that establishment, a well-known haunt of radical sympathisers, to convey a message that he wanted a meeting with 'a Jacobin leader'. The proprietor had protested to Dubois his ignorance as to how this message could be conveyed, but nevertheless had managed to convey it. In a short time Dubois would be brought to the apartment by Buonarroti's minions and the reason for his unexpected request would then be made known.

Buonarroti rose and crossed over to the dormer window. He pressed his forehead reflectively against the cold glass and gazed down at the streets of Montmartre. Soon his reflections had turned to a determination that his escape from prison should not have been in vain. He continued staring down. The Faubourg Montmartre was so representative of the rest of Paris. And Paris so representative of the other cities of this world. It mattered not who ruled, kings or first consuls. It was always the people who suffered.

Take France, for example. The start of a new century; yet, despite Napoleon's rhetorical promises, the plight of the people was little improved from their condition in the years before the Revolution.

There was still little or no work for them. The result was bottomless poverty. Only last year, at the height of the famine, many Parisians – some living within sight of the Tuileries Palace – had been forced to eat the carcasses of diseased war horses to stay alive. The resulting death toll had been heavy.

The capital itself, with its 600,000 population, was still an undeveloped place of almost mediaeval mystery, a labyrinth of streets and alleys in which countless heaps of rubbish piled up before the doors, waiting for the next thunderstorm to spread the muck over the middle of the road and turn it into a slough of mud. All this and the fact that the houses had fallen into neglect, their walls unplastered, their roofs unrepaired, had combined to give Paris the ruinous, maudlin aspect it presented to Buonarroti on this morning of Thursday 6 May.

And what was Napoleon's feeling about the conditions of his people? Was there any compassion? Through a servant, a Jacobin agent planted in the Tuileries, the personal views of the First Consul – as distinct from his public utterances – were well known to Buonarroti.

"As long as I am in power," Napoleon had said only recently to his guests, seated around a lavish meal, "these dregs of society shall never again be given a chance for revolution. They know what stuff I am made of and that I shall always be ready to crush them if I find them up to any tricks."

As long as he is in power!

Then we shall see.

Such a man must not be allowed to govern.

Will not be allowed to govern.

For the revolution is not over.

It continues.

45

It continues the world over.

And will always continue while dictators live and the people are kept in subjection.

One day . . .

One day, to *us*, the Illuminati, will be the power. The power! *The power!!*

For the good of the people.

Buonarroti heard footsteps ascending the stairs. He turned and crossed to the table, where a pistol lay. He picked it up, cocked back the hammer and moved to position himself against the rear wall, behind the door. Into the room, thrust by unseen hands, stumbled the Prefect of Police for all Paris. His hands flew to his face and tore the blindfold away from his eyes, to see Buonarroti's pistol pointed at his chest. Nervously Dubois wet his lips and waited. Buonarroti pointed towards a chair pushed under a wooden table in the middle of the room. Dubois sat down heavily.

It was a square room, dim and dark. The uneven wooden floor was bare of any covering. In the corner was an unmade double bed, the blankets rumpled untidily across it, the stale smell of sleep still lingering in the air.

Buonarroti pulled back another chair and sat down to face Dubois, still pointing the pistol across the table at the prefect's heart. Feigning unconcern Dubois looked back and saw a person of no great height, dressed only in a shirt, breeches and boots. In his early forties, olive-skinned, with aquiline features, his hair was long and black and his dark, deepset eyes studied Dubois with a cool and easy authority. Without a doubt this was a man used to command.

"Now, Citizen Dubois," said Buonarroti, slowly and deliberately, "to what do I owe this visit?"

"I have information which should be of interest to you." Dubois eyed the pistol apprehensively.

Buonarroti smiled. A contemptuous smile. "The pistol is making you nervous?" He lowered the gun but kept his hand loosely on the butt. He looked straight at Dubois, the glimmer of amusement fading from his eyes. "Citizen Dubois, you intrigue me. In the hour since I was told you wanted to see me I have given much thought as to your reasons. That you have information to sell seems to be the most obvious conclusion: your position as Prefect of Police provides you with a wealth of detail which, no doubt, organisations such as ourselves may be anxious to buy—"

"I am not here to sell," interrupted Dubois. "The information is free."

"Free? The Prefect of Police for all Paris risks his life to bring information to a Jacobin terrorist! And with no thought of gain?"

"I think only of France and its security."

"Ah, I see! A patriot! And the information you hold relates to the security of France?"

"Not only its security, but its very future."

"Its future?" Buonarroti leaned forward quickly, his eyes almost hypnotic as he gazed deeply into Dubois's face. "Then, Citizen, I suggest you proceed; but let me warn you," and Buonarroti touched the gun, "the consequences will be unpleasant if your account does not ring true."

Dubois cleared his throat nervously then began, with a forced calm, to recount the details of Napoleon's invasion plans, with special emphasis on the danger to France if the plan failed. Buonarroti listened without interruption, his dark eyes fixed on Dubois's face. When, some ten minutes later, Dubois had concluded his story Buonarroti did not make any immediate reply but came to his feet and paced the room. He stopped suddenly and looked up. "Citizen, there are a number of matters which puzzle me. Not about the genuineness of Napoleon's plans – they sound typical of that betrayer of Jacobin principles. No, my problem concerns yourself, Dubois. In particular, your motive in bringing these details to me."

"I will answer all your queries."

"Then first tell me how you came by your information?"

"From the Minister of Police."

"Ah! The honourable and noble Fouché! Joseph with the skin of many colours. And how came Fouché by it? Bribery, no doubt?"

47

"No, he was told by Bonaparte himself," replied Dubois, his voice reflecting a growing confidence.

Buonarroti turned suddenly. "Tell me then, Dubois, why bring this information to the Jacobins? Our aims are the very antithesis of all that the present government stands for? Why come to us with your story?"

"Whom else should I turn to?" pleaded Dubois, hands upraised. "The generals? Then which one? Which general can I trust not to betray me to Napoleon? Their aims will be military and no doubt in line with Napoleon's. Should I turn to the Royalists? But not many years ago I fought to remove them. I come to you because it is well known that my political loyalties have always been to the Jacobin cause. We may not agree as to methods but our aims are the same. I accepted office as Prefect of Police because this is how I can best serve the *right* and *proper* France. For this same reason I come to you now and ask for your help."

Buonarroti took a moment to reply. Finally, "Let us say, Dubois, that I accept your explanation. Have you worked out a plan to stop this invasion?"

"There is only one way. Napoleon must be killed and France returned to Jacobin rule."

"But the assassination of Napoleon has been tried many times. Each attempt has failed. Why should we succeed now?"

"Because this time you will have the Prefect of Police on your side, providing you with information and help."

"Such as?" asked Buonarroti.

"With respect," answered Dubois, "I suggest that you first put my proposal to your fellow Jacobins. If they agree to it, then is the time to work out the details."

Buonarroti looked carefully at Dubois before replying. "So be it," he said; "and now, before you leave, describe to me again these invasion plans, so that I am quite clear . . ."

Dubois left under escort to be returned to the Café des Bains Chinois. Philippe-Michele Buonarroti crossed to the far wall of the garret. He opened the door to an adjoining room and called in two men. Pierre-François Réal's longish hair was now so white that it contrasted sharply with his dark coat and breeches; the second man, Pierre-Marie Desmarest, was slightly taller than Réal, with notably penetrating eyes. All three sat down at the table.

"You heard?" asked Buonarroti.

"Every word," said Réal. His voice was without emotion.

"And?"

"Dubois is Fouché's puppet. I am inclined to believe the details of Napoleon's invasion plans but I do not for one moment believe his motive in bringing them to us."

"I agree. But what does Fouché hope to gain? Surely he realises that if we collaborated to bring about Napoleon's death this must inevitably lead to our return to power?"

"Ah, Philippe," Réal answered, looking reflectively at Buonarroti, "to penetrate the mind of Joseph Fouché one must work with him day by day as I am forced to. Consider the repercussions if the Jacobins agree to kill Napoleon. We will have assassinated the 'beloved First Consul of France'! Then ask yourself, Philippe, will this not present Fouché and his army friends with the ideal opportunity to rid themselves of us once and for all? A sprinkling of money in the right places and a cry for vengeance will rise up from the streets of Paris. With one act Fouché will have removed both Napoleon and the Jacobins – leaving a clear field to further his personal ambitions. For have no doubt, Joseph Fouché's greed is bottomless. A far cry from his days of Jacobin fervour." Réal turned to Desmarest. "Do you not agree with my theory, Pierre?"

Desmarest's smile did not reach his eyes. "It would be in keeping with what we know of the man." He turned to Buonarroti. "But give me one week and I will find out. I will use only those men I have personally recruited. The slightest hint of betrayal will be brought back to me."

"If so," said Buonarroti, "then they will live to regret it."

"I ask you, Minister, I plead with you. Have done with your scheme before it's too late!" Dubois's hands were shaking.

"My good Dubois," Fouché replied, "you really must learn to control your fears. I can assure you they are unfounded."

"With respect, Minister, you were not there. This was no ordinary Jacobin. The certainty is heavy within me, they are planning something."

"Let them plan, Dubois, they can do nothing without us. They have no recognised leader."

"They have one now. This was a man of considerable authority. In fact—"

"Dubois, you are mistaken. Rest assured, the old Jacobin leaders are either deported to the Seychelles, or like Buonarroti, safe in prison on the island of Oléron. No, Dubois, your fears are groundless; any new leader, whoever he is, must be inexperienced. My scheme will continue. Let us be rid of Napoleon Bonaparte before it's too damned late."

CHAPTER 5

The coach rumbled to the brow of the hill, slowed down, and stopped to give the horses a brief respite before they took the strain of the heavy vehicle's long descent into Bristol.

Richard Machen brushed away the dust which lay thick and white across the front of his greatcoat, turned down his collar and looked through the open window. After the deafening clatter of the coach wheels, there was silence broken only by the panting of the horses and the clinking of their harness as they shuffled their hooves on the ground.

Dawn was breaking. Forward lay Bristol, covered in a thin blanket of mist which was already dissolving to uncover the city's dark mass of rooflines and spires, the tall masts of ships anchored in its port, and the broad rolling channel beyond.

Machen drew back inside. Across that channel, but half a day's journey now, lay the isolated Gower peninsula and home. Summer would soon be here, and with it Jane Ashford. He dwelt on the thought of warm, balmy days on a lonely peninsula, far away from the sound of guns and the smell of war, and the company of a beautiful young woman to share it with; what more could a man ask for?

Gregor opened his eyes and looked across at him, a half smile on his lips. The other passengers, a pompous old lady with a spoilt lapdog on her knee and a red-faced fat man, whose breath reeked of the brandy he had consumed since joining the coach at Bath, still had their eyes shut tight.

"You are still thinking of Despard?" asked Gregor, his voice kept to a whisper.

His mind still preoccupied with thoughts of Jane, Machen only half shook his head, intending to show that Despard was the last person on his mind.

"Absolutely," said Gregor, misinterpreting the motion, and still eager to remedy any residual effect of his loose tongue. "After all," his face showed deliberate contempt, "whatever his ambitions, how on earth can an unemployed Irish colonel and a handful of disgruntled soldiers possibly cause harm to a great and powerful country like England?"

Machen looked back through the window. The rolling countryside unfolded more clearly now as the dawn light increased. It looked rich, fertile, solid. Over the channel the mist had almost dispersed and on its shining surface a number of ships were already under sail, heading for the open sea.

Gregor was right, Machen readily agreed to himself. What possible harm could this impregnable land suffer from a motley band of melodramatic desperadoes. And with pleasanter thoughts on his mind, he really did not want to talk any more on the matter.

Part Two

Rousseau was my master. The dogmas of popular sovereignty inflamed my being. From then on I had the deep conviction that it was the duty of a man of means to work towards the overthrow of the social system which oppresses civilised Europe and substitute an *Order* which would conserve the dignity and happiness of all.

Till I cease to live I will ever conspire against tyrants.
                                                Philippe-Michele Buonarroti

CHAPTER 6

In France, on a lonely beach outside Calais, the keel of a rowing boat rasped against the shingle.

One of the rowers leapt into the water and held the boat steady for two men to jump on to the sands. A clink of coin and the boat turned into the waves. Slowly, to the fading splash of oars, it disappeared back into the grey mist.

Despard and Macnamara swung round, ploughed through the loose shingle, and headed towards Calais. Paris was now but 340 kilometres away, a coach journey of just under three days.

In Paris Joseph Fouché awoke, and in the light of dawn he turned and looked around the large bedroom. The air was heavy with the sound of breathing. His wife, the pious Bretonne Bonne-Jeanne, lay beside him, and beyond, his four children who, at the insistence of their doting father, slept in the same room.

Five more years and he would have sufficient wealth to enable him to retire to his estate in the country, taking his dear family with him.

But first, Napoleon Bonaparte must be removed. And those troublesome Jacobins.

His plan was proceeding well. Dubois had already established contact with the leader of the revolutionary party. And only yesterday Fouché and General Bernadotte had met for further discussions. Of necessity, much of the conversation

55

had been by inference only, but Fouché was a past master at this type of exchange, and there was no doubt that Bernadotte had been receptive to his proposals.

It would not be long now.

Once the generals were in power there would be no more foolish plans of invading England. His financial ambitions could then be realised.

Fouché nestled into the feather mattress, pulled the bedclothes about him, and closed his eyes with satisfaction.

Philippe-Michele Buonarroti opened his eyes and turned to his mistress.

Thérèse moved nearer and nestled into him. The early light of dawn crept into the room. Buonarroti moved his head to look up at the cracked ceiling. In its jagged damp-stained lines he could trace a map of France.

Out there in that country's towns and cities were the discontented masses. After years of repression it would take little to start the new revolution. The last two years had been spent effectively spreading the seed. Underground movements had been established around Paris in a band 100 miles wide, reaching to Le Havre, Dieppe and Arras in the north, to Reims and Troyes in the east, and as far as Caen and Le Mans to the west. In the south the organisation extended more than 100 miles, forming a wedge into the very heart of France, with Tours and Dijon as the western and eastern points and then sweeping down the Loire Valley and past, to the city of Lyon itself.

Six months from now – with or without Dubois's plan to assassinate Napoleon – France would be theirs.

The cracks in the mottled ceiling now took on in Buonarroti's eyes the outline of Britain, then the whole of Europe. Soon, he thought he could make out the map of the world.

The vision was inspirational, almost a sign of his predestined purpose!

To help create one vast people's republic in which all men would be equal.

*　　*　　*

56

Sunday evening, and the diligence from Calais arrived at the Paris coaching station in the Rue de Bouloi. Colonel Edward Despard and Conor Macnamara alighted and set off for the Faubourg Montmartre.

As they made their way through the narrow alleys and teeming lodging houses Macnamara absorbed the familiar scenes. It was good to be back.

On Monday Despard, after a day spent at the Ministry of War without receiving audience, returned frustrated and angry to the lodging house on the Rue Marivaux.

From his own experiences in Paris some years before, Macnamara knew there was only one antidote to the colonel's dark mood. Thus it was that the evening found the two men at the Café des Bains Chinois on the Rue Marivaux. There, in heady conversation with men of similar radical persuasion – conversation which ranged from the theoretical interpretation of Thomas Paine's *The Rights of Man* and Rousseau's *Social Contract* to the practical methods by which these views could be implemented into society – Despard forgot his frustration and fury, became mellow and, as the evening progressed, expansive.

During the discussions one of the group rose and quietly left the café, to return a short time later accompanied by a man in his early forties, olive-skinned and with distinguished features. As the debate continued the newcomer had much to contribute; in particular, his views on revolutionary military tactics were so novel that Despard kept him in conversation into the small hours of the morning long after the café had closed.

In addition Despard found the man to be a most sympathetic listener.

CHAPTER 7

In the deepening gloom of evening Buonarroti and Pierre-François Réal sat hunched in conversation on opposite sides of the bare, wooden table set in the middle of the garret apartment.

If any man knew Buonarroti well it was Réal. His companion was now six months into his forty-first year. Descended from the same family as the painter Michelangelo, also surnamed Buonarroti, he had been educated first at a Jesuit school in Florence, then as a law student at the University of Pisa; by the time he left university Buonarroti's only aim in life was, to quote his own words, "to rescue the masses from tyranny and slavery" whatever the personal risk.

When the French Revolution broke out Buonarroti made his way to Paris and immediately aligned himself with the Jacobin party. He was soon noticed by Robespierre and appointed a Member of the Military Council of the French Army in Italy and later, Agent of the French Republic in all conquered countries.

When Robespierre was brought down Buonarroti managed to avoid the guillotine. Instead he was imprisoned in Les Plessis prison, in Paris, where he met François-Noël 'Gracchus' Babeuf, the editor of a radical paper called the *Tribune of the People*. They used their time to plan armed revolution.

As soon as they were released they formed a military council of Jacobin extremists, under the generalship of Buonarroti, to

58

agree the tactics to be used on the day. But they were betrayed by a police spy named Grisel. On 10 May 1796 Buonarroti and Babeuf were arrested. They were taken, first, to the Ministry of Police for interrogation then, fearing reprisals from Jacobin militants if the trial was held in Paris, the authorities moved them to Vendôme, a provincial town in the Loire Valley.

Pierre-François Réal was chosen to defend them.

At the time of the trial Réal was thirty-nine years old. Born in Chatou, the son of a royal gamekeeper, he began practising as a lawyer in 1788, becoming a Jacobin activist shortly after. His ardour was quickly rewarded and Réal soon rose to be a man of influence in France.

At the trial Réal sat back and allowed Babeuf to condemn himself by his inflammatory and self-incriminating statements from the dock, for the authorities had been crying out for blood and Babeuf made an excellent scapegoat. As a result he was found guilty of treason and guillotined.

But with Buonarroti, Réal used a different strategy. Five of the witnesses called by the prosecution were persuaded to abscond, four others were similarly influenced not to testify, including Grisel, who had first betrayed the conspiracy. Grisel now reversed his position to state, under oath, that criminal fraud had been perpetrated, Buonarroti's name having been added to the original deposition after it had been declared and sworn. Réal's tactics paid off, Buonarroti escaped the death sentence, and was committed for life at Fort National, a prison on a barren island off Cherbourg.

Réal went back to Paris where he used his extraordinary political skills to manoeuvre for himself the position of Administrator of Police for the Department of the Seine, the top police post in Paris, next only to the Minister of Police himself. Admittedly this had given rise to rumours of strong influence being brought to bear to secure him the situation, but for someone to have made open accusation against Réal would have been an act of folly.

A month after his appointment he travelled to Cherbourg and in a private meeting with Buonarroti in prison he at last explained why such efforts had been made – and money changed hands – to save his life. The Italian's genius for revolutionary warfare, first displayed when serving with the armies of France, had been recognised by those who had secretly plotted the Revolution seven years before. Now a second revolution was being planned to wrest control of France back into their hands. It required a three-man Military Council to decide its tactics; two men had already been chosen, Buonarroti was being invited to be the third. If he accepted, his release from prison could easily be arranged.

Buonarroti accepted.

In February 1800 Réal placed a proposal on the desk of Joseph Fouché, who had recently been appointed Minister of Police. It recommended that for security reasons the political prisoner, Philippe-Michele Buonarroti, should be moved from Cherbourg to another prison on the island of Oléron, off the west coast of France. Fouché first consulted with the Head of the Sûreté, who seconded Réal's proposal, and eventually Fouché agreed.

In March 1800, under armed escort, Buonarroti left Cherbourg . . .

The apartment grew darker.

"Think of the coincidence," Buonarroti argued. "It is as though the gods had decreed it."

"I agree." Réal was emphatic. "Any English revolutionary movement must be encouraged. It has long been awaited. And even if it fails it could inspire others in that country to follow Despard's example. But why should it affect our own plans for France?"

A single candle cast a bright glow on to Buonarroti's wide, arched forehead.

"Pierre, my meeting with this Irish colonel is bound to affect our thinking. The Illuminati's aims are universal. France was chosen first because of all the countries in Europe only here were the conditions suitable for revolution. That the Supreme Council was correct was borne out by their success, but then Robespierre wrecked it all and overnight all that the Illuminati had been working towards collapsed. Now, through this Irish colonel, the lost years can be restored . . .

"Just consider the coincidences. People. Dates. Events. See how they fit into a pattern. First, there are our own plans for France, set for November. Then, through Dubois, we hear of Napoleon's plans to invade England. Again, set for November. Finally, we have the one factor to unite all these plans and divert them to our cause. Yesterday, in the Café des Bains Chinois, I hear a man tell of his plans for the revolution of England. The date set for this uprising is 23 November." Buonarroti paused to give effect to his words. "I tell you, Pierre, this coincidence of dates and events must be made to work to our advantage . . ."

Réal stood up and paced the floor. With the first finger of his right hand Buonarroti drew the numeral one in the thin coat of dust which lay on the surface of the table.

"First, our plans for France must be postponed." Buonarroti looked up at the Administrator of Police. "Instructions to that effect will be sent to all the lodges. However, they are to hold themselves in readiness for the new day, which will not be too long delayed. Meanwhile," Buonarroti drew the numeral two on the table, "on 23 November, the revolution planned by Despard will begin in London and the major cities of England. There is little chance of him succeeding, but his uprising will at least provide a diversion for Napoleon's invasion; for a while the defence of the south coast will be forgotten. Thus, while their backs are turned," and slowly the revolutionary traced the third numeral in the dust, "Napoleon's forces will be able to land unopposed. A day to establish a beachhead and then the short march on London. Within three weeks England will be under French control."

Buonarroti looked at his companion's face to study the effect his words had had. Réal's eyes gave no indication that he was being swayed by the force of Buonarroti's argument.

"Then?" he asked.

Buonarroti's hand flashed across the surface of the table, sweeping a wide passage through the dust and obliterating the three Roman numerals.

"Napoleon will return to France to seek the adulation he so craves. Instead, he will be greeted by the second French Revolution and his own assassination. The Illuminati will then take over the government of France. Our occupation army in England will give us control of that country and once we have gained the support of the English working classes, no nation on earth will be able to stand against us. Think of it, Pierre: all our aims achieved within our lifetimes . . . not after our deaths."

The room was plunged into silence as the ambition of Buonarroti's plan overwhelmed both men.

"Philippe," said Réal, "your proposals go so far beyond the bounds of reason that my first reaction is to dismiss them out of hand. And yet – the audacity of the plan! Perhaps it *might* work . . ."

"It *will* work," Buonarroti insisted, "but only if we can find a way to influence the date of Napoleon's invasion. It *must* take place on the days following Despard's uprising."

"And as the First Consul and the Illuminati are hardly on intimate terms that would seem to nullify further discussion," Réal said drily. "But first, tell me, why is Despard in Paris?"

"He seeks financial backing for his revolution and hopes to obtain it from the government of France."

"Is he aware of your identity?"

"Identity? But Pierre, I am a prisoner on the Island of Oléron! Surely as Administrator of Police you know that!"

Pierre-François Réal smiled, for he knew that the threat of retribution conveyed infinitely more dread if it were made not only against the individual concerned, but also against his family. Such a threat, supplemented by generous bribes, had been made to ensure the co-operation of the guards chosen to convey Buonarroti to his new prison. On the way to Oléron an ardent Illuminati had been substituted for Buonarroti, a man who bore him a remarkable resemblance and was prepared to await the coming revolution to be released from prison.

The Administrator of Police returned to his question. "Then how does Despard regard you?"

"As a Jacobin sympathiser, understanding his cause."

"And you told him nothing of the Illuminati or their plans?"

"Nothing."

"All to the good," said Réal, "for secrecy and security walk hand in hand." He paused, thoughtfully. "So, Despard looks to France for financial support? We must ensure he obtains it—"

Buonarroti interrupted. "But what of Fouché?"

Réal sat down. "Yes, Philippe, I had not forgotten *Citizen* Fouché! The man is quite definitely planning something. Desmarest had him followed. Twice last week he had secret meetings with Bernadotte. I'm certain they are part of a conspiracy to remove Napoleon and lay the blame at the feet of the Jacobins. If we are to pursue this plan of yours they must be prevented. Without Napoleon there will be no invasion. And no invasion means no more plan."

Réal looked carefully at his revolutionary friend. "But the crux of the matter is the *date* of the invasion. If Despard's revolution is planned for the 23 November the invasion must *not* take place before then. Somehow this must be conveyed to Napoleon, and in such a way that the question of Fouché and the generals, and the finance for Despard, can be solved at the same time."

Réal smiled. "It is at moments like these," he said, "that one appreciates the benefits of being in high office. Two reports from the Sûreté should solve all these problems." He paused as he heard the sound of footsteps ascending the stairs. The door of the apartment opened and both Buonarroti and Réal turned to greet Pierre-Marie Desmarest, Head of France's Sûreté Générale, and the third member of the Illuminati's Military Council.

WEDNESDAY, 12 MAY 1802

Pierre-Marie Desmarest, Head of the Sûreté Générale, France's Secret Police, was thirty-eight years old, from an old bourgeois family. Originally ordained as a priest in 1789, he joined the French Revolutionary Army and was promoted to the rank of sergeant-major during the war against Austria. On his return to Paris, he was elected President of the Society of Friends of Liberté and Égalité. A versatile, clever man, gifted with an excellent memory and a penetrating observation of people, he was recommended to Réal, by then Administrator of Police. The two men immediately discovered that they shared a political affinity. Thus when Fouché was appointed Minister of Police in August 1799 and began his reorganisation, Réal proposed Desmarest as Head of the Sûreté Générale and Secret Police, which was confirmed two months later. It was during Desmarest's period of office that the files of the Sûreté were built up to include detailed reports on everyone of the slightest importance in France.

On the morning of Wednesday, 12 May, Desmarest sat at his desk overlooking the Quai Malaquais. Around him the walls of the large room were covered from floor to ceiling by dark, wooden shelves, each shelf weighed down by hundreds of files, rows of brown folders tied with black ribbon. Despite the mid-morning heat of an early summer's day the room's only window was closed.

Desmarest was reading an interrogation report from the Temple prison when he was interrupted by his second in command, a sly, apparently obsequious man named Pâques.

In his hand Pâques held some papers. He approached the desk with a certain trepidation for his superior was not a person who tolerated being disturbed at important work. He coughed discreetly and with a frown Desmarest looked up.

"Your pardon, Monsieur. I regret having to disturb you but these two reports arrived but a moment ago. Attached is a communication recommending that they should be acted upon immediately."

Without making any reply Desmarest stretched out his right hand, took the proffered documents, read them in silence, then looked across at the clock on the mantelpiece.

"Is the Minister available?"

"I believe so, Monsieur Desmarest."

The Head of the Sûreté fell silent, tapping his fingers lightly against the desk top as he pretended to consider his next action. With a sudden movement he rose to his feet, picked the reports up from the desk, and walked briskly out of the room.

Desmarest realised that the first report was greatly affecting the Minister. The knuckles of Fouché's hands grew whiter as he tightened his grip on the papers. At least two minutes passed before he spoke:

"The first report, Monsieur Desmarest? Does it give all the names or are there others to follow?"

The three conspirators had fully discussed the question of whether to betray Fouché's involvement. On reflection – especially taking into consideration that a new Minister of Police would probably appoint his own supporters around him and dismiss both Réal and Desmarest – it had been felt prudent to have Fouché remain in office . . .

Desmarest therefore replied, "No, Minister, as I understand it, no one else is involved."

Fouché turned and looked into the room. "Have you confirmed the details of this report?"

"Not yet, Minister, but there can be little doubt. As you can see, the information is quite detailed. Dates. Times. Names. And previous reports from this agent have proved to be most accurate."

The Minister was swift to reply this time:

"Monsieur Desmarest, in our profession we must be certain. I have no desire to trouble the First Consul without just cause. Therefore, until the facts have been verified I think this report should be withheld."

"With respect, Minister," Desmarest's voice was cold and insistent, "the question of evidence is for the First Consul to decide. Our instructions are to convey all suspicions to him in our daily reports. For myself there can be no question of withholding this information. It must be included in tomorrow's despatches to the Palace."

THURSDAY, 13 MAY 1802

It was a nervous Minister of Police who was ushered into Bonaparte's presence the next day. As he had feared, the two reports lay on the desk.

"Monsieur le Premier Consul—" Fouché's formal greeting was cut short as Napoleon came right up to him and thrust the papers into his face, scratching his skin.

"Well, Fouché, well?" The First Consul's voice was pitched

high with intensity, the eyes gazed hypnotically at the Minister. "Did I not say they were plotting against me? Bernadotte, Decaen, Lannes, Brune. At last, through the vigilance of Monsieur Desmarest, we have the proof. Now we can act against them."

Fouché drew his face away. "The evidence has not been verified, General," he was quick to reply. "There could be a logical explanation for these meetings. Army matters, for example. I am of the opinion that the Sûreté should be given time to confirm."

An immediate look of suspicion came into Napoleon's eyes.

"Fouché," the deliberate, soft tones which the First Consul now used held a distinct threat. "Why should you, my Minister of Police, choose to defend traitors rather than confirm a report from one of your own Departments? Why should that be, eh, Monsieur Fouché?" and Napoleon thrust his face close up to the Minister's.

Fouché replied, almost too hastily, "General, you know only too well that my loyalty is to you."

Napoleon glared at Fouché, his eyelids unflickering, the look unbroken. The First Consul of France had no doubt of the Minister's complicity. But at this moment Fouché's talents were much needed. The scheme for trade consul spies to be sent to England was already being implemented. The men were all chosen, briefed, and sworn to silence. In a few days' time they would be ready to travel. But for the plan to succeed it would require Fouché's genius for administration. Furthermore Fouché already knew too much of the invasion plans, and with the new English ambassador shortly to arrive in Paris it would be dangerous to have Fouché as an enemy. Napoleon knew he had no choice but to pretend to believe in the Minister's loyalty. Nevertheless, the man must be taught a lesson:

"Then I invite you to prove it, Monsieur Fouché," he said, in an even more whispered, almost sinister tone.

"My General, you have only to ask."

Napoleon's smile was extremely hard-edged:

"The generals, Monsieur Fouché, those who have been plotting against me, I wish them dismissed. As Minister of

Police the responsibility for effecting this order is yours. See to it . . . personally!"

The First Consul's face gloated as he stepped back and deliberately allowed the silence to emphasise his triumph over the Minister of Police. Fouché said nothing, and a long moment passed before Napoleon referred to the next document, in his left hand.

"Now, as to the second of the reports from Monsieur Desmarest, the one on this Irish colonel, Despard . . . ?" Napoleon's voice was normal again.

"Yes, General?" Fouché's voice was compliantly subdued.

"It would appear that the man has a burning zeal to create revolution in England and is in Paris to seek financial aid." Napoleon's gaze on Fouché was narrow and watchful. "See that he obtains it, Fouché. His plans could be a considerable help to my invasion."

Napoleon jabbed at the report with the first finger of his right hand. "We are set for November. Despard's revolution, the twenty-third of that month. The conclusion is obvious. If our assault forces are held back until after that date . . ."

Fouché was relieved by this shift in the conversation. "General, that is a stroke of genius! The invasion cannot fail. Is Colonel Despard to be told of your plans?"

"Of course not, Fouché." Bonaparte's voice held a note of exasperation. "The less this military novice knows the better."

Fouché was emboldened enough to continue his pretence. "Surely, General, hardly a novice. The man's plans appear to be well thought out."

"Nonsense, Fouché!" Napoleon's voice was contemptuous. "Why, take his plans to assassinate the King of England. The whole thing is almost . . . symbolic. The end of the Monarchy, the beginning of the Republic. Now a true strategist would realise that there are other English leaders whose deaths would be of much more value . . ." Napoleon suddenly paused in mid-sentence, crossed to his desk and abruptly sat down. For some minutes he remained there, motionless, then he looked up at the Minister of Police.

"Fouché," he said, his eyes feverish with excitement, "that

could be the culmination of my plan. Imagine it. Addington, their Prime Minister. The English Cabinet. His advisers from the War Office and the Admiralty. William Pitt. Members of Parliament. Generals. Admirals. The execution of such men would leave Britain leaderless; and with Despard's revolution taking place at the same time, why, the success of my invasion would be assured . . ." Napoleon Bonaparte paused to contemplate the vision.

Fouché almost shouted his objection. "But, General, it would be impossible to carry out such a——"

"You forget," Napoleon sprang from his chair and brought the reports around the desk to brandish them before Fouché's eyes. "The date Despard has chosen for his revolution is the day of their ceremonial opening of Parliament. All these men will be at the ceremony. A perfect situation for any assassination plan."

"General! Consider the repercussions . . . !"

Napoleon turned his fixed gaze on the Minister. "You still do not appear to share my vision, Fouché. So as of this moment, this extension of my plan will be Monsieur Desmarest's responsibility. As a reward for his vigilance he is now empowered to conduct the negotiations with this Despard. The Colonel is to be given all that he needs. Money. Arms. Men, if needs be. But only on this condition: he *must* adopt my assassination plan as being essential to the success of his revolution . . ." Napoleon laughed . . . "temporary though it will be."

Bonaparte walked over to the desk. With his back still to Fouché, he said, "Give my gratitude to Monsieur Desmarest. Two excellent reports."

Suddenly he half turned. "Oh, Fouché . . . now that he is back on shore, Nelson should be among those present at Westminster. Instruct Desmarest to add the creature's name to the list. It will add greatly to my pleasure to know we will soon be avenged for the defeat he inflicted on us at the Nile." And with a dismissive gesture of his right hand Napoleon brought the meeting to an end.

*   *   *

Bernadotte's Chief of Staff and many of his minor officers were arrested and imprisoned without trial. His regiment was shipped across the Atlantic to Santo Domingo. Bernadotte himself was saved from banishment only through the intervention of his wife, Désirée, who had once been betrothed to Napoleon.

General Decaen was sent to the colonies. General Lannes to Lisbon, Brune to Constantinople.

The lesson was not lost on Fouché. From that day Napoleon's plan to send military and naval spies to Britain in the guise of trade consuls received his undivided attention.

CHAPTER 8

As he rode north out of Paris Buonarroti pulled his coat tight around him; but the rain lashed in even under the broad brim of his hat and inside his collar. Before long he was wet through.

It was back in Florence, in 1786, when he joined the freemasonry movement, that Buonarroti had first heard the rumour being whispered among his brother masons of a secret, select, worldwide society operating within the movement; membership of it was apparently restricted to men in authority who first of all were freemasons, and secondly who subscribed – no, more than subscribed, were dedicated – to the republican ideal of world government.

It was said that the original, worldwide movement had once included the American politician Thomas Jefferson who, as American Ambassador to France, had actively helped Robespierre draft his Declaration of the Rights of Man.

But in 1776 when Jefferson composed the American Declaration of Independence, he acknowledged the authority of God and thereby alienated the leaders of the European Illuminati – in particular Adam Weishaupt, then a Professor of Canon Law at the University of Munich, who took the exact opposite stand. "This pretended religion of Christ," he protested, "is nothing else than the work of priests, of imposture and of tyranny, being founded on lying, error, chimera and imposture. I intend to deliver, one day, the human race from all religion."

At a meeting in Ingoldstadt, in Bavaria, Weishaupt was

appointed Head of the European Illuminati, and given five years to devise a plan whereby their form of republicanism could be brought about in all the countries of Europe.

Exactly five years later, in 1781, Weishaupt called his second conference, this time in Wilhelmsbad, also in Bavaria, to put his proposals before them.

First: The aim of the Illuminati was to transform not only Europe but the whole world into one vast, people's republic in which all forms of religion would be banned.

Second: The implementation of that aim should start in Europe.

Third: The method of takeover would be by organised revolution. An Illuminati Inner Council would be co-opted and sworn-in in all European countries. Each Council would be given the responsibility of orchestrating dissension amongst the people of its country. After the success of the planned revolution the Council would take over the government.

Fourth: Final authority over the Inner Councils and over the whole movement was to be vested in a seven-man Supreme Council, called the Areopagus, meaning 'a council whose judgments are without question'.

The conference having passed these proposals unanimously, Weishaupt continued to explain his plan.

Like most bold schemes it was basically very simple. Without the knowledge of most of its members, Weishaupt proposed taking control of the freemasonry movement. As he informed the Wilhelmsbad conference, it had the three essentials required.

First, the movement was long established.

Second, it was worldwide.

Third, it was a closed body.

This proposal was also unanimously accepted.

In effect the Illuminati would become a secret society working within freemasonry, using the movement to their political advantage: first to recruit men of like mind, second to place Illuminati members in positions of responsibility throughout each country, ready to take over when the day of revolution came.

According to Weishaupt, if this plan was implemented, then

71

the whole of Europe could be in Illuminati hands within fifteen or twenty years.

One of the French Illuminati, a twenty-three-year-old advocate named Maximilien Marie Isidore de Robespierre, proposed that France should be the first country chosen. The detailed plans were agreed, and eight years later the Revolution took place.

But, because the French Chapter had not first established administrative control over France they did not immediately achieve ascendency, and it was only through the instigation of his Reign of Terror that Robespierre – under the Jacobin mantle – eventually came to power. He was not elected President of the Convention until June 1794.

It was then that he committed his fatal error.

For Robespierre, when he was recruited into the ranks of the Illuminati, was already a freemason, and secretly subscribed to the freemasonry doctrine of the Supreme Being, in violation of Weishaupt's directive given at the Wilhelmsbad conference.

Four days after being elected President, Robespierre asked the French Assembly to accept the Cult of the Supreme Being as the new civic religion of France.

From that moment on Robespierre became an object of ridicule and his political enemies were thus able to secure not only his downfall, but the downfall also of most of the Jacobin leaders. Less than two months later he went to the guillotine, taking Saint-Just and many of the French Illuminati with him. And the Illuminatis had been forced to start their plan to control Europe all over again . . .

In accordance with the Illuminati's rule, Buonarroti did not reach the château until it was dark. The servitor led him into the Black Room and within minutes the Illuminati's seven-man Supreme Council filed in, dressed, as always, in black habits, their faces permanently hidden by their cowls. They took up their places before the long oblong table draped in black.

The one in the centre – Buonarroti knew him to be Adam Weishaupt, although that fact was never openly acknowledged

– raised his right arm. His fellow Council members followed suit, and the opening ritual began:

> Brothers, we are witnesses to the signs of the Illuminati, by which name are the Enlightened Ones known.
>
> To the one Cause, we of the Areopagus, the Illuminati's Supreme and High Council, dedicate ourselves.
>
> The triangle is three. The world is three. Earth, sea and air.
>
> The square is four. The world is four. North, south, east and west.
>
> The triangle and the square together are seven. The world is seven. This is the number of its continents and seas.
>
> The triangle is three. Man is three. Body, mind and free spirit. In this present world all three are kept in subjection by the evil lies of the Church which through a crucified Jew has ever sought to impose its blasphemies. By this the Church shows itself to be at enmity with the true nature of man and must be destroyed.
>
> The square is four. Man's desired freedoms are four. Freedom from want, freedom from fear, freedom from kings, freedom from existing governments. In this present world all four are kept in subjection by the evil oppressions of autocratic regimens and aristocracies. By this they show themselves to be at enmity with the true estate of man and must be removed . . .

The ceremony continued, finally drawing to its conclusion by their repetition of the Illuminati oath:

> *I honour the sword. It is a quick and essential medium of removing from earth those who oppose the truth and those who try to take it from our hands.*
>
> *Always I shall reveal to the Illuminati all that I have heard or found out, and I shall seek out and observe things which might otherwise escape me.*
>
> *Together we stand.*
> *Ourselves Alone.*
> *To the fulfilment of our Cause.*
> *Liberty! . . . Equality! . . . Fraternity!*

The seven men sat down. The spokesman lifted his cowled head and addressed Buonarroti. "You are alone?"

73

"Yes."

"Proceed."

Speaking in brief but weighty sentences Buonarroti told of all that had happened over the past week . . .

Of Dubois and his proposal for Napoleon's assassination.

Of Napoleon's plans to invade England.

Of Colonel Despard's intended revolution in that same country.

Then taking pains not to exclude a single detail, Buonarroti carefully explained his proposal that the second revolution of France should be postponed, in order that the plan of the Illuminati might be extended to include also Britain, a country in which their movement was already well established.

The Supreme Council approved Buonarroti's plan. The following day the names of the French trade consuls, as provided by Desmarest, were forwarded to their Inner Council in England, with the request that any information which could assist Napoleon's invasion plans should be passed on direct to his spies.

PART THREE

'Tis all a Chequer-board of Nights and Days
Where Destiny with Men for Pieces plays:
Hither and Thither moves, and mates, and slays,
And one by one back in the Closet lays.
Edward Fitzgerald, *The Rubaiyat of Omar Khayyám*

CHAPTER 9

The cottage stood defiant against the sea at the edge of the
lonely headland, where the sands met the flat-lying rocks. A
long grey, limestone-walled dwelling, its low roof-line ended
in a wide stone chimney which rose up out of its side wall.
Surrounding the cottage was a large, stone-walled, stone-
flagged quay which jutted out 100 feet or so towards the sea.
The front wall of the dwelling, with its central, sea-bleached,
wooden door and two small-paned windows to either side,
faced inwards towards the sanded sweep of Port Eynon Bay.
Across the far waters a headland rose sharply out of the sea and
moved inland, forming a horseshoe of low hills and falling back
into the sea again to the rear of the cottage, where it met the
sheer cliffs at the southern tip of Port Eynon Head. Between
the Head and the cottage lay a flatland of rough grass and
ferns.

It was early evening. Machen and Gregor were standing at
the very edge of the quay, looking out to sea. The turning high
tide lapped against the stone walls some distance below their
feet. Behind them the sun slowly settled, silhouetting the
mansion of Culver Hall which stood near to the cliff-edge, with
its wide view of the Bristol Channel and the ocean beyond.

Out on the waters the white sails of Sir John Lucas's
schooner, *Conjurer*, filled out as they caught the stronger
mid-channel breeze outside the bay. Machen and Gregor
continued to watch as the vessel – carrying Lucas to visit his
estates in Ireland – sailed towards the blue-grey evening haze

which curtained the horizon. Gregor eventually turned to Machen.

"That," he said with a regretful sigh, "marks the end of a busy, but pleasant, two weeks. I am grateful to you for your gracious hospitality. Such proximity to Sir John enabled our business to be swiftly concluded, much to everyone's satisfaction."

"Why not stay a day longer?" Machen felt obliged to suggest as they turned to walk back across the quay towards the cottage.

"Alas, my negotiations are complete, the contracts have been signed, and I have no excuse to send to the Admiralty to justify an extended stay." Gregor gave a wry smile. "No, Mr Machen, tomorrow I must regretfully start my journey back to the noise and bustle of London."

"The loss is mine," Machen responded politely. "Still, the fact that your Admiralty negotiations turned out to be with Sir John, at least enabled our brief acquaintanceship to continue. And no doubt you will be back for further talks twelve months from now?"

"Even sooner, if this peace with France turns out to be as precarious as I suspect."

A stone seat extended out of the cottage wall. The two men sat down. Gregor turned to Machen. "Tell me, Mr Machen, how did the Lucases come to their present position and fortune?"

Machen's left arm swept the channel. "As with most things on Gower, it began with the sea," he replied. "The first John Lucas, who started it all, lived during the reign of King Henry VIII. He was a privateer and apparently in league with the King himself, for half his plunder went to Henry, leaving Lucas and his men to share the rest. His ventures became so profitable that here, on the very site of this cottage, he built a stronghold which he named Salthouse, because at high tide the sea reached half way up the walls. For years, Lucas controlled all the smuggler gangs which operated out of the Gower coast, sharing his profits with the poor of the area until he was revered by them like some sort of Robin Hood. It is always said locally that he built Salthouse at this point because he discovered a natural cave which led underground from the cliffs below

Culver Hall and emerged at the point on which this cottage now stands—"

"Why was Salthouse pulled down?" Gregor interrupted.

"It was destroyed in the Great Storm of 1703."

"But the ventures of this first smuggler baron created the vast Lucas interests?" asked Gregor curiously.

"Yes, all of them," replied Machen. "Their plantations in the West Indies; the Swansea copper works with which you have negotiated the supply of bolts and sheathing for the Navy; and their shipping fleets. All built on so-called illegal profits."

"So-called! Such words are indictable!" Gregor laughed.

"Not to the Lucases. To them, smuggling was a way of life: a legal industry. To their way of thinking it was the government which was in the wrong, not they."

"No wonder," said Gregor thoughtfully, "the present Sir John was such a hard negotiator."

"In such matters I imagine he could be. But to me, as a child, he was always kind and gentle. My mother died when I was born, and my father – who was captain of one of Lucas's merchantmen – had already died some months previously. I was brought up by my grandparents, and I remember my grandfather telling me one day that some illness had prevented Lucas from ever having children. Maybe the desire for a son had something to do with his interest in me, but, whatever the reason, he ensured that I wanted for nothing, sent me away to school at the age of nine, and secured my appointment as a midshipman." Machen reflected for a brief moment. "Yes, I have much to thank Sir John for."

Beyond the horizon, where the waters of the Bristol Channel met the rollers of the cold Atlantic, and out of sight of the watchers on the shore, Sir John Lucas ordered his crew to alter *Conjurer*'s course. Its new passage would take it around the protruding tip of Cornwall and towards the north-western corner of France.

The darkness crept over the still waters of the bay. Inside the cottage the only light came from the dying fire as Machen rose from the wooden settle in order to escape to bed.

"To continue our discussions of the last few days," Gregor persisted, remaining seated, and disregarding Machen's obvious lack of interest:

"A great change is coming over this country of ours. Imprisoned on your floating wooden island as you have been these past years, you will know little of how Britain is changing, with industry taking over from agriculture as the main employer of labour. Men, women, whole families even, are moving from the country to the cities in search of work, with the result that the populations of our major cities are rising by leaps and bounds. The result is unemployment, low wages, food shortages and such terrible living conditions that I would not be surprised to hear of even further rioting . . ."

"Rioting?" Machen felt obliged to ask.

"Last year and the year before. Mostly food riots but the government must heed the signs. For while our friend Despard merely talks about his ambitions, other more determined men have already been using these problems to foster discontent for their own political purposes."

"There have always been riots." Machen sought to conclude the conversation, bored with Gregor's constant talk of revolution. "When I was a child my history lessons were littered with them. But they were rarely premeditated – the riots, I mean."

"Ah, but today's movements are better organised. Thankfully they appear to be localising their activities, but heaven help us if they ever combined into one national movement." Gregor took from his pocket a creased folded paper which he handed to Machen. "Let me show you an example."

It was a handbill, with a bold heading, which Gregor read out:

FELLOW COUNTRYMEN

How long will ye quietly and cowardly suffer yourselves to be imposed upon, and half-starved by a set of mercenary slaves and Government hirelings?

80

Can you still suffer
them to proceed in their
extensive monopolies,
while your children are
crying for bread? No! Let
them exist not a day
longer. We are the
sovereignty, rise then
from your lethargy. Be at
the Corn Market on
Monday.

"A strange document to be carrying on your person,
Mr Gregor?" said Machen reflectively, despite his previous
indifference.

"As you will have realised by now, I find such matters of
great interest. I have other similar examples amongst my
papers. This particular one related to a meeting a year last
September in London's Corn Market."

"What happened?"

"For six days there were disturbances in the Market.
Eventually the military had to be sent for. Unfortunately that
did not stop it, for less than a month later similar handbills were
being distributed calling for a meeting on Kennington
Common. Again the military had to be summoned."

"Then the troubles are confined to London?" Machen
commented in a tone which suggested that Gregor was making
much of a small issue.

"On the contrary." Gregor protested, 'During the same
period reports came into the Home Office showing the unrest
to be widespread. The worst trouble spots were in Notting-
ham, Lancashire and the West Riding of Yorkshire. There
were rumours of people arming themselves with weapons and
enrolling in secret societies – even taking oaths of confederacy.
The United Englishmen, the United Britons, the United
Irishmen, the Black Lamp, the Friends of Liberty, the English
Jacobins: the names of these movements came to the knowledge of the authorities and finally the House of Commons
appointed a Committee of Secrecy to enquire into them. Their
findings were sufficiently serious for the government to

re-enact the Seditious Meetings Act, banning all gatherings which could in any way be regarded as being of a rebellious nature. That was in April 1801 – only last year."

Machen picked up a poker and prodded out the fire.

"Relax, Mr Gregor; time to worry if these movements ever joined up!"

"But that is my one great fear," replied Gregor. "If just one of these organisations was able to extend its activities and connect with the other bodies to make one united movement . . ." Gregor paused, his abrupt silence giving effect to his misgivings.

"Perhaps my years at sea have set me apart," said Machen, moving towards his bedroom, "but somehow I cannot see this country as a republic, with heads rolling from the guillotine. I would gamble that Britain, its monarchy, and its method of government, will continue for many years yet to come."

"On such unbounded optimism," said Gregor resignedly, taking the hint and rising from his chair, "I will follow your example, I have a long journey before me on the morrow. But Mr Machen take it from me," he said with final emphasis, making it sound almost like a threat, "one day you will remember all these things I have been saying."

MONDAY, 24 MAY 1802: ROSCOFF, FRANCE

The evening was drawing to a close as the *Conjurer* entered the channel which would carry it into the port of Roscoff. This small fishing port on the Brest peninsula, on the north-west corner of France, was approached by two channels, neither of which was simple to negotiate. But Sir John Lucas had sailed these waters for many years. Even so, in the approaches, the tide streams ran transversely across the schooner's bow and demanded all of his concentration. He eased the boat into the channel known as the Passe de Benven, where the ebb stream began about an hour and a half before high water and for which the final marker was the square grey tower on the south side of the harbour.

Before him, to both sides of Roscoff, lay a flat, windswept

countryside, with few trees and very little shelter, a land open to the sea winds and dangerous later in the year.

But long before the coming of autumn, thought Lucas, he would be gone.

CHAPTER 10

Conor Macnamara woke in the dingy lodging-house room. He closed his eyes again and reflected on the meetings of the previous week between Despard, himself and Desmarest at the offices of the Sûreté. So anxious had the Frenchman been to accede to Despard's request for finance and arms that yesterday the colonel, well satisfied, had been able to start back for London.

Meanwhile Conor was remaining in Paris to discuss the shipments of arms – dates, times and landing points – and also to plan the attack on Westminster, a condition which Desmarest had insisted upon as part of the negotiations.

As Macnamara lay there his thoughts drifted back to the small monastery school in Dublin and the gnarled old Jesuit priest who had brought Irish history to life for him, as he recounted to his charges the injustices which their country had suffered over the years at the hands of the English.

Young Conor – the second son of an Irish solicitor – had absorbed every word . . . about the dark days when Cromwell had come with 10,000 trained soldiers to the land of kings and princesses, warriors and bards, and within months had subjugated it . . . and when the priest told of Drogheda, where Cromwell's army came upon a church full of women and children and burned it down to the ground, young Conor's anger had known no bounds . . . Years later, in 1688, had come the revolution, when the Irish rose as a man, in an uprising such as had never been seen before, and carrying all before them drove the English nearly into the sea, before William III – God curse him to Hell! – brought the glory to an end by winning the Battle of the Boyne. Since then the pattern of Ireland had been woven by the English into enormous estates given to absentee landlords, men with so little interest in the country of their inheritance that many had not even seen their lands.

From then on there had been no need for history lessons: Conor and his elder brother John had joined the revolutionary movement, the United Irishmen, as it was formed, eleven years ago in 1791. From the beginning, Conor possessed a brand of dedicated ruthlessness which enabled him to regard all English life merely from the point of view of whether or not it was an obstacle to Irish liberation. When called upon by the movement, Conor never hesitated to put his convictions into practice and in only a few years he had risen to some prominence as a trusted lieutenant of its leader, Wolfe Tone. When, in 1796, Tone journeyed to France to raise support from the French government for his planned revolution, Conor had travelled with him.

Four years ago, in 1798, when Conor was thirty, the revolution had taken place. Led by Conor and men like him the Irish of Wicklow and Wexford had risen with a fervour which could be compared only to religious fanaticism, until their English oppressors had quenched the uprising in blood at the appropriately named Vinegar Hill.

Wolfe Tone had been captured. To avoid being questioned by the English he cut his own throat. Conor and his men had dispersed to fight underground. When Colonel Despard came recruiting to Ireland, Conor and his brother had joined him. And now the French had extended Despard's plans to include an attack on Westminster, on the very day of the Opening of Parliament when most of England's leaders would be there. Desmarest had even provided the list.

Conor Macnamara looked up at the ceiling and vowed. For Drogheda, for all the countless injustices which Ireland has suffered. *Vengeance is mine. I will repay . . . !*

*   *   *

"Only one thing remains to make it feasible," Desmarest stated.

"That is?" questioned Fouché. It was early morning and the Minister of Police had summoned Desmarest to his apartment to discuss the progress of Napoleon's latest plans.

"A permanent base, Monsieur, somewhere for Despard to store all the arms we have agreed to supply him. And from where they can be distributed with the minimum risk of discovery. Of necessity it must be secluded. You will remember, Monsieur, that when the Great Revolution first broke out we received a flood of support from all over Europe, and among them were many from England, from men of backgrounds as diverse as their poet, Wordsworth, and the politician Charles Fox. All those letters were kept and filed away. Among them will be many from men sympathetic to a revolutionary cause like Despard's."

There was silence as Fouché considered Desmarest's proposal. "I pray you are successful in your search, Monsieur Desmarest. Let me know the outcome."

Pâques entered Desmarest's room and placed two files on the table. Desmarest looked up questioningly.

"The indexes you asked for, Monsieur," Pâques explained.

With a flick of his right hand Desmarest dismissed his subordinate. He reached for the top index, headed "British Sympathisers", opened the file and began to read the pages of handwritten notes. One of the entries suddenly took his interest. He stood up and walked slowly along the walls of shelves, his eyes searching the files. He stopped, reached up, took down a file and opened it, read the first two pages, then went back to his table and, placing the file upon it, returned to the main index. After two hours of intense concentration five files reposed on the table for further, detailed perusal.

The Head of the Sûreté now picked up the second index; its title was "British Trade Connections". An hour passed, during which time another three files had been removed from his shelves to add to those already on the table.

Desmarest now pulled the eight personal files towards him,

opened the first and began to read again. It took him another hour to read them all, during which time five of the eight had been rejected and returned to the shelves.

Three files now remained on Desmarest's table.

He took more care over this second reading, poring over the pages, taking notes, and referring to a map he drew from the right-hand drawer of his table.

Suddenly he picked up the file headed, "British Trade Connection – Lucas", and looked at his pocket watch. It was three o'clock in the afternoon. Fouché would be in his office. Desmarest rose and left his room.

He placed the file in front of Fouché. "I've found it. The ideal hiding place," he announced. "A large, isolated estate, convenient for both France and Ireland, with miles of its own coastline, perfect for the shipment and storage of arms. It answers all the requirements."

Fouché opened the file and began to study the details. Desmarest continued. "The estate is situated on a small peninsula called Gower, on the south coast of Wales." He hesitated. "There is, unfortunately, one problem."

Fouché looked up.

"The owner, Sir John Lucas, is far removed from being a potential revolutionary. However, from our information, it would appear that he is open to persuasion."

"Persuasion?" Fouché questioned. "You mean bribery?"

"No," replied Desmarest slowly, "threat." Desmarest gave a thin-lipped smile. "In many ways, this could be preferable to involving a sympathiser. There would be no need to confide in the man, merely enforce his co-operation."

"And how is this to be done?" asked Fouché, with little enthusiasm.

Desmarest dropped his voice to a half whisper, almost conspiratorial in tone. "Tell him that unless he agrees to collaborate," Desmarest raised his right hand and pointed his thin right-index finger at the file, "most of the documents on this file will be sent to his government. Minister, there is enough evidence here for the British courts to condemn him without question. If Lucas values his freedom he is unlikely to refuse."

Fouché returned to the papers. "Exactly what is he guilty of?"

"Smuggling." Desmarest answered in a brief word.

"But in England smuggling is not regarded as a serious offence," Fouché objected. "And the man probably has friends in high places with influence to enable him to refute the charge."

"With respect, Minister," replied Desmarest, "the man's smuggling activities are conducted through the port of Roscoff. And the evidence proves that it continued throughout the war. A clear case of fraternisation with the enemy, as I think you will agree."

Fouché's air of puzzlement faded, to be replaced by a look of resigned comprehension. He read the documents with a reluctant interest, and conceded, "As you say, the man probably has no choice but to agree."

Fouché knew this, for it was he who had first conceived the scheme. Throughout the recently ended war the French government had allowed the fishing village of Roscoff to remain an open port. Its main activity was its regular trade with British smugglers. However, unknown to the smugglers, the contraband sold at Roscoff was not supplied by local traders but by the French government itself. The income derived from such sales was used by the French authorities to supplement the wages of their armed forces, in particular the wages of the invasion corps garrisoned on France's northern coast, that known by the title "The Army of England". That Lucas's money had been used for this purpose would not read too well in an English courtroom.

"Furthermore," said Desmarest as Fouché continued to read, "if he considers prison more agreeable than co-operation, he has a wife whose life we can threaten. Once he hears of the many slow and painful methods we have perfected, he will soon agree to our demands."

Fouché looked up. "Despard's demands," he corrected. "Take especial care, Monsieur Desmarest. The peace with England demands that France cannot show herself to be openly involved." Fouché paused. "I assume the next thing is for Colonel Despard's lieutenant, this . . . ?"

88

"Macnamara," said Desmarest.

". . . this Macnamara to go to Wales, meet Lucas and – persuade him to agree."

"Yes, Monsieur, except that there will be no need for Macnamara to travel abroad. At this time of the year Lucas can be found in Roscoff, buying and organising his supplies for the coming year. Macnamara will be there in fewer than three days."

FRIDAY, 28 MAY 1802: PARIS

Desmarest continued to study the Irishman, taking in the pale determined face of a man who would afford his enemies no compromise, and above all his cold slate-blue eyes. The implementation of Napoleon's plans, the assault on the British Houses of Parliament, and the assassinations of the country's leaders, could not be in better hands. Macnamara's cold-blooded desire for revenge ensured the plan's success.

"What if Lucas refuses?" asked Macnamara.

"It is hardly likely," Desmarest replied, "but if he does, you need only remind him that he is on French soil, where a fatal accident could so easily befall him. And in addition you can assure him that his wife will still die."

"What about servants? Neighbours? Friends?"

Desmarest replied calmly, "This estate was chosen because of its complete isolation. There will be no interference from neighbours."

When, on Saturday, 28 May, Macnamara rode out of Paris, he took with him a large chest. It contained the money for Colonel Despard to ensure the success of his revolution.

CHAPTER 11

SUNDAY, 11 JULY 1802: PORT EYNON, GOWER PENINSULA
Richard Machen shielded his eyes with his hand and watched the schooner sail into the bay.

Five days earlier the agent to Sir John Lucas had arrived from Swansea and, after serving notices of dismissal on all the staff at the Hall, had then come to the cottage to inform Machen that his tenure there could also be in doubt. The problem was that Sir John, in his instructions as to the leasing of his estates, had not referred to Machen's occupancy of the cottage. No doubt it had been forgotten in the negotiations.

"What negotiations?" Machen's question was abrupt.

"I promise you the whole matter has been of great surprise to me," the agent had replied, "but Sir John has agreed to lease Culver Hall and all its lands to a chapter of the Benedictine Order—"

"Monks?" Machen interjected incredulously. "Lucas is letting his home as a monastery?"

"Those are my instructions in Sir John's own hand," said the agent. "He instructs me to obtain the transfer licence from the Mansel-Talbots of Penrice Castle. There is also a missive from the incoming prior to myself, emphasising the need for Sir John's instructions to be implemented before their arrival, sometime within the coming week."

"Am I allowed to read them?"

"Certainly: they are my authority to present to any who may question my acts over the next day."

Machen accepted the papers, glanced at the official licence

from Penrice Castle, then turned to the letter from Sir John Lucas. It was a long communication, written in Lucas's own hand. In addition to instructing his agent, Lucas explained that the existence of the new peace had decided him to sail to France and spend some time there.

During his stay he had been privileged to meet a Benedictine Father, an Irishman of great learning and compassion, who had explained how, some 200 years earlier, the church of Clancy, in north-eastern France, had given the properties of their monastery at Dieulouard to the English Congregation of the Benedictine Order. From that time, British adherents to that Order had been taught at Dieulouard, and at the conclusion of their training were sent back by the Benedictines to serve in their own native land. This branch of the movement was known as the Mission to Britain, being divided into two chapters, one for the north and the other for the south.

But the outbreak of the Revolution, and with men such as Robespierre and Saint-Just in power, had led to the persecution of the Christian religion in France, and the work at Dieulouard had suffered. In September 1793 Robespierre had secured a decree against the monastery from the Paris Convention and, on 12 October 1793, it had been executed, with the result that the Father and his fellow monks in Dieulouard had been imprisoned. They had been released only after Robespierre's death.

Now, since Napoleon's rise to power, a new tolerance was being shown towards religion. Last April, only three months ago, France and the Roman Catholic Church had been officially reconciled in a religious Te Deum in Notre-Dame cathedral. And although the work of the Benedictines this side of the Channel had continued throughout the persecution in France, the task of increasing the evangelisation of Britain had assumed paramount importance in the mind of the Irish Father.

It appeared that when the holy man had spoken to him of his personal experiences and faith, Lucas had slowly come to realise the emptiness of his own life; to the extent that he had actually suggested a new, independent Mission to Wales, and, in the knowledge that he was without children to succeed to his title and estates, had offered to lease Culver Hall to the Benedictines, at a peppercorn rent.

The agent was instructed to assist the Order by implementing the requirements of the Father whose testimony had so impressed Lucas.

Machen turned to the second letter.

In it the Father introduced himself as the president of the newly formed Welsh Congregation, emphasising the Benedictines' insistence on maintaining themselves by their own labours; therefore he deeply regretted that none of the staff of the Hall could be kept on after the new prior and the appointed monks arrived in the company of Sir John to take over the Hall.

Machen looked up from his reading.

There was no mention of his own occupation of the cottage but Machen's thoughts turned to Lady Lucas, a solitary figure often seen walking along the headland, passing time until the return of her husband. What was her reaction to this news?

"She has refused to leave," the agent replied. "In a personal letter Sir John requested that she travel to their home in London and await him there, but she has determined to ignore his instructions, convinced that his decision may be attributed to some illness. With only her maid to attend her she awaits his return at Culver Hall."

Minutes later the agent departed, leaving Machen considering his position, and the bitter disappointment that Jane's visit would now be cancelled. His immediate thought was to call on Lady Lucas and discuss the matter with her, but then he changed his mind. He had no wish to intrude on a woman certain to be distressed by the unexpected loss of her home. Instead he decided to follow her lead and await Sir John's return.

That was five days ago; time spent waiting, sitting on the quay looking out to sea, or sailing his grandfather's small boat which, on his return home, he had discovered in the dunes above high-water mark and, with a few minor repairs, had made seaworthy.

Now he watched the schooner drop anchor some distance from the shore. Minutes later the long boat made for the beach. Rowed by two sailors, it carried a number of black-robed monks and in their midst he could make out the figure of Sir John. Machen climbed down the stone steps to the side of the quay, and crossed the sands towards where the boat would beach.

An incoming wave lifted the boat and carried it, roller-high, into the shallows, where it rasped against the sands and slid to a halt. The foremost of the two sailors leapt out, splashed his way forward to the prow and held the craft steady against the incoming tide.

Two of the monks clambered out, their robes falling into water up to their knees, then they offered their hands to Lucas. Slowly, uncertainly, he climbed over the side and, with the two men on either side, splashed his way laboriously through the water towards the beach, followed by the remaining monks. Then the long boat made its way back to the schooner.

Lucas looked up and saw Machen waiting. He turned and said something to the monk on his right side. Machen crossed to meet them, and clasped Lucas's hand, shocked to see that his face was white and drawn and his eyes lined grey with suffering.

"Richard!" Sir John's voice was little more than a whisper. "It is good to see you again, though somewhat unexpected." His eyes avoided Machen's face. "I thought you would be well gone by now."

"I was unsure what to do, Sir." Machen's voice betrayed his concern. "You gave your agent no specific instructions as to myself or the cottage."

"My apologies, Richard. He should have realised that my decision affected you as much as the others. My gift to the Benedictines includes the cottage. But" – he looked questioningly at one of the monks – "Lieutenant Machen can stay the night?"

Machen turned to the man for his answer and found himself looking into the coldest eyes he had ever seen.

"I regret that is not possible."

The monk's voice held no emotion, offering no explanation. He took hold of Lucas's arm and turned to continue up the beach, then he paused and looked back at Machen.

"As you can see, Sir John has not been well these last days.

Because of this he has asked that he be granted seclusion with us for a while. In the meantime it would be appreciated if you could vacate the cottage. Before midday."

There was a cutting in the sand dunes which led to the grasslands beyond. It was not until Lucas and his new companions had passed through it that Machen realised he should have told Sir John of his wife's continued presence in the Hall.

Well within the hour Machen had packed his long-bag and was ready for departure. It was a good march over the hills and moors of Gower to Swansea, where he would find lodgings until the Admiralty recalled him to duty – an unknown length of time because of the peace. He hoped his money would last out.

He threw his long-bag over his shoulder and walked hurriedly out of the cottage, across the quay and on to the shore. The tide was going out and he turned to walk along the still-wet sand.

For some reason the solitude of the long, curving bay increased the emptiness within him, and on impulse Machen turned away. He climbed over the dunes and made his way through the rough grass and thick ferns, following the paths made over long years by the wild horses which roamed the peninsula.

To his left stretched Port Eynon Head, its eastern slopes facing inwards towards the bay, rising gently at first but becoming progressively steeper as they approached the rim, and hiding most of Culver Hall from his view; the only part he could see was the very roof of the keep.

Silhouetted against the white-flecked, blue sky, seagulls wheeled and dived in the air currents created by the headland.

It was a familiar scene and of such utter peace and tranquillity that Machen could scarcely bear to leave it. He stood there for some moments silent, saying goodbye to the place, and to his dreams of Jane Ashford. Then he turned and continued along the narrow pathway, his face set towards Swansea.

*   *   *

From the roof of the keep Macnamara looked down on Culver Hall with a feeling of satisfaction. The place appeared to have been built more as a stronghold than a private residence. The high square-shaped keep was obviously the original fortification and many centuries old. Below it stretched a large, hard-earthed courtyard encircled by buildings added on by past generations of owners. To Macnamara's immediate right was the chapel and the thickness of its walls showed it to have been planned more as a last line of defence than a place of worship. Past the chapel and extending from it at a right-angle was the south wing of the Hall – the staff quarters and kitchen – its outer walls erected almost at the edge of the cliffs. Across the courtyard stood the main Hall itself – a solid, grey-stoned, three-storeyed edifice – while to the left, completing the square, were the gatehouse, outbuildings and stables.

The keep – as befitted its original purpose as a watchtower – was so much taller than the surrounding buildings that Macnamara was able to see over the roofs; his gaze followed the headland as it curved inland around the bay. He saw a man striding along the foot of the headland, his bag slung over his shoulder. Macnamara's eyes narrowed as he studied the man's walk.

There was no doubt, his suspicions were confirmed . . . it was the same man he had observed at the Golden Cross in London, the one who by his interference had almost allowed the guardsman to escape. Now, for a second time, he had become involved in their activities. How?

Instinctively Macnamara's hand fell to his side. But he had forgotten he was wearing a monk's habit, and his fingers closed around some meaningless cross instead of the knife he expected there.

He turned from the turreted wall, forcing away all thought of Machen by reminding himself of Colonel Despard's first words when he had delivered the money-chest into his hands: "Now that we have the means *nothing* must be allowed to interfere with the success of our mission!"

CHAPTER 12

SUNDAY, 11 JULY 1802: CLAPHAM
It had been a long, slow Sunday. This was the way Sir Robert seemed to prefer to spend his rest days away from the Admiralty, especially since Jane's mother had been taken ill during that long spell of midwinter some six months ago. She had died within a matter of days and with Jane still over three years away from her twenty-fifth year, the terms of her late father's Will had come into force. Noble became her guardian and, very mindful of his responsibilities, a stern guardian he had proved to be.

It was during the course of the evening meal, eaten in silence as usual, when Jane suddenly looked up and reminded Sir Robert that in but a few weeks she would be journeying to Gower to spend the latter part of August and the whole of September with Uncle John and Aunt Katrine at Culver Hall.

Noble carefully laid both knife and fork down on his plate and looked across at her, his narrow face adopting a mild, authoritative expression.

"I regret I must forbid it," he declared in the clipped, precise, naval manner he always used when exercising his role of guardian.

Jane immediately protested. "But, Uncle Robert! For the last ten years, ever since father died, Mother and I always spent this time of the year on Gower. Mother drew such strength and comfort from her visits home. Why should you wish to deny me the same privilege?"

"My dear Jane," Noble replied, his voice taking on the reproachful tone of a man unkindly criticised, "you know that

I am obliged to offer no reason other than the right of guardianship vested in me by the terms of your father's Will. However, I had hoped that by now you would have come to realise my decisions are influenced only by those factors which I consider to be in your best interests. In this respect I cannot but deny I have never approved of Sir John Lucas, nor that I have my suspicions as to certain of his activities. For your mother's sake I did not previously voice these opinions, but, now that you are my responsibility alone, I am obliged to declare them openly. I must ask you to abide by my decision, and trust there will be no more talk of Culver Hall."

And with a continued air of hurt dignity Sir Robert Noble resumed his attack on the slices of lean beef covering his dinner plate.

Jane flushed with anger. How *dare* you! her mind cried out, this is *my* home! And in three years' time, when your guardianship ceases, it will become my property by law. And then, my dear, dictatorial Uncle Robert, from that moment I will be my own mistress and make my own decisions!

But discretion prevailed and Jane kept her thoughts to herself.

When her father, William Ashford, a prosperous young city merchant, had married the beautiful and headstrong Sarah Lucas, he brought his young bride to the romantic old black and white timber-beamed house he had purchased for her on the southern slope of the common in Clapham. It was surrounded by open countryside which he knew she loved, yet it was also only a carriage ride from his city business.

Two years after the marriage, when Jane was born, the family solicitor advised that a Will be drawn up to protect the interests of both mother and child. The terms he advised, and which were accepted by the young William Ashford, robust and in good health and hardly anticipating death, gave the interest in the estate to his wife during her lifetime, and after her death to his daughter absolutely. However, if Sarah Ashford died before Jane reached the age of twenty-five, then a guardian was to be appointed until that day arrived. William Ashford appointed his first and only cousin, Robert Noble, then signed the Will, left it in a deed box with his solicitor and put it out of his mind until the arrival of a second child – and, he hoped, a third and a fourth – would cause the Will to be amended.

But William and Sarah Ashford's desires were not fulfilled. Jane remained the only child and as a consequence received the full outpouring of her parents' love.

In truth, Jane now admitted to herself, she was thoroughly spoiled. Nevertheless she could look back on those years with happy memories: the games on the lawn, the tea parties, the carriage rides, but best of all following her father when he went out riding, trying to keep up with him on her little short-legged pony.

But then, when he was returning from the city one evening in spring a stray dog attacked the horses pulling his carriage; the horses bolted, the carriage overturned, and William Ashford lay dead by the side of the dusty road, his neck broken.

Wife and daughter were devastated; and from that day on Sarah Ashford evidenced her grief by rarely wearing clothes other than in dark colours. Her only true moments of happiness during the years that followed were the summer months she spent on Gower with her brother, John, and Katrine, his young wife. There, at Culver Hall, she seemed to gather the strength needed to sustain her through the remaining months of each year.

Then, three years after the death of William Ashford, Robert Noble – or Sir Robert as he now was, and captain of a British ship of the line – was invalided home from active service with wounds received during a skirmish with the French.

He dutifully came to visit them in Clapham and was graciously invited by Sarah Ashford to remain a while at their home. But during what was intended by her mother to be a brief stay, Noble used his family influence to secure himself a position with the Admiralty in Whitehall . . .

That year the Navy had set up its relay telegraphic service, linking its ports at Portsmouth and Deal with two shutter rooms set up on the very roof of the Admiralty Building. Noble was appointed the officer in charge of this department.

And thus he remained living with them in Glebe House, daily journeying to the Admiralty by chaise; and one evening a week to attend meetings at his London freemasonry lodge, which he joined soon after ceasing active service.

But Jane, retaining her intuitive judgment of the people who had surrounded her as a child, found herself unable to respond in friendly fashion to her uncle, and little understanding existed between ward and guardian. However, there was one compensation to her uncle's presence within the household: at least he provided her mother with a certain companionship, and although no hint of romance ever existed between the two, Noble proved to be an acceptable chaperon, attending Sarah Ashford and Jane to various functions, dinners and theatres, all of which helped to make her mother forget her grief. For this at least Jane was grateful and as a consequence she had endeavoured to conceal her own lack of affection for Noble.

And, she had always had her yearly visits to Culver Hall to look forward to. Until now.

Angry and bitterly she bade her guardian good night and went up to her room. She thought about Richard Machen, imagining him to be at his cottage eagerly awaiting her arrival. It took her a long time to fall asleep.

When she opened her eyes the following morning her thoughts were still of Richard Machen. The light told her it was early. A strong breeze was blowing in through the open casement.

Shivering, she rose and pulled the window closed, then stood there for a moment looking across the park. Past tended lawns, carefully planted trees now in full leaf, and beyond the stream which skirted the edge of the grounds, was nothing but luscious farmland and open fields right away to Streatham. Over it all lay a haze as the ground slowly awoke to the rising sun.

Turning and diving back into her bed, Jane lay there listening to the sounds of the household awakening and suddenly she made up her mind to defy her guardian. She would not accept this restrictive atmosphere he was placing about her. As a child she had been brought up in a household of love; so much so that this emotion was an essential part of her nature. Deep within her there was a large capacity to give and crave affection, and although through the bitter experiences of the deaths of both her parents she knew that love must sometimes bring pain, nevertheless she saw the pain of real love as a pain of caring, and that with it there would also be a giving, a receiving, a sharing which would make it all so worth while. For this reason alone she could no longer remain here with Noble, the recipient of his constant strictures, or her very soul would wither away.

Somehow she must find her own way to Culver Hall. Once there she could tell Uncle John and Aunt Katrine of her life since Noble had become her guardian and ask that she be allowed to remain with them at Culver Hall for the next three years, until she became of age to inherit.

But how to plan it? Why, simply by pretending until mid-August – by which time her uncle should have returned from France – to accept her guardian's will. Then on a weekday, while Noble was at the Admiralty, one of the grooms could drive her into the city. Once there she would make her way straight to the Golden Cross, book the first available seat on the Swansea coach, and write a hurried letter to Uncle John – which he would not receive until after she had left, thereby preventing him from sending an acknowledgment for Sir Robert to read – telling him of the time of her arrival. After that she would return to Clapham and quietly await the moment of her departure.

The coach to Swansea, she knew, left early in the morning. She would be on her way long before Noble had woken up, leaving a letter to her guardian, explaining where she was going, and why. This should ensure her an uninterrupted stay at Culver Hall, for Sir Robert's pride was such that it would never allow him to follow her, nor would he wish to face the wrath of her Uncle John.

And so long as the peace between Britain and France continued to prosper, Richard and she would have a much longer time in which to learn to know each other properly.

CHAPTER 13

Napoleon Bonaparte read Fouché's morning's reports with growing exhilaration.

The first communiqué, from Monsieur Desmarest, Head of the Sûreté, enclosed Colonel Despard's own assessment of his progress.

With the financial support France had given him, Despard had already made contact with most of the secret political organisations in Britain in all the main areas of the country. All had agreed to unite in the common cause. A national revolutionary council, the Secret Committee of England, had been formed with Despard as its head.

The plans for London and the Home Counties were now nearing finalisation. Despard claimed to have some 40,000 supporters in the capital alone. The prime targets would be the Houses of Parliament – where the leaders of the government would be assassinated along with the king – the Tower of London and the Bank of England. Arms from the Tower and the Bank would be distributed to the people, and by nightfall of the first day, 23 November, London would be in the hands of the Commander-in-Chief, Despard, and his Executive and National Council.

At this stage the country's communications would be cut by smashing the Admiralty's semaphore towers and by stopping all the mail coaches. This last action would act as the signal to the various organisations up and down the country that the takeover of London had been successful. They would then rise up and assume authority in the areas delegated to them. Within days, according to Despard, the whole of Britain would be under their control. Napoleon doubted it, but it would certainly place the country into chaos. He reached the end of this report and looked up at his Minister of Police: "It would appear, Monsieur Fouché, that my invasion cannot possibly fail!"

"No, General, and that view will be especially strengthened after you have read the second report. It comes from one of our trade consuls in London. The details were passed on to him in secret by someone who had access to such information, an Englishman much taken with our method of government, so it would seem."

Napoleon turned to the document eagerly.

At the beginning of that year, according to the report, when the two countries were still at war, Britain had a total of 505 ships in sea service. However, after the signing of the Amiens peace treaty, the Admiralty, under the direction of the British government, had been forced to implement financial retrenchment. Many of the ships had been recalled, others – the report named the vessels – soon would be. By the end of the year, of the 126 ships of the line originally in sea service no more than 30 would remain. And the 379 other ships – one-deckers, sloops and the rest – would be cut back to about 170.

A total reduction of 300 ships! And that was not all. The report went on to detail the strength of the armed forces based on British soil. It appeared that the country had fewer than 200,000 soldiers to defend it, and many of these were no more than volunteers. Nor were they concentrated on the south coast as the French had supposed, but were dispersed evenly throughout the land.

"All this means," Napoleon declared, "that they have hardly enough troops to cope with Despard's uprising, let alone my invasion forces. Fouché," he exclaimed, "we will land virtually unopposed! And what is more, it seems that while you and I are preparing for war, the English admirals and generals are exercising all their energies on enjoying the peace, attending functions, parties, receptions, and all that sort of thing."

"Really, General? Quite unbelievable."

Napoleon's face reflected a brief, cynical smile.

"Why, the mood even extends to that one-armed, one-eyed Nelson; he is apparently accompanying a Sir William and Lady Hamilton on a tour of South Wales . . ."

CHAPTER 14

Swansea was crowded. The people were thronging Wind
Street, the main thoroughfare, waiting for Lord Nelson to
emerge from Worcester House, the mansion next to the old
castle which dominated the town, and the home of one
Thomas Morgan, steward to the Duke of Beaufort, where the
portreeve of Swansea was holding a banquet in honour of
Britain's most famous admiral.

Machen looked all about him. The excitement was infec-
tious, it showed in all the faces, from the smart dandy to the
shabbiest ruffian, from the ladies in all their finery to the old
crones peddling their wares amongst the crowds. The noise,
the bustle, the laughter, the cries of children and the barking of
dogs mingled into a continuous uproar.

He noticed one rider forcing his horse through the crowd,
leading two other horses, one side-saddled and riderless, the
other a pack horse. The man's face seemed familiar. Where
had he seen it? Recently? Yes. Machen suddenly remembered
the schooner anchored against the broad sweep of Port Eynon
Bay, the bowed figure of Sir John Lucas, and the monk who
assisted him ashore, with eyes the colour of blue ice in
midwinter.

It was the same man, of that Machen was certain. But what
was he doing in Swansea and dressed, not in his monk's habit,
but in a gentleman's well-cut dark coat and breeches? He
followed the horseman down the street.

*   *   *

Macnamara was briefly curious about the reason for the mass of people filling the streets, then he dismissed it from his mind.

Over the heads of the crowd he could see the name of the Mackworth Arms, the coaching inn the Ashford woman had mentioned in her letter received only yesterday, addressed to Sir John Lucas. Alongside the hotel was the tunnel that led to the livery stables; he would leave the horses there while he enquired whether the London stage was likely to arrive on time.

Inside Worcester House, Vice-Admiral Viscount Nelson, Duke of Brontë, Knight of the Bath, and now Freeman of Swansea, was embarrassed.

The cause was Emma Hamilton. Happy though he was to be the object of her passion, he wished she would confine her hero-worship to the bedroom, and not display it so blatantly in public.

A sumptuous meal having finally reached its conclusion, the voluptuously built Emma was standing before the assembled guests singing Horatio's praises in her own inimitable manner. The tune was that of the National Anthem, the words she had composed herself:

> Join we great Nelson's name,
> First on the Roll of fame,
> Him let us sing.

She sang on with uninhibited gusto:

> Spread we his praise around,
> Honour of British ground,
> Who made Nile's shores resound,
> God save the King.

Nelson remembered the difficulty he had experienced in persuading Emma to mention the king in the last line. During the verses that followed the vice-admiral thankfully turned his thoughts to the tour on which he and the Hamiltons were engaged.

They had left Merton, Nelson's home outside London, in two heavily laden carriages, on Tuesday, 20 July 1802. Sir William Hamilton was to visit his estates at Milford Haven, Nelson to prepare a report for the government on the harbours of South Wales and to inspect the Forest of Dean with a view to its timbers being used for ship-building. Their journey to Milford had taken them through many of the towns of South Wales, and everywhere a rapturous welcome awaited him.

The Swansea dignitary sitting next to him cut across his thoughts:

"There will be a triumphal drive through the streets. The people have come from miles around to pay homage to you, My Lord. You are much loved here in Wales."

Nelson smiled, "You are very kind."

He listened again to Emma. To the great delight of her audience she was now singing the tune of "Rule, Britannia!", but again the words were her own.

Outside, the whole population of Swansea seemed to be celebrating the visit of Lord Nelson. The people cried his name in the streets and exulted in his victories over the French. Even the ostler in the Mackworth Arms – after confirming to Macnamara that the London stage was not expected for some hours – wanted nothing other than to talk about the honour that the great man had bestowed upon Swansea by becoming a freeman of the town. Macnamara escaped to the Plume of Feathers, but there the man who served him – introducing himself by the name of Tom Cleaves – boasted to the revolutionary:

"I was once a bosun of Lord Nelson's. As soon as the Admiral starts his drive through the town I'm going to march in front of the carriage, to salute him with my bosun's pipe. Such an honour, heh?"

Macnamara was relieved to find the Blue Boar Inn and the company of men of like mind to himself, with nothing but contempt for the hero-worshipping mob outside. Nor did the patrons of the Blue Boar refer to anyone as Lord.

As they sat talking in an upstairs room there came an exultant roar from outside.

Macnamara crossed to the window to see the carriage passing below. He looked down at the small, frail figure of Nelson sitting in the open coach, dressed in his naval best and bedecked with his various medals and honours. By his side sat a round, more-than-full-figured woman; together the two waved to the cheering crowds, veritably glorying, it seemed to the Irishman, in the public adulation. To complete the way in which 'the common man has this day betrayed himself' – the words were those of a Welshman standing alongside Macnamara – a group of local sailors had taken the place of the horses and were bodily pulling the admiral's conveyance along the street. Before them strode the puffed-up figure of Tom Cleaves, blowing on his pipe.

"Come the day of retribution," said the voice at Macnamara's side, "warmongers like Nelson must be the first to go."

Without turning, Macnamara agreed.

He studied the slight figure below. Nelson, with his reputation of ruthlessness in battle, was every inch the confident, superior Englishman, so typical of the race which had caused Ireland such pain. And so representative of the way the English Establishment protected its own.

Why, just compare the treatment meted out to Nelson and Despard. Two men who once, in Nicaragua, had fought shoulder-to-shoulder; but the Englishman had prospered, while Despard, the Irishman, after years of faithful service in the West Indies, had been unfairly held responsible for a wave of unrest which passed over the island of Honduras. He came to London in the year 1790, personally to plead his innocence before the Secretary of State, but that *gentleman* had been too busy with important matters and years had gone by with no interview. When a decision was finally made Despard was told that the case against him had been dropped, he was absolved of all blame, but the position of Superintendent was now abolished! However, he was assured his past services would not be forgotten and he would be duly rewarded.

But being Irish – there was no doubt this was the reason – the Colonel had received no money, and no new post. Instead, he heard news of the promotion and progress of others – Englishmen of course – who had not served Britain half as well as he. Finally, in 1798, the English authorities had arrested him as a subversive and locked him away without trial in the House of Correction at Shrewsbury. But Despard's years in prison had given him the opportunity to plan, and the time for Nelson and men like him was not far away now. Three months to be precise. For when Despard's uprising took place on 23 November, Nelson being a peer of the realm would take his place with all the other peers inside Westminster for the ceremonial Opening of Parliament.

Macnamara suddenly remembered Desmarest's final briefing . . .

Even Napoleon himself considered Nelson's death to be essential. On the First Consul's list the admiral's name had been placed above all the others.

As the sailors continued to pull the open carriage through the cheering crowds in the direction of Swansea harbour, Conor Macnamara took a last look down at Nelson. And in that tiny fraction of time he felt a sudden, vivid awareness of his own destiny . . . a cold certainty that when Nelson died it would be by his hands.

Late in the afternoon it turned to rain. Nelson and the Hamiltons were driven away and the crowds slowly dispersed, leaving the cobbled Wind Street wet and forlorn.

Huddled in an alley opposite the Blue Boar, Machen pulled up the collar of his faded old naval jacket. The steady drizzle had saturated his hair so that it hung wet and dark on his forehead, but he made no attempt to brush it away, nor the drops of water that ran down his brow.

His attention was on the front door of the inn. The monk's appearance in Swansea and the question of his clothing still puzzled him, and in spite of the weather he was determined to find the answer.

From the northern approach to the town came the muffled rumble of an approaching coach. Machen drew himself deeper into the shadow of the passage wall. With a clattering roar the

Royal Mail swept past the alley and drew to a halt in front of the Mackworth Arms.

Moments later the monk appeared in the open doorway of the Blue Boar; he looked over at the coach and made his way across the street towards it.

Three of the passengers had already descended from the coach and were standing about waiting for their baggage to be handed down. One of them, a young woman, stood looking about her, obviously searching for someone she had expected to be there to meet her. Despite the distance there was no mistaking her.

As Machen stepped out of hiding to run across the street, the monk reached the coach and went straight up to her. Instinctively Machen drew back. He watched as they briefly conversed for some moments, then the man indicated the hotel as though asking Jane to go inside. She shook her head. The monk turned to accept a travelling case which the guard was holding down to him. Having caught it, both he and Jane then made for the tunnel which led to the stables behind the hotel.

The episode increased Machen's curiosity. Although the reason for the two extra horses was now evident, why was Jane Ashford journeying to Culver Hall? The place was now a Benedictine monastery. What was more, to return to the original mystery, why was the monk dressed in a gentleman's coat and not his monastic habit?

Think! Think carefully. There must be a logical explanation, otherwise a man as strict as Jane's guardian would never have allowed her to travel.

In the first place, Jane's arrival must mean that Sir John and Lady Lucas were still at Culver Hall. But how? And *why* was Jane joining them there?

Machen concentrated, desperate to find the answers, and suddenly it all seemed obvious. The legal papers to transfer Culver Hall to the Benedictines would have taken weeks to prepare, consequently the Lucases had delayed their departure until everything was signed and sealed. And with a thousand and one things to be done – the removal of their personal possessions, together with all the furniture, paintings, ornaments and the like – what could be more natural than for Jane to journey to Culver Hall to assist her aunt?

Even so, that still left the question of why had the monk changed to normal clothing? But again there was an obvious answer. In a town crowded with people come to see Lord Nelson, and with very few Roman Catholic monasteries established in Wales, the monk had probably not wished to draw attention to himself, and had therefore borrowed one of Sir John's old suits.

That was it. Both questions logically answered. No mystery after all.

Machen looked up. The rain clouds were passing away. It was going to be a fine evening. Tomorrow he was due to sail from Swansea as an officer on board one of Lucas's merchant vessels. Three weeks earlier, bored after a fortnight's idling around Swansea, Machen had sought employment with Lucas's agent. The 60-foot, 94-ton brigantine *Elisabeth Kate*, bound for Liverpool with a cargo of copper patent bolts and returning via the South Lancashire coalfield and the copper smelting works at Amlwch, on the island of Anglesey, had admirably suited his purpose. Altogether Machen expected to be away some two months, which meant that long before he returned Jane Ashford would be back in London and the opportunity to continue their too-brief acquaintanceship lost.

His thoughts were suddenly interrupted by the sharp clatter of hooves from the tunnel of the Mackworth Arms. He looked across to see the monk emerging, leading the pack horse with Jane's luggage tied across its back, and finally Jane herself, riding side-saddle.

Machen hesitated. Should he run across to her? But to what purpose. Tomorrow he would be gone. And despite her obvious pleasure at seeing him again in London, what possible hope could there be for him, a penniless naval officer, to even try to win the affections of an heiress like Jane Ashford? He had nothing to offer her but the clothes on his back. Dismiss the thought that she might return his affections. With a sinking heart he realised that from the very beginning it had all been but a dream.

He watched as the train made its way up the empty street, the iron shoes of the horses clip-clopping with a hollow clatter on the wet, grey cobblestones.

They turned the corner at the top of the street and passed out of Machen's sight.

As they crossed the headland towards the Hall, Macnamara, her uncle's new secretary – as he had introduced himself to her outside the Mackworth Arms – eased his horse down to a walk. Jane did the same.

It was a calm evening. The setting sun behind them cast a majestic fan of red-flecked clouds across the sky and lighted a crimson path across the waters of Port Eynon Bay. Below them and near to the foot of the headland stood Richard's cottage. Bathed in the red glow, the building and its surrounding quay appeared warm and inviting against the background of the flat, shining sea.

Would he be as glad to see her as she was to see him? Tomorrow she planned to awake with the dawn and ride down and surprise him. She could feel her heart race away at the thought that Richard was now but a stone's throw away.

Pointing towards the cottage she turned to Macnamara. "Do you know whether Lieutenant Machen rises early?"

The man did not even follow the direction of her out-stretched hand.

"You must enquire of your uncle," was his toneless reply.

Out of the corner of her eyes Jane studied the man's unforgiving, hard profile. Throughout the journey his mood had been one of flat, awkward silence. What had possessed her uncle to engage such a person?

They reached the Hall and by the hands of persons unseen the heavy, double gates opened slowly inwards. As soon as the gap between the doors was wide enough Macnamara nudged his horse forward. Jane followed.

As the doors closed behind her, Jane half turned in the saddle and saw two black-robed monks leering up at her. Startled, she looked towards Macnamara for explanation, but he kept his back towards her and continued across the courtyard, to dismount at the foot of the stone steps leading up to the main building.

He turned away from his horse and walked back towards her.

Striving to appear calm, Jane unhooked the back of her right knee from around the pommel of her side-saddle. She prayed there would be no trace of fear in her voice as she asked, "Why are there monks—"

Before she could complete the question, Macnamara grabbed her left wrist and pulled her bodily off the horse. She cried out in pain but Macnamara ignored her. He pulled her up the stone steps towards the main door of the hall . . . up the main staircase . . . along the wide gallery . . . and down the landing to the door of her Aunt Katrine's bedroom. Macnamara unlocked the door, pushed her into the room, and slammed the door shut behind her.

"Jane!"

Aunt Katrine rose out of a high-backed chair facing the window and the view over the Bristol Channel. Arms outstretched she ran across the room, and clasped Jane tightly.

"Jane! Whatever possessed you to come here? Are you alone, or is Sir Robert with you?"

Jane did not reply but pretending a calmness she did not feel she led Katrine back to the chair, knelt beside her, and took hold of her hands.

"Aunt . . . take your time . . . but tell me, what is happening here, who are these people, and what are they doing in Culver Hall?"

Katrine closed her eyes, concentrating on composing her thoughts, and then began to relate what Sir John had told her in the brief time they were allowed together before he was incarcerated in the keep.

That summer Sir John had taken advantage of the new peace to visit the French port of Roscoff. About a week after his arrival he was approached by a man with an Irish accent – the leader of the men now in possession of the Hall – who, after claiming to represent the Benedictine Order in Britain, had asked Lucas to lease Culver Hall to the movement. Naturally, Sir John had refused. The Irishman had then showed his religious claims to be false by threatening Lucas with prison, and then when this failed . . .

". . . He told John that wherever I was," Katrine whispered, "be it in Gower or London, if he did not co-operate my life would be forfeit."

The crew of his schooner were sentenced to Brest prison on false charges of stealing, she continued, and the boat manned by French sailors. They set sail for England, where they anchored off the Romney Marshes for a week while the Irishman delivered a large chest to London. When he returned they sailed for Ireland and at a lonely cove not far from Wexford they took twelve men aboard, then headed back to Britain and Gower. One day out from Port Eynon the leader and his twelve companions changed into monks' clothing. The following day they arrived at Culver Hall, and Sir John's schooner, *Conjurer*, then sailed back to France. Since that date Culver Hall had been run, ostensibly, as a monastery, part of preserving that appearance to the outside world sustained by a number of monks who worked daily in the kitchen garden.

"But what do they want with Culver Hall?" Jane repeated.

"Its seclusion," Katrine replied. "There are few places so isolated as Gower. They are storing arms here and distributing them."

"Arms!" Jane rose to her feet. "But for what purpose?"

"John thinks it to be revolution—"

"Revolution!"

"It is the only explanation, Jane."

"Then they allow you to see Uncle John?"

"Every day, for ten minutes. When John returned from France and found me still here, awaiting his return, he told the Irishman that only if he saw me and received my daily assurances that I am unharmed would he continue to co-operate."

Jane crossed to the window and looked out on a peaceful scene. The sun had long since fallen behind the hills but by the light of a full moon she could see the calm waters of the bay and out in the channel the white sails of three ships. "Poor Uncle John!" she whispered. "And yourself, Aunt?"

Suddenly Katrine, her emotions pent-up over the long weeks, broke down in an outpouring of tears. Jane held her aunt tightly in her arms, Katrine's head against her shoulder until the trembling subsided. Only then did she ask the question uppermost on her mind, yet dreading the answer.

"And Richard? What have they done with Lieutenant Machen?"

"Have no fear, Jane," her aunt replied, keeping her voice steady. "He vacated the cottage the day they arrived, and should be safe well away from here."

Jane closed her eyes and thanked God for that one mercy. Then she reopened them and, remaining by her aunt's side, looked out of the window. In the cold clarity of the moonlight Jane knew, without any doubt, that when these men had no further use for the place, any promise they had made to Sir John would be worthless. On the day of their departure three bodies would be left behind at Culver Hall.

CHAPTER 15

After a three-month voyage, lengthened by north-westerly gales which had forced her to shelter in Amlwch harbour for much of October, the brigantine *Elisabeth Kate* returned to Swansea and her crew was paid off.

The agent to Sir John Lucas looked across his paper-littered desk at the seated Machen.

"Certainly I can offer you further employment," he said, "but after nine years of fighting, why be so anxious to deny yourself the life of well-deserved idleness?"

The view from the office was towards the warehouses which surrounded the harbour. Over their roofs could be seen scores of top-masts silhouetted black against the grey, November sky.

"I could pretend that idleness breeds boredom," Machen answered, "but, in truth, if I stayed on shore I should soon be without money. The Admiralty's half-wage would barely pay for my lodgings."

"You have my sympathies," the agent replied. "In all honesty, if these rises in food prices continue they will force me to approach Sir John to increase my own fees."

"Force!" Machen smiled. "I would not have thought Sir John a difficult man to appeal to?"

"Not in the past," the man agreed, "but ever since this religious mania took hold of him, he seems to have changed completely."

"In what way?"

"It is difficult to explain," said the agent hesitantly, "but each time I see him at Culver—"

"Culver Hall!" Machen's voice was incredulous. "Is he still there?"

"Certainly."

"And Lady Lucas?"

"No. At least I do not think so. In all my visits to the hall, I have never set eyes on her. I assume she is at their London home."

"How often do you meet with Sir John?"

"Every Friday," the agent replied. "There are always documents requiring his personal signature."

"Is his health improved?" he asked.

"It would seem to be . . ." the agent paused in his answer ". . . physically at least . . ."

"Then what . . . ?" Machen left the question open for the agent to volunteer what was troubling him.

"It is difficult to explain, but we are never left alone. The abbot in charge of the monks attends our every meeting."

"But why?"

"Goodness knows, but his presence behind Sir John, listening to everything we say, is disconcerting to say the least." The agent shrugged his shoulders philosophically. "Still, it is not for me to ponder on the peculiarities of the nobility. My task is to accept instructions and ensure they are carried out."

The man stood, the conversation over, and held his hand out to Machen. "Call in again on Monday. By then I should know the *Elisabeth Kate*'s sailing date."

Machen had one further question:

"What of Miss Ashford, Sir John's niece from London? She arrived at the Hall some three months ago. Did you meet her on any of your earlier visits?"

The agent looked surprised. "No. I was not aware she had ever been there."

Subdued and thoughtful, Machen emerged from the building and stood for a moment in the street. Suddenly he turned right to stride up Wind Street, towards the Mackworth Arms and its stables where the inn kept a number of old hacks for hire.

Two hours later, as he neared Culver Hall, Machen reached the point where to ride any further along the headland would bring him in sight of the keep. He dismounted, led his mare into a near-by coppice and secured the reins to a branch.

It was still too light to make any move. Machen settled down to wait.

Hardly daring to breathe Jane Ashford tried the bedroom door. She was right, her ears had not deceived her! The guard had for once forgotten to lock it!

She whispered to Katrine to remain in the room, then slipped through the open doorway and out on to the landing. Taking care to make no sound she made her way to the top of the stairs and leaned over the gallery balustrade.

The murmur of voices drifted up from the library, but otherwise the hall was wrapped in silence. The meeting taking place behind the closed doors explained the guard's thoughtless haste to return downstairs after delivering their meal.

Jane returned to the bedroom door, and with finger on lips beckoned her aunt.

Together the two women made for the stairs.

They *must* escape, Jane thought. After twelve long weeks of imprisonment this was their first opportunity; and almost certainly their last. That afternoon, from their bedroom window, they had watched the *Conjurer* sail into the bay, and the subsequent atmosphere and bustle within the Hall told them that the departure of Macnamara and his men was not far away.

Slowly and silently they descended the long flight of stairs, and eventually they reached the ground floor. It was late afternoon and the inner hall stood in semi-darkness. The library was on their right, its door closed; from behind it came the sound of a solitary voice.

Jane signalled to her aunt that it was time to put their hurried plan into action. Katrine nodded in acknowledgment, then turned, crossed the hall and entered the long passageway which led to the kitchens.

Jane left the inner hall and made for the main entrance, opened the door slightly and peered out towards the roof of the keep. The guard was at his post. It was her responsibility to divert his attention.

She turned her gaze to the left to study the route Katrine must take. The kitchen exit was in the far corner of the courtyard and the door to the stables in the opposite corner. Between them stood first the chapel and then the keep. Once out in the open Katrine would be in full view from the turreted wall if the guard looked directly down.

Jane saw the kitchen door begin to open and the brief flutter of Katrine's handkerchief. It was time!

Hiding the short iron poker from the bedroom in the heavy folds of her skirts, Jane crossed the terrace and descended the steps into the courtyard. Struggling to control her trembling legs she walked slowly towards the gatehouse. Every evening both she and Katrine had been allowed to walk around the courtyard for some ten minutes or so, and she prayed that the guard would assume she was following this familiar routine.

From the corner of her eye she saw she had the man's attention.

Long before she reached the gatehouse she was rewarded by seeing Katrine reach the stable door and squeeze inside.

Jane's mouth felt dry. The next five minutes would be the most dangerous of her life. On the outcome depended their whole escape plan . . . and although the criminals would obviously have fled before the local militia could reach Culver, surely they would not wish to add murder to their crimes, and Sir John would be found still alive?

Jane reached the gatehouse and knocked. The door opened and the guard stood framed in the portal, his eyes wide with astonishment when he saw her.

Jane said, "I have been instructed to . . . entertain you." She deliberately paused to leave no doubt as to her meaning, then brushed past him and, turning slowly to face him, she raised her left hand to her bodice and began to undo the buttons. The man's unbelieving stare changed into an immediate leer; as he moved to close the door, his back was turned to her, his eyes on the latch.

Jane stepped forward. Bringing out the poker from her

folded skirts and holding it in both hands, she struck him with all her might across the back of his head. She both felt and heard the sickening thud before the guard collapsed senseless, perhaps dead. Jane staggered and leaned against the wall for support, fighting her rising nausea; then, her mind and body once more under control, she turned to face the door, eyes averted from the body sprawled across the floor.

Opening the door no more than an inch or so she looked up towards the keep, where the other guard was staring in perplexity towards the gatehouse. Soon he would feel constrained to act, she feared.

Hurry, Katrine! Please hurry!

How long did it take to bridle and saddle two horses? Jane could hear dimly the sounds of restlessness from inside the stables, the thud of the horses against their stalls, and the occasional whinny. The guard walked to the corner of the keep and looked down; but deciding that the animals must be merely restless he straightened up and returned his gaze towards the gatehouse.

How much longer . . . ?

The stable door slightly opened and Jane detected a brief wave of a white handkerchief from inside the building. Katrine was ready.

Jane opened the gatehouse door and stepped out into the courtyard. With an air of casualness, she closed the door behind her, then turned to her right and walked towards the main gates. With a few steps she was under the stone archway and out of view of the guard. Now she dropped all pretence and threw herself at the doors. They towered above her, heavy and solid, and secured from the inside with a large, sliding beam of wood. She pulled at it. The bar refused to budge!

She heard the guard on the keep shout out . . .

With a feeling of desperation bordering on panic she tugged at the bolt.

The guard yelled, louder.

The bar started to move; slowly it slid across until after one final, violent pull, the gates were free. Jane grabbed with both hands at the iron ring on her right. She pulled at it and slowly the heavy door began to swing open, scraping against the uneven floor. A space appeared between the doors, enough for Jane to see out to the headland.

Behind her she heard a bellow of anger. Half turning she saw Macnamara run out of the Hall, followed by the rest of his men.

From the direction of the stables came the clatter of iron hooves . . . Desperately Jane turned back to the gate, pulling with all her weight on the iron ring, and forced open a gap large enough for a horse to pass through.

She looked back towards the Hall. The Irishman stood in the centre of the courtyard, arms upraised before the rider and the two approaching horses; while Katrine, bent low over her mount and leading the second animal, rode straight at him. Macnamara waited until the last moment, then calmly stepped back a pace, and grabbing at the lead rope of the trailing horse, tore it from Katrine's hand.

Katrine turned her mount's head and made for the open gateway.

Behind her the Irishman leapt on to the back of the other animal.

As Katrine approached her, Jane saw her look over her shoulder to see how far the man was behind her. There was no time to pause and pull Jane up . . .

Jane stepped aside and cried out, "Ride on! Don't stop!"

Katrine gave her horse its head. She swept past Jane with a despairing glance, and then she was through the gate and out on to the headland.

In the courtyard Macnamara pulled at his horse's bridle. He pointed towards Jane. "Take her! I want her unharmed!" Then he kicked his mount forward once more.

Jane put her shoulders to the gate, trying to force it shut, but its weight was too much, and the Irishman swept on through the gap.

Moments later the first of the men reached her. He forced her arms behind her back, then he smiled down at her as his right hand slid slowly down to caress her breasts over her velvet bodice.

"You have some pretty petals, my unplucked English rose," he whispered, "some very pretty petals. But do not fret. Once

Conor has given the word it will be my pleasure to deflower you completely!"

And with a wink to his friends, and amid laughter, he propelled Jane across the courtyard and back to the Hall.

She looked up at the keep.

From the window of his cell her uncle's white face looked down on her, his hands gripping the bars in frustrated rage.

The shadows crept over the headland, it was time to move. As he stood to his feet Machen heard the approaching drumming of hoofbeats.

He parted the branches and looked up at the headland. Within moments the horse appeared. The rider was a woman, leaning forward and spurring her mount on to greater speed.

A second horse came into sight. The rider was one of the monks, in apparent pursuit, bent low over his horse, forcing it on faster.

As the riders drew nearer, Machen recognised the woman to be Lady Lucas, and the monk was surely the one who had met Jane Ashford off the London stage! The pursuing animal was gaining; slowly, inexorably, it drew alongside the first one.

But her flight was taking Lady Lucas too near to the edge of the plateau and with growing apprehension Machen saw that the monk's steed was leaning into the first horse, forcing it nearer and nearer the steep slope below. Already Lady Lucas's horse was rebelling, pulling nervously against the reins, then, suddenly, without warning, it dug its front hooves into the mountain turf and slid sharply to a halt.

Lady Lucas tried desperately to stay seated but was thrown forward on to the horse's neck. The animal bucked in fear, and catapulted its rider over the edge of the headland.

Machen watched helplessly as Lady Lucas plummeted down, her arms and legs thrashing helplessly. Within seconds it was over. She fell on to some protruding rocks, her head jerked back sharply, and suddenly all resistance ceased. The body rolled on and came to a halt against the trunk of a tree, no more than ten feet from where Machen stood.

Instinctively Machen remained hidden, knowing there was

nothing he could do. She must have died the instant her head struck the rocks.

On the rim of the headland the monk brought his horse to a halt. He looked down at the body, then stood up in his stirrups and stared around him, his eyes sweeping the open countryside.

Satisfied there were no witnesses, he rode his horse across to Lady Lucas's mount, gathered up the loose reins and headed back towards Culver Hall.

From his cover Machen looked appalled at the pathetic, lifeless figure. Lady Lucas's death had been no accident! The monk had deliberately pushed her horse to the edge.

But why? And why had she tried to escape?

Who were they, these monks who had persuaded Sir John to lease Culver Hall to them; who had such a hold over him that the abbot in charge attended every meeting with the agent?

Machen searched for an answer. Could it be that Sir John was now so much under their influence he had agreed to assign even more of his wealth to them, but Lady Lucas had objected and . . .

What of Jane?

There was only one way to find the answer, and that was to get inside Culver Hall. He crossed to the body of Lady Lucas, gathered her up in his arms, and began the long sad walk across the grasslands to the cottage.

CHAPTER 16

As Machen approached the cottage a man's cough intruded on the stillness. The sound came from beyond the sand dunes.

Machen laid the body on the ground, then, keeping low, he ran to the back of the quay. Pressing himself against the wall, he peered through the dusk.

High up on the beach stood a large stack of boxes and casks. Alongside, a number of pack horses stood patiently in line, panniers strapped across their backs, onto which four monks were loading supplies, securing each item with ropes.

He looked to the boat anchored in the bay and saw that it was Sir John Lucas's schooner.

One of the monks pulled a string of six horses away from the others and led them across the beach, towards the cutting in the sand dunes.

Shielded by the hollows Machen raced towards the cutting, his feet making little sound on the dry sand. He reached it before the pack-train and hid behind a hillock, looking up at the dark sky: clouds dominated and the moon was still hidden. After some moments he heard the horses plod by. He waited until they had passed, then, climbing over the hillock, he walked alongside the last animal, his hands feeling the canvas-wrapped packages. Recognition dawned: he knew the feel of muskets well enough.

Machen watched the train fade into the distance, now convinced that the men occupying Culver Hall were not even monks. Then who were they? Smugglers? Gun-runners? One thing was certain: they were extremely well organised as well as

123

ruthless. But why choose Culver Hall as a base for their operations? It had required a great deal of forethought, planning . . .

And Jane could well be in the hands of these men! He mastered his rage. What was needed now was a plan of campaign, and a calm mind to implement it.

Retrieving Lady Lucas's body, he made for the cottage, crept up the quay steps, and along the rear wall of the dwelling. He opened the scullery door and stepped inside. Musty air declared the cottage empty and unused. Machen carried Lady Lucas into the second bedroom and placed her gently down on the bed.

Minutes later he descended the quay. In his right hand he carried an unlit lantern. Tied to it with cord was a pistol-shaped object.

He ran across the sands, skirting the far edge of the dunes, and made for one of the many overgrown thickets immediately behind the cottage. Easing his way quietly through the thick undergrowth he reached a particularly large bush, knelt down, and parted the long grasses and ferns beneath it. At that moment the clouds broke and the moon appeared, its light revealing a small opening in the ground, normally completely hidden by the abundant vegetation that surrounded it. It was over twenty years since he had accidentally discovered the opening and – as is the way of a child – had kept it his secret.

It looked no more than the entrance to an animal hide, but Machen knew that the burrow, though narrow at the opening, grew larger and wider as it sloped downwards, passing through the rocks beneath, until it reached a larger tunnel, which fitted in with local legend as the one used by the first John Lucas, those many centuries ago.

Machen lowered himself into the hole, pulling the lantern after him, and, searching with his feet for niches in the rocks, he began the descent.

Minutes later he reached the main tunnel. In total blackness he untied the pistol-like object, and holding the handle he pulled the trigger. The mechanism of the strike-a-light was the same as that of a flintlock pistol: a flint held in the cock struck against a raised steel plate, throwing a spark on to an attached small box of tinder. The tinder ignited, and Machen lit the lantern.

Holding it up before him, Machen started along the tunnel. At first the cavern stretched out level under the flat grasslands, but then it reached into the headland and began to climb. Every so often there would be a small flight of man-made steps, hewn into the rock floor, while elsewhere the tunnel narrowed to little more than the width of a man's shoulders.

Where the natural fissure ended were two long, steep flights of steps which climbed into the blackness above. Machen took the one to his left. Here was further evidence of the interference of man, for the stairway had been chiselled out of the rock to afford passage, and he counted ninety steps before the lantern showed he had arrived at the top.

He now stood in a recess about five feet long. Three of its walls were of large roughly cut stones, while the fourth was a cobwebbed panel of solid oak. Machen listened, his ear against the panel until he was satisfied that the room behind was vacant. He extinguished the lantern, placed it with the strike-a-light on the floor, then felt along the right wall, found a metal lever and pulled on it. The panel – seemingly unused since Machen had found it all those years ago – finally creaked open under the pressure of his shoulders.

He was in the chapel of Culver Hall.

At the front of the chancel a door led through a carved wooden screen into the stone-floored nave of the chapel. In the half light of the moon Machen could see stacks of supplies piled high across the nave: boxes of food and meats, some recently opened; and mountains of arms, muskets, pistols, sabres – an unimaginable arsenal. He threaded his way between them towards the building's only exit, a solid oak door bearing a thick wooden beam.

He passed through the open door into a square room, similarly built and with an even stouter door which Machen knew led out into the courtyard. This was the ground floor of the keep, the original fortification of Culver Hall, built in the twelfth century by the Welsh Prince Eynon.

He began to climb the well-worn stone steps, lighted by torches in iron sconces, until he reached the old prison cells on the third floor. From here a short flight of steps led through a trap door on to the keep roof, the best vantage point from which to look down on the Hall and find out exactly what was happening.

"Richard!"

Machen started. He was on the first step leading up to the roof.

"Over here!"

He looked down the torchlit landing. Pressed against the small barred grille in one of the cell doors he could see the face of Sir John Lucas.

Machen sped to the door, utterly confused by all that had happened within the last two hours: the death of Lady Lucas, the discovery that arms were being smuggled into Culver Hall; and now Lucas himself being held prisoner in his own keep.

"Sir John! In heaven's name, what—"

"No time for explanations, Richard," Lucas interrupted, "Jane is in terrible danger. A few hours ago she and Katrine tried to escape. Katrine's horse was brought back without her and I can only guess as to her fate . . ." his voice broke ". . . but now you are here, together there may still be a chance to save Jane."

Machen hesitated, not knowing how much to reveal, but Lucas continued: "First you must get the keys from the guard – on the roof of the keep. Then, by using the tunnel perhaps we can—"

Through the cell window came the sound of raised voices. Lucas half-ran across the room to look down on to the courtyard, immediately he spun around.

"Too late!" His voice was desperate. "It's a pack-train. Quick, Richard, get to Jane before they enter the chapel . . ."

"I'll be back," Machen promised. He tore down the three flights of stone steps, through the chapel and into the chancel. Having found the disguised release catch, he passed through the hidden door and closed it behind him.

He relit the torch, and descended through the bowels of the cliffs. At the bottom he crossed to the other flight of steps, which he remembered led upwards into the main hall itself, coming out inside the central supporting wall of the building which was twelve feet thick.

Machen placed the torch in an iron ring secured to the inner cliff wall; its reflected light would be sufficient for the rest of his journey. The dancing flames searched upwards into the blackness, illuminating the rocky walls of the tunnel. Machen gave a silent prayer of gratitude to the long-dead Lucas who had thought to provide himself with this further bolt-hole if his stronghold ever came under attack, and turned to the steps.

He reached a recessed landing inside the inner wall of the main building. On his left was a panel of solid oak which he knew formed the back of a section of the library bookshelving. From the library Machen heard voices raised in conversation, but his fear for Jane's safety was such that he had no time to listen.

Turning away from the recess he began to climb the final flight of stairs.

In the library Macnamara concluded the meeting:

"We will be gone by first light, the arms left in the chapel are for distribution to your cells throughout South Wales. That gives you five days to remove them before Lucas's agent returns."

"And the signal?" asked one of the Welsh revolutionaries.

"The detailed instructions will be issued by your own Military Councils. But by the evening of 23 November London should be in our hands. All stagecoaches out of the city will then be stopped. That will be the signal to you to rise; and to other organisations throughout the land—"

"And then heads will roll," a second Welshman interjected, with enthusiasm.

"Like they did in France with the bastard guillotine!" shouted another.

A general outburst of approval greeted his last sentiment.

Macnamara turned to one of his own men.

"It is time to rid ourselves of Lucas," he said. "Have him brought here. In the meantime as I find no pleasure in taking a woman unless it is reciprocated, you and the others may have his niece and dispose of her as you will."

In the bedroom above the library Jane turned from fingering the coverlet of the square, four-postered bed, and under the watchful eye of the guard moved to the large wardrobe nearer the window. She opened it and gazed at Katrine's clothes without seeing them. She felt numb inside.

Her grief on being told by the Irishman of Katrine's death had brought with it the realisation of her own situation. If she was to escape even fouler treatment, only one course of action was open to her. She must take her own life. She tried to prepare herself for the moment when she must fling open the casement and jump.

She moved slowly to the window and placed her hand idly on the latch, but immediately the guard was behind her. He threw both his arms around her waist and pulled her back into the room. As she fought desperately to free herself, over the man's shoulder she saw a door in the wall panelling open.

In an instant Machen was across the room. He raised his right arm and brought the hard edge of his hand down like an axe on to the back of the guard's neck. Jane heard the bone crack, and the body suddenly crumpled to the floor at her feet.

Machen gave her his hand. She desperately wanted him to hold her, but instead he said, "There's no time to lose," and led her towards the secret door.

As they entered the recess Machen halted and walked back to the bedroom door, he turned the key, then opened it slowly and peered through. Satisfied that no one was on the landing, he threw the door open, and returned to Jane's side.

"Why leave it open?" she whispered.

"To make them think you have escaped that way," he explained.

From downstairs came the sound of voices as the library door opened, and then the footsteps of someone coming up the stairs.

Machen closed the panel.

Shoulders touching, they stood in the semi-darkness of the

walled recess, the only source of light being from a flickering glow on a wall some way below them.

Suddenly from inside the bedroom a voice was raised in anger.

They ran down the long stone steps until they reached the level floor. To her left the torchlight revealed to Jane what appeared to be a natural cavern, and to her right a second flight of steps leading upwards. Machen collected the torch from its bracket and turned left to enter the tunnel.

Jane asked, "What of my uncle?"

Machen stopped. He had forgotten about Lucas. Torn between his loyalty and affection for Sir John and the necessity to warn the authorities about the activities at Culver Hall, he hesitated, but then looked down into Jane's imploring eyes.

Pausing only to explain the way out of the tunnel, Machen told her that if he did not return within half an hour she must make her own escape, and raise the warning. He then handed her the torch and turned to the steps that led up to the chapel; he reached the panel and eased it open.

The pack-train must have been unloaded, for the chapel, bathed in a red glow which came in through the slit-windows from the courtyard outside, was empty. Machen passed into the nave and made his way between the stacks of arms towards the door, which suddenly opened and a man in a long monastic habit entered.

He saw Machen, but before he could shout for help Machen drove his foot up into the man's crotch. Breathless, in agony, the man dropped to his knees, hands already between his thighs, clutching at his pain. By Machen's side was a stack of sabres; he grabbed one and drove it into the kneeling man's chest.

Machen looked up, but there was no sound from the keep. Still clutching the sabre he crept towards the door. He looked into the room; it was empty, but the outside door was wide open, revealing the square outside lit by torches held in iron rings on the surrounding walls.

A number of men, some in black robes, others in more homespun clothing, were searching the stables and out-buildings. The hunt was obviously for Jane.

Slowly Machen closed the door and drew the heavy wooden bar across it. That would withstand hours of battering. There remained only the guard on the keep roof to overpower, then take his keys, release Lucas and escape through the chapel and into the tunnel where Jane was waiting.

Machen reached the third-floor landing. The door to the cell stood wide open. Even before looking inside he knew that Lucas was gone.

Now what . . . ?

Above Machen's head the guard stamped his feet on the floor, trying to keep warm against the cold, November winds. The sound was magnified between the bare, stone walls of the passageway, and as Machen looked upwards a sudden idea came to him.

Swiftly he climbed the steps and knocked on the underneath of the trap-door. The locking bar was pulled back and the trap-door began to open. The guard, unsuspecting, was bending over to his task, when Machen slammed the door upwards and hurled himself through the opening. The man toppled backwards, completely off balance, his musket still on the floor beside him. A powerful blow to the head, and the guard fell back unconscious.

Machen crept to the turreted wall and looked over in time to see a man in monk's clothing emerge from the main entrance of the hall, walk to the top of the steps and shout down:

"Any sign?"

There was a chorus of negative replies.

"Keep searching. She cannot have got far." The man had a distinct Irish accent.

It was time, Machen thought, to make his presence and demands known. He stood up and shouted, "Here!"

Every eye swung upwards. There was a still pause and then the Irishman tore down the steps, across the torchlit courtyard and to the door to the keep. He tried it, and finding it locked stepped back some feet into the courtyard and looked up at Machen. Even through the flame-broken darkness, Machen recognised him; three times he had seen this man before: on the beach the day they had taken over the Hall, then meeting Jane off the London coach, and lastly when he had killed Lady

Lucas. He was obviously the leader, the man with whom he must negotiate for the release of Sir John.

"So she is with you?" Not waiting for a reply the man continued, "And what will this avail you? Our gunpowder is stored separately from our other supplies. It will take but a moment to remove this door."

"I think not – an explosion in the middle of the night would inevitably draw someone's attention. Port Eynon is not that far away."

The Irishman looked down on the floor, pondering the situation. He lifted his face again, and even at that distance Machen could feel the cold ferocity of the man's eyes:

"What is it you want?"

"Sir John Lucas."

"Lucas! Now why should I give him to you? You are shut in a building with no possible means of escape, protected only by a door which can soon be broken down."

"The man guarding the keep . . ."

"What about him?"

"I have him; unconscious, but alive."

"And?"

"I will exchange him for Lucas."

The Irishman looked up at Machen in silence; then without moving his head he shouted, "Have Lucas brought here."

One of the man's original accomplices – conspicuous by his monk's habit – turned and ran across the courtyard, up the steps, and disappeared inside the hall. A strange eerie silence descended over the courtyard as the flames from the many torches cast dark, dancing shadows across the surrounding walls.

Lucas appeared in the open doorway, his hands tied behind his back. His guard pushed him down the steps across the courtyard to his leader's side.

The Irishman looked up. "A life for a life?" he asked.

At his words Lucas raised his eyes and searched the keep, and saw Machen.

The courtyard was hushed; no one moved.

"You have your answer."

And in one swift movement the man took a knife from his belt and slit John Lucas's throat.

The Irishman wiped the blade on his robe and replaced the knife in his belt. To the man standing next to him wearing a brown homespun suit, he said in a voice loud enough for Machen to hear, "Wait only until we have sailed, then break the door down and dispose of them."

And totally ignoring Machen he turned away and walked towards the hall.

Machen heard a slight sound behind him. He spun around. The guard had regained consciousness and was slowly rising to his feet, his eyes fixed on Machen, his right hand groping for his musket. Machen took one step forward and stamped on the man's outstretched fingers. The guard screamed out in pain. Machen bent down, picked up the musket and held the barrel to the man's temple.

"And now, my friend," Machen hissed, "if you value your life, you will tell me all you know."

The guard was only too anxious to comply. When he had finished, Machen asked, "Is that everything?" The man nodded.

Machen pulled the trigger, then made for the steps.

As he broke the news of her uncle's death – but omitting the barbaric way in which it had been perpetrated – Jane swayed and would have fallen had Machen not caught her. She clung to him, her face buried against his chest, her whole body shaking with grief, and he did his best to comfort her.

Slowly her grief subsided. Machen picked up the torch, held her hand and led her into the tunnel. Eventually they reached the cavern.

Machen found a flat rock on which he made her sit. Then he removed his naval jacket, placing it over her shoulders to help keep out the cold.

"I will not be long," he told her.

"You're leaving?" she asked fearfully, half rising to her feet.

"Only to reconnoitre our escape," he answered, "and find my grandfather's boat."

Machen crawled out of the shaft and, remaining within the protection of the thicket, peered through the branches, and beyond the open space between the cottage and the end of the dunes.

Dawn had broken. The sea was mildly choppy. John Lucas's schooner rode at anchor in the bay, and a long boat was making for the beach, where Conor Macnamara – as Machen now knew him to be – and eight of his companions stood waiting. The long boat grounded on the sands and then took them out to the schooner, which upped anchor and sailed proudly out of the bay.

The mast of his grandfather's boat showed above the bank where he had last beached it. Machen studied how far the waves had advanced towards the dunes. He reckoned that high tide would be in about two hours' time.

A few hours later they crossed the Bristol Channel to Minehead. By midday they were in Taunton; and one hour later they began their long coach journey to London.

At each stage-halt they found a corner to be alone. By the time they reached London Jane had told Richard all she knew. Of her uncle's experiences in Roscoff. The money chest which had been delivered to London. The Arms brought into Culver Hall and the long months of distribution.

To Jane's account Richard was able to add what the guard had told him. That the revolution was planned for 23 November, now only eight days away. The leader was a Colonel Despard, aided by two Irish brothers named Macnamara. The younger one, Conor, the leader of the band who had occupied Culver Hall, was the man who murdered both her uncle and her aunt.

Retribution would follow, Machen assured her. The guard had given him vital information. Tomorrow evening, at the

Oakley Arms in Lambeth, Colonel Despard was holding his final briefing. Not knowing that he and Jane had escaped from Culver Hall, Conor Macnamara would obviously be at the meeting.

As soon as the stagecoach arrived in London, Machen said, he would go straight to the authorities and tell them all he knew. The police would descend in force on the Oakley Arms; the revolution would be over, the ringleaders arrested, and Conor Macnamara would hang for his crimes.

However, one aspect of Jane's story remained an enigma to Machen. The money chest which Macnamara had delivered to London? Why should France – a country which had long since abandoned its revolutionary principles – finance a radical like Colonel Despard? Or more to the point, why should Napoleon Bonaparte want to support the man?

What did the little corporal hope to gain?

In Paris, Napoleon Bonaparte was putting the final touches to the speech he intended to make to the Assembly on the morning of Thursday, 25 November, the day after his invasion army had sailed. He read the closing sentences out loud:

> My armies are the best in the world. Who can withstand them? Certainly not your wretched English troops who do not know how to fight. Three days' forced march and we shall be in London, and then I shall acquire the rights of a conqueror. Treaties, constitutions and all other agreements will cease to exist. I, Napoleon Bonaparte, am no longer bound by them.

CHAPTER 17

The Admiralty commissionaire apologised that David Gregor was not in his room; an orderly had been sent to find him; in the meantime if First-Lieutenant Machen would care to sit in the waiting-room?

Machen agreed and then added, "Could you inform Sir Robert Noble that I am here. I carry a message from his ward."

"Very good, Sir."

The waiting-room had only one occupant, a young naval officer who stood by the near wall, nervously spinning a globe of the world supported on a large wooden stand. The orb's finger-stained surface bore testimony to the thousands of other young officers – himself included – whose temperament had not allowed them to sit still while waiting through long periods, sometimes days, often weeks, to hear of when they would receive their next ship's appointment.

Machen crossed the floor and sat down in a long-backed leather chair, one of three grouped in the far corner of the room.

He did not have to wait long before Sir Robert Noble appeared in the doorway.

Machen walked over to him. In character, Noble immediately confronted him.

"Mr Machen, I understand you have a message from my ward. After three months of silence I consider it about time. Had my duties at the Admiralty not prevented me, I might well have made the journey to Gower before now . . ."

At that moment David Gregor walked into the room, a smile of welcome on his face, which died away when he saw Sir Robert. He hesitated, then indicated he would wait until the conversation was over.

"Sir Robert!" Machen said urgently, "forgive me, but I have much to do and little time in which to accomplish it. Miss Ashford arrived with me in London but minutes ago. You will find her waiting in the coffee shop of the Golden Cross. She is distressed but, as you will discover, her experiences of the past three months . . ."

Sir Robert turned away and strode out of the room. Gregor moved from the doorway and crossed to Machen's side. He shook Machen's hand.

"Mr Machen! What brings you—"

"Mr Gregor," Machen interrupted, shrugging off Noble's insulting behaviour, "I desperately need your help." And taking Gregor's arm he led him to the group of chairs in the far corner of the room.

By the time Machen had finished Gregor's face was pale and his voice reflected extreme concern:

"But this is unbelievable . . . the country but seven days away from revolution and the authorities with not even a whisper of it . . ." Gregor rose to his feet. "We must warn them . . ."

"Mr Gregor, this is why I am here. Two hours from now Colonel Despard is holding his final briefing at a tavern in Lambeth known as the Oakley Arms. If we act swiftly he and his ringleaders can be caught red-handed. To which of the authorities should the message be . . . ?"

"The Police Office in Bow Street, without doubt."

"Will you take it?"

"Of course. But why?"

"I intend keeping watch on the Oakley Arms. If the meeting disperses before the Bow Street officers arrive—"

"But Mr Machen," Gregor objected, "even if it does, it will not take the police long to discover where Despard lives. And once they have him in custody they will soon obtain the names and addresses of the other ringleaders."

"Except perhaps Macnamara's. Remember how you first

136

described him to me: a man of the shadows? What if he is staying at some lodging-house unknown to Despard? When he hears of the Colonel's arrest – the news will spread like wildfire through Lambeth – Macnamara is bound to make a run for it. I made a promise to Miss Ashford and cannot take the risk of him escaping. He must be brought to justice for murdering Sir John and Lady Lucas."

"So you intend to play the hero and follow him back to his lodging-house?"

"Only if he is accompanied; but if he's alone I will take him myself."

"That could prove dangerous, Mr Machen."

"Nevertheless if it must be. Now, Mr Gregor, where is the Oakley Arms?"

Lambeth's narrow streets were unlit and dark but, following Gregor's instructions, Machen came to Oakley Street. It was little more than a lane, leading nowhere, and eventually petered out into open market-garden ground and fields. The Oakley Arms stood at the far end of the street.

Machen entered a vegetable-patch, and lay down on the muddy ground at the foot of the hedgerow to keep watch on the front door of the inn.

During the course of the next half hour the dim light filtering out of the windows enabled him to count some forty men entering the Oakley Arms, among them Colonel Edward Marcus Despard, conspicuous by his erect walk and the umbrella carried under his arm.

But there was no sign of Conor Macnamara.

Perhaps he is not coming, Machen thought. But then he rejected his doubts. No, this meeting was Despard's final briefing: nothing would keep Macnamara from it.

Machen stood up, pushed his way through a gap in the hedge and crossed over to the inn. He peered through windows: only three men in the bar-room, just two in the tap-room, all apparently regular customers.

Machen considered: Despard had obviously hired a private room, probably on the first floor. If the inn had a separate back stairs Macnamara would almost certainly have entered that way. But there was no way he could keep watch on both doors . . .

Machen took off his old naval jacket, turned it inside out to show the torn, threadbare lining and threw it over his shoulder. He looked down at his shirt and his mud-covered breeches. One thing was certain: no one in the bar-room of the Oakley Arms would take him for any kind of officer, naval, military or otherwise.

But once inside, what then?

One step at a time, he thought, and walked into the Oakley.

The landlord, who was pouring a drink out of a large earthenware jug, looked up from behind the crude, thick-planked bar. Seeing that Machen was not one of his regular customers he said casually, "If you're for the meeting, it's upstairs, in the clubroom."

Machen hesitated, fractionally, then thanked the man, and made across the sawdusted floor to the narrow stairs. No challenge came, and he reached the landing. It was very dim, the only light being that seeping up from the floor below.

A veritable babel of voices was coming from behind the door of the room at the far end of the corridor. Machen crept towards it, hoping to hear the sound of Macnamara's Irish voice.

Half way along the landing, he heard two men talking in another room, but with the noise from down the corridor it was impossible to make out the words.

Machen opened the door to the adjoining room, which in the light from the landing proved to be a small lumber room. It had no window. Machen closed the door slowly and drew the wooden bolt across. In the blackness he pressed his ear against the dividing wall to the next room and found he could hear the speaker fairly clearly:

". . . You can inform your Committee that the arms have all been distributed. Once the signal has been given by halting the stagecoaches there will be no stopping the revolution. In less than a week, Colonel, the government should be firmly in the hands of the Executive Council."

138

The title given him confirmed the listener to be Despard and the speaker was quite definitely Irish! But the latter was asking the Colonel a question:

"And the takeover of London? Is everything as planned?"

"There have been a few minor alterations," Colonel Despard replied. His voice had a rasping edge. "But in essence it is the same plan we discussed in Paris some months ago. Because of their arms stores the Bank of England and the Tower are still our main military targets, Conor."

Conor Macnamara! But he was asking Despard another question.

"And the King?"

"I intend to do this with my own hand," the Colonel answered, his voice flat and emotionless.

"Have you devised the method?"

"Yes, in this we have been most fortunate. The procession from St James's Palace to Westminster will cross Horse Guards Parade. The First Battalion will line the route and one of our members, John Wood, is serving with them. On the Parade a huge cannon captured in Egypt is displayed as a trophy of war, and Wood has been chosen to stand guard alongside it. On the night before the Opening he will load it with chain-shot. The following morning, as the procession makes its way towards Westminster, I will position myself at this point and fire the cannon at the King's carriage . . . and be damned if that does not send mad George, and all those around him, straight into hell . . ."

Machen stared into the darkness.

"One thing further, Colonel, before you go into the meeting . . ."

"Yes?"

"The assault on the Houses of Parliament. I will need at least 300 of your best men. More if you can release them. With this number I guarantee that, within a quarter of an hour of the attack beginning, not one person attending the Opening will be left alive."

"Then I can promise you that the Committee will agree to your request. Remain here, I will be back to confirm it as soon as the meeting is over."

Machen heard Despard walk out of the next room and into the corridor.

Machen sat still, his mind in a tumult, not daring to move in case Macnamara heard him. Despard's ambitions were far greater than he had ever imagined.

The King, the Lords and the Members of Parliament, all to be assassinated! Leaving Britain leaderless; and the revolution gathering momentum as the news spread across the country!

The whole affair was unbelievable.

Thankfully Machen recalled that by now Gregor must have reached Bow Street, and that the police forces would already be on their way.

Hardly daring to move, he reconciled himself to remaining in the lumber room until they arrived.

Suddenly Machen heard the sound of urgent footsteps on the stairs.

"Ah, John," Despard's voice carried down the corridor. "Better late than never. The meeting is well in progress."

John? It was a common enough name but could the newcomer be John Macnamara, the man he had fought with on the gallery of the Golden Cross?

"I was late returning from Chatham, Colonel." The voice had a definite Irish accent. "I have a message for you."

"Out with it, man. No secrets here."

"With respect, Colonel, but it's personal."

Despard declared his annoyance at the interruption, but followed the man out on to the landing, pulling the clubroom door closed behind him.

"Well?"

"It's a good thing I was late, Colonel! There is a man at the back of the Oakley. Says he must have words with you."

Despard swore. "Will it not wait, John?"

"Apparently not, Colonel. He said to tell you it was urgent."

Despard hurried along the landing and down the stairs. The door next to Machen's opened and Conor Macnamara's voice called out:

"John, in here."

Machen heard him enter the room.

"Who is it wants to speak to the Colonel?"

140

"I don't know, Conor, he's a stranger to me."

"Did he indicate what it was about?"

"No – he just insisted on seeing the Colonel."

Then came the repeated sound of footsteps hurrying up the stairs. In the next room the pacing ceased. Despard's voice came clearly from the adjoining room:

"Conor! Who the hell is Machen, and why did you not warn me about him?"

Machen gave a start as he heard his own name. And a sudden silence descended next door. Finally came Macnamara's low voice, only two words, controlled and yet full of menace:

"Why, Colonel?"

"Conor, do not attempt to outface me. The man outside has told me everything."

"And?"

"This Machen and the woman you thought to be imprisoned in Culver Hall have escaped and are now in London. It seems Machen knows all about us. He planned to send for the authorities and have us arrested while at the meeting . . ."

"*Planned*, Colonel . . . ?

"Fortunately for us Machen went to the wrong place for help. The police have *not* been called."

Machen sank against the wall, his mind in utter confusion. Since arriving in London he had spoken to only one person about Despard, and that was David Gregor! Which could only mean that the man outside the Oakley Arms, the sympathiser who had come to warn Despard, *must* be Gregor. It seemed hardly credible . . . and yet . . . Machen suddenly remembered their past conversations which had shown Gregor's intimate knowledge of political groups like Despard's.

How could he have been so trusting, Machen despaired? The police were not on their way to the Oakley Arms after all. The only two people – outside of those involved – who knew of Despard's plans were still himself and Jane Ashford. How could they, only two of them, stop the revolution!

At this, Machen accepted that the capture of Conor Macnamara was no longer important compared to his patriotic responsibility. He must leave the Oakley Arms at once and get to Bow Street. Despard and his revolutionary plans had to be defeated at all costs.

In the meantime the conversation within the next room was continuing:

"But with seven days still to go, Machen can warn the police himself!" Conor Macnamara was stating the obvious.

"Yes," Despard replied, "if we allow him to escape."

Machen paused to listen:

"Escape . . . ?"

"It seems, Conor, that the man is determined to bring you to justice. To ensure this he is at the moment hiding somewhere within sight of the Oakley Arms, waiting for you to appear."

Conor Macnamara cursed loudly. "I ought to have killed him the day we arrived at Culver Hall!" There was another string of invectives. "When we catch him, I swear I will personally avenge myself for all his interference."

John Macnamara asked, "What about the woman, Colonel?"

"Lucas's niece? She has already been taken care of."

The shock of the reply caused Machen to stumble. He fell back against the wall, and although the sound he made was only slight, it was enough to alert the men in the next room. He heard them walk hurriedly across the floor.

Machen shot to his feet and threw himself on to the narrow landing. But the three men were already in the corridor, with John Macnamara leading. Machen cannoned into him with his shoulder, hurling him back against the other two. But his own impetus carried him too far forward and, before he could recover, a number of men rushed out of the clubroom. They took one glance at the situation and within seconds Machen was overpowered.

Conor Macnamara walked slowly towards him, a long-bladed knife in his hand; there was no mistaking the venom in his voice as he recognised his antagonist:

"Machen!"

Macnamara came nearer. As Machen awaited the thrust of his knife, there came a sudden commotion from downstairs, and a voice called out to reassure the locals: "Do not be alarmed! We are police officers!"

Machen felt his arms released, and threw himself backwards, away from the upward swing of Macnamara's hand. The blade, aimed to enter under his rib cage, missed only by inches. As he fell against the wall Machen heard the pounding of many footsteps on the wooden stairs.

He turned his head and saw Despard and his committee members rushing back into the clubroom, while Conor and John Macnamara slipped into the other room, slamming the door shut behind them.

Machen pushed his way to the door and kicked it open. John Macnamara was already clambering through the window and up on to the roof of the inn, Conor preparing to follow. Conor turned and, as he saw Machen, his right hand sped behind his back and reappeared holding his knife.

The passage resounded with running feet, and shouts of panic from the clubroom.

Machen said, "You're done for, Macnamara."

In one movement Macnamara hurled the knife and turned for the window. Machen dived to one side and the knife went past his shoulder. Macnamara was nearly through the window when Machen threw himself forward and grabbed him by the ankle. Macnamara kicked at his face with his other foot. Machen rolled away from it. From the corner of his eye he saw a uniformed man standing behind him, a thick, wooden stick in his raised hand.

In the split second between the blow and oblivion he felt Macnamara's ankle slip away from his grasp . . .

The policeman looked down at the senseless figure and turned as a companion walked into the room. "Would you believe it? Fighting over who was to escape first, and me no more than two feet away."

CHAPTER 18

Machen came to slowly. After a while he realised that the thunder came from the wheels of a horse carriage. He opened his eyes and found himself lying on the floor of some closed conveyance. Around him were men in rough clothes, despondently regarding a number of police officers holding drawn batons.

Machen pulled himself to his feet and explained who he was to the nearest officer.

The solid custodian of the law looked at Machen's clothing and replied, "Yeah, and I'm the King of England."

They arrived at the prison. There were a number of carriages and some thirty to forty prisoners, including Despard, still walking proud and carrying his green umbrella with the hooked yellow handle.

But there was no sign of either Conor or John Macnamara.

The prisoners, Machen included, were held over for interrogation the following morning at Union Hall, Southwark, and then removed to the cells.

Machen was unable to sleep.

Heavy of heart, he was barely conscious of the other prisoners lying about him in the darkness – and all chained, as was he, to their hard wooden beds.

He lay on his back and looked through the barred window to the sky, his thoughts of a brave and beautiful young woman, his mind refusing to accept that she was dead . . .

Why had God allowed it to happen? Permitted Gregor to carry out his treachery; taking the life of an innocent woman instead of contenting himself with simply warning Despard . . . ?

But if Gregor had warned Despard – and as hard as he tried he could reach no other conclusion – then how was it that the police had still arrived at the Oakley Arms? If Gregor had not given the alarm, then who had . . . ?

Machen forced his mind to wrestle the problem, but was unable to provide an answer. Eventually he fell into a restless sleep.

At dawn the prisoners were given a meagre breakfast, then loaded into closed coaches and driven to Union Hall. Starting with Colonel Despard they were taken out for interrogation, but it was almost midday before Machen was called.

His questioner introduced himself as one John Stafford, Chief Clerk of Police at the Hall.

Machen gave him a brief statement which included no more than his name, naval rank, and an account of David Gregor's part in the conspiracy. More than this he refused to say, explaining that he had information relating to Despard's plans which could only be given to someone in the highest of authority.

At first Stafford refused, but Machen's insistence was such that he eventually agreed and Machen was placed in a separate cell away from the other prisoners. It was a small room, cold, with only a narrow wooden bed, a plain wooden table, and two chairs.

Machen paced up and down.

Hours passed. Suddenly the door opened, and a tall, grey-haired man of distinguished appearance walked into the room. With him was a young man wearing a guardsman's uniform, and an attendant police officer.

The tall man turned to the soldier and asked, in a low, cultured voice, "Well, Windsor? Do you know the man?"

The guardsman replied, "No. I've never seen him before in my life."

The tall man gave a curt nod, at which the police officer led the soldier out of the cell.

145

Taking the chair nearest the door, the tall man sat down, removed his hat, placed it carefully on the table, and said, "My name is William Haswell. I am one of the Private Secretaries to Lord Pelham, the Home Secretary." He indicated the chair on the opposite side of the table. "Please sit down."

Machen did as invited. Haswell cleared his throat:

"Mr Machen . . . Mr Stafford communicated your request to the Home Office and it has been agreed that I should hear your statement, once we had established that you were who you claimed to be, and that you were not yourself involved with Colonel Despard. On the first matter, enquiries at the Admiralty have at least confirmed the brief details you gave to Mr Stafford. On the second, the soldier I brought into the room was Guardsman Windsor, who until yesterday was a member of Colonel Despard's Revolutionary Committee. At the eleventh hour he decided not to go through with it and informed us of the meeting at the Oakley Arms . . ."

Machen recollected the evil look on Macnamara's face and the knife in his hand. Thank heavens for Guardsman Windsor, he thought.

". . . Windsor's confirmation that he has never seen you before means that I am now prepared to take your statement. Please tell it in the strict sequence of events, and take your time, omitting not the slightest detail."

Machen began from when he had first met Gregor, Despard, and John Macnamara, at the Golden Cross . . .

He concluded: "And then last night in prison, it occurred to me why Bonaparte might be financing Despard."

"And what is your theory on that score, Mr Machen?"

"A revolution such as Despard was planning would give Napoleon the ideal moment at which to invade us. Just imagine it. The whole country torn apart from within; its leaders assassinated; the Navy with most of its ships in port. In such circumstances a large attack on our shores could hardly have failed."

The Private Secretary rose to his feet. "An interesting supposition, Mr Machen, and one we might well discuss in more detail at a later meeting . . ."

Machen leapt up to face Haswell. "Later meeting! But surely I can be released now?"

"Unfortunately not. You will appreciate that before this can be authorised, there are aspects of your story still to be checked . . ."

"Then check them with David Gregor. Force him to talk!"

"I'm afraid that is not possible, Mr Machen . . ."

"Not possible! To force a traitor to talk? You will be telling me next that he is not even to pay for his crime!"

"He already has, Mr Machen," Haswell replied calmly. "In confirmation of your earlier statement a police officer was sent to the Admiralty to arrest the man. He returned with the information that Gregor's body had been found earlier this morning, stabbed to death."

Haswell paused to allow Machen to absorb the shock, then continued. "I can only assume that after warning Despard of your presence at the Oakley Arms, Gregor must have taken cover somewhere within sight of the inn to assure himself that you would be found. Instead of which he witnessed the police arrive and then – if I am correct in my conjecture – the escape of the Macnamara brothers. In which case he must have made himself known to them, offered them help. As they approached Charing Cross, your friend Conor Macnamara must have decided it was too dangerous for him personally to allow Gregor to live. Apart from yourself, Gregor was now one of the few men who could identify him. Consequently, as they passed the warehouses of Great Scotland Yard, Macnamara must have disposed of him . . ."

Haswell turned to the door, leaving Machen still stunned.

". . . But do not concern yourself, Mr Machen, I will return with your release papers as soon as the Home Secretary authorises them."

CHAPTER 19

A large fire burned in the ornate fireplace of the study of Number 10 Downing Street. Henry Addington, the Prime Minister, sat in the depths of a leather high-backed chair, drawn close up to the hearth. Lord Pelham, the Home Secretary, sat opposite.

Between their two chairs stood a small side-table, bearing a crystal-glass decanter half filled with port, and two goblets also half filled.

"Well, will *The Times* co-operate?" the Prime Minister asked.

"Yes, Henry," Lord Pelham replied. "It will print nothing until tomorrow, and then will give only the briefest of details."

"Good." Addington sighed with relief. "If the government is not to fall it is essential that we play down this damned affair. In no way can we admit the country was but seven days from revolution and we knew not a blasted thing about it. Already the city is abounding with rumours—"

"With so many carriages and police officers pouring down Whitehall," Lord Pelham intervened, "that is hardly to be wondered at."

"Quite," said the Prime Minister. "In which case, imagine the outcry if the city knew the truth. A conspiracy of colossal proportions, supported by workers' underground movements, and all of them – if this Lieutenant Machen is to be believed – armed to the very teeth . . ."

"And financed by France!" the Home Secretary added.

"Quite," said Henry Addington. "Why, the whole country would be in uproar."

"At least it confirms the suspicions of our military spies," said Lord Pelham. "The 90,000 or so men that Napoleon has barracked in secret camps around Boulogne, Calais and Étaples *must* be an invasion army after all."

"You really think that Napoleon means to send them across the Channel in these barges?"

"I do, Prime Minister."

"The little man must be mad to think he could get away with it."

Lord Pelham coughed discreetly. "He almost did, Henry. Furthermore, Despard's failure is no guarantee that he will cancel his invasion plans."

The Prime Minister leaned forward in his chair. "Then let him try, Pelham; just let him try. With the number of ships of the line we now have patrolling round, why, they'll all be blasted out of the water long before they reach mid-Channel! I doubt that even *one* French soldier will survive . . ."

"But can we afford to let Bonaparte make the attempt, Henry?" the Home Secretary asked quietly.

"Why ever not, Pelham? Barges will present no danger to our ships! And think of the celebrations if we present our people with such a victory. It would certainly make them forget all about Despard!"

"On the other hand," Lord Pelham objected, "it could look bad if it ever became public knowledge that the invasion and Despard's revolution were connected. In addition, Prime Minister, do not overlook the fact that since the peace was declared thousands of British subjects have journeyed across to France: some for business reasons, others to visit relatives and friends, or simply for pleasure. If we allow the invasion flotilla to proceed and then destroy it, Napoleon might well be constrained to take his revenge against every English man and woman found within his jurisdiction. If that happened I shudder to contemplate the depths to which our esteem would sink."

"H'm," sniffed the Prime Minister. "Yes, Pelham, I take your point. But damn it, if the man is determined to invade us, how do you suggest we stop him? Will diplomacy do any good, that's the point?"

"Ambassadorial channels, Henry. Send word to Paris. Let it be whispered to those who have Bonaparte's ear that we know of his invasion plans; make him appreciate the catastrophe that is awaiting the flotilla if he is foolish enough to attempt it."

The Prime Minister considered the proposal. "Agreed," he finally conceded, with evident bad grace.

Lord Pelham relaxed. He leaned across to the side-table, picked up the goblet nearest him, sipped appreciatively at its contents, and then turned to the Prime Minister:

"With a detail on its way to Gower to dispose of the Lucases and Miss Ashford buried away in Clapham that leaves only *one* person to consider."

"Quite," said Henry Addington. "This damned Machen!"

"Exactly, Henry. The question is, how do we deal with him? He knows so much about the affair that it could cause us considerable embarrassment if his version ever became public knowledge. It would contradict our own statements of it being only a localised uprising."

"And don't forget," the Prime Minister added, "that Machen overheard Despard's plans to assassinate the King and the Members of the House of Lords and the Commons."

"If that got out it would be *catastrophic*!" the Home Secretary said vehemently. "He *must* be sworn to secrecy before he's released."

"But we know nothing about him, Pelham. The man's a damned sailor, an ordinary First-Lieutenant, and probably fond of the drink. Too much ale, a loose tongue, and it would all be out. Why, he knows almost as much as we do, and what he doesn't know he seems to have guessed . . ."

"Napoleon's invasion plans?"

"Exactly."

"Then what do we do with him?"

"Let's sleep on it for a few days, Pelham, and then decide. After all, we can't have the government brought down just because of one man's loose tongue. At a time like this the fate of the country is more important than one bloody naval lieutenant."

*　　*　　*

150

Henry Addington accepted the copy of Saturday's *The Times* from the Home Secretary, opened it up, and read the report out aloud:

> Colonel Despard was brought to the Office and remained there a long time, but underwent a very short examination before the Council. He was fully committed to Newgate to take his trial, but not for High Treason, as it has been reported, in plotting against the life of His Majesty – no evidence to that was adduced. The crime he was accused of is seducing some of the Guards from their duty and allegiance. It has been idly rumoured that more than two hundred of them were seduced, but we can assert, from unquestionable authority, that the number does not exceed ten.

"That's good," the Prime Minister commented, with undisguised satisfaction. "Even denies it was treason. That should keep the talk down."

Henry Addington spread the open newspaper across his lap. "Now, Pelham, what about the date of the trial?"

"I thought we'd leave it a few months, Henry. Let it first become a matter of history, allow the hysteria to die down."

The Prime Minister nodded his approval.

"What does Attorney-General Perceval think of the case for the prosecution?"

"Cut and dried, Henry, especially now that Guardsman Windsor has persuaded others to turn King's Evidence."

"Good. I think it imperative, Pelham, that Perceval's opening speech state the government to have been apprised of Despard's intentions months before he was arrested."

"I quite agree, Prime Minister," said the Home Secretary. "He could add to it that we deliberately delayed action until their final meeting when we knew that all the Committee members would be gathered together under the one roof."

"Absolutely, Pelham," the Prime Minister beamed, then moved on to his next question:

"Who has been chosen to act for the defence?"

"Mr Serjeant Best."

"Couldn't be better. Have you had the opportunity of speaking to him yet?"

"Early this morning."

"And?"

"He has agreed, but only after much convincing that it was in the country's best interest. However, he has made certain conditions."

"Such as?"

"Only Despard and six of his lieutenants are to be tried . . ."

"And the others?"

"To be set free after the trial."

"And what does he offer in return?"

"That he will present no case for the defence . . ."

"But that's no use," Addington objected. "The man must appear to do something, if only for appearances' sake."

"Mr Best suggests that he be allowed to call witnesses forward merely to attest to the characters of the seven on trial; and then, on the strength of this, to beg the court's mercy."

"Which will be refused, of course?"

"Naturally, Henry."

"Then in those circumstances, it is agreed. Have the other six defendants been chosen?"

"Yes, Henry. As part of our strategy to make this appear a localised uprising we selected Despard's first-lieutenants in London. Their names . . ." Lord Pelham consulted a list held in his hand, ". . . are Graham, Wratten, Broughton, Francis, Wood, and a man named John Macnamara, who as yet is still at large."

"Presumably Irish," the Prime Minister remarked.

"Yes; believed to be a member of the United Irishmen."

"Then make sure you apprehend him. We could do with an Irishman, especially with the present unrest over there. The execution of one of their own could well make them think twice before starting another revolution."

Henry Addington leaned forward, the newspaper rustling as he pressed against it:

"Has anyone been found willing to attest to the character of any of these men?"

152

"Only for Despard thus far, but I guarantee the name will come as a shock to you."

The Prime Minister waited.

"Nelson!" said the Home Secretary.

"Great heavens!" Addington exclaimed. "How long has Nelson known Despard?"

"Twenty-five years, Henry. Apparently he fought alongside Despard during some expedition in the West Indies."

"But not since then?"

"It would appear not. Nevertheless he has expressed a desire to testify to the character of his once friend."

Henry Addington rubbed his chin thoughtfully:

"We'd better be careful on this one, Pelham. Let's not forget that Nelson's a bloody hero. We don't want any of his glory rubbing off on to Despard, or the jury might be persuaded to recommend clemency. I think you should instruct both Perceval and Best to be careful as to the questions they put to him."

"Yes, Henry." The Home Secretary paused a moment, then said, "To return to the question of Lieutenant Machen, Prime Minister. He cannot remain in custody much longer. We must either charge him or let him go."

Henry Addington looked straight into the other's eyes. "I'm glad you raised the matter, Pelham, for I have been giving it much consideration over the last two days. It seems to me that we have only Machen's word he was not involved with Despard. After all, he *was* arrested at the Oakley Arms, in circumstances which could only lead one to suppose he had been attending the meeting. Do you not agree?"

"Absolutely."

"Furthermore, in the delicate political situation in which the government finds itself, it could endanger public morale if such a man were allowed to broadcast his knowledge before the trial. Especially if his conversation, by some unfortunate stroke of bad luck, came to the knowledge of a member of the Opposition. Such an event could prove deuced embarrassing. And what this country needs most, in this moment of her history, is stability."

"Quite," agreed Pelham. "And a man like Machen . . . D'ye

know, Prime Minister, the more I think of it, the more convinced I become that he must have been involved."

Pelham then made a suggestion. "Henry, why not let a judge decide?"

The Prime Minister considered the idea. "Yes, yes, I think that would be best. And we'll make it as soon as possible, get the matter over with."

"What about first thing tomorrow morning?"

"Tomorrow is Sunday, Pelham."

"That's of no consequence, Henry. Leave it to me, I will arrange it. After all, in a free land like ours a man should not be forced to spend a moment longer in prison than necessary . . . unless he's guilty, of course."

MONDAY, 22 NOVEMBER 1802: LONDON
Late afternoon.

The dismasted *Justitia*, once a proud ship of some 260 tons, was doomed to spend the rest of her life as a prison hulk, permanently at anchor in the mainstream of the River Thames, between the two points known as 'Gallions' and 'Barking Reach'.

In this the *Justitia* was not alone; there were many ships like her, housing on an average some 250 prisoners, criminals whose offences in years past would have warranted being deported to the American colonies. But with the transportation system having completely broken down because of the War of American Independence, and Australia and Botany Bay being so far away, the popular sentence of the British courts for a man committed to a short term of imprisonment was – Machen could still hear the judge's awful words ringing in his ears – "hard labour in the raising of sand, soil and gravel, and cleansing the River Thames, or any other service for the benefit of the navigation of the said river".

Early on Sunday morning Machen had found himself brought before an empty courtroom and charged with 'inciting unrest'. Despite his protestations of innocence he had been found guilty, taken to Newgate prison for his ankles to be fettered, and then chained to those of a man so sick in appearance that he looked hardly able to survive the day. The following morning Machen found himself one of a tightly guarded party of twelve transported from Newgate to Woolwich. And now they had been conveyed to the *Justitia*, there would be no chance of escape.

Under the eyes of the guards – seven of them, rough and brutal in appearance, who patrolled the open deck with cutlasses drawn, looking devoid of all feeling – they were made to strip, wash themselves down in a large tub of water, and forced to put on a suit of coarse slop clothing. They were then re-fettered, and taken below deck into what seemed like a veritable hell hole, a foul, stenching darkness, where the prisoners were packed together, and where there was the constant noise of rattling chains.

Machen and the man fettered to him were directed to their allotted space in the centre of the deck, one narrow straw bed on the wooden floor which their joined chains would force them to share.

Night-time came but Machen was unable to sleep. He lay on his back looking up into the darkness . . .

Three long years lay before him, three never-ending years of hard labour. But already he had determined that during no part of it would he allow his mind to dwell on the injustice of his sentence. For brooding would inevitably lead to despair and Machen knew enough of the reputation of these prison ships. Many of those condemned to them lost all sense of purpose, and simply gave up, to become prey to the diseases which walked hand in hand with such terrible conditions.

They died. Rumour had it that more than one in three men sent to the hulks never finished their sentence.

However, to look at it another way, almost two in three did survive.

Machen was determined that he would be counted with this number. Every day he would labour until tired – but not exhausted – in order to find sleep. He would eat all he could whatever the taste, and after years in the Navy he was inured to bad food; avoid trouble so as not to undergo punishment and its weakening effects. And slowly, hopefully, if he could but retain his sanity, the days would pass into weeks, the weeks into months, and the months into years.

And when the day of his release finally came, he would begin the fight to prove his innocence.

With both Jane and Gregor dead, there was only one man who could give evidence on his behalf . . . provided that Jane, before she met her death, had told him the full story. That was Sir Robert Noble.

CHAPTER 20

The Sessions House in Newington came to a hush as the Crown's indictment of treason against Colonel Edward Despard, John Macnamara, and their fellow conspirators was read out to a crowded courtroom. Named the leader of the uprising – as the British government had now publicly admitted it to be – a gaunt, white-faced Despard had entered the court shabbily dressed, his hair cropped short, and with a cotton handkerchief around his neck.

With but one exception, the entire gaze of the thronged public gallery was fixed on Colonel Despard. That exception was a man dressed in a dark suit, his slate-blue eyes fixed on John Macnamara. It was two and a half months since Conor Macnamara had last seen his brother, who now was on the immediate right of Despard as the prisoners stood to hear the charges:

First Overt Act: That the prisoners on the sixteenth day of November in the forty-third year of His Majesty's reign . . . did traitorously conspire, combine, consult, consent and agree and attempt and endeavour to seduce divers soldiers and persons serving the forces of the King by sea and land, and particularly one Thomas Windsor, to unite themselves to and join and associate with and be aiding and assisting to them, the prisoners, and divers other false traitors, in a wicked and traitorous attempt to be by them made with force and arms to subvert the government and constitution of the realm and to depose the King . . .

Conor's mind went back to when they had escaped from the inn on the Tuesday evening. John had found them refuge with one of the lesser members of the movement, a chandler with a shop in Swan Yard, opposite Somerset House. Their plan was to remain hidden for at least a fortnight, until the hue and cry died down; then to make their way overland to a small fishing village on the west coast of Wales from where they would buy passage to Ireland.

But on the Friday, when the first report about Despard appeared in *The Times*, the chandler became noticeably quiet and subdued; a short while later he left the shop, promising to return within the hour.

He was as good as his promise, except that he was accompanied by three Bow Street police officers and a guardsman. The police officer in charge held a warrant for the arrest of one John Macnamara. He held no papers for Conor.

The guardsman, Thomas Windsor, was brought forward and asked to identify the prisoner. This he did, stating John's face to be familiar to him as one of Despard's leading lieutenants. He added that he had never before seen Conor.

John Macnamara was manacled and taken away. The chandler – who had obviously thought that both brothers would be arrested – immediately scuttled into his shop and barricaded the door to escape Conor's revenge.

The Irishman stood there, looking at the barred door, and giving the matter much angry thought. But then he decided that to take the man's life might well prejudice John's case, and walked away.

The next two and a half months he spent in a back-street lodging-house run by an Irish widow named Bridget, who helped Conor through the lonely nights of that long, cold winter by sharing with him the warmth of her bed.

During the times of Bridget's accomplished ministrations the fears had been blotted out; but slowly, inexorably, the morning had arrived . . . Monday, 7 February, the day of the trial, the day that would mean life or death for John.

Macnamara brought his mind back to the court proceedings. The Crown was represented by nine counsel, led by the

Attorney-General, Spencer Perceval. Chief counsel for the defence was Mr Serjeant Best . . .

The prosecution rose to present its case, and the trial began: "May it please your Lordship." The prosecutor bowed to the Right Honourable Lord Ellenborough who was leading the four presiding judges. "Gentlemen of the jury, it is so obvious that attention is excited in proportion to the importance of the subject to which it is to be directed, that I cannot permit myself to entertain a doubt but that you are already sufficiently acquainted with the important nature of your present enquiry, to insure to my address, and much more to the evidence which will follow it, the utmost attention you can bestow. I say the importance of . . ."

Macnamara was furious at the man's pompous manner, and the way he was pacing the well of the court, gesturing, posturing . . . all an act, a grand performance put on for the jury, to persuade them, to cajole . . .

Take heed, you *English* jury. John is not a traitor. He is an Irish patriot who carried the fight on to your soil. He is a soldier fighting for his country's freedom. It is under those conditions that he was captured. He is therefore a prisoner of war! It is in that capacity he should be tried by the court; as a military protagonist worthy of that standing. Not as a traitor!

Macnamara forced his attention back to the drama being enacted in the court. Eventually the prosecuting counsel drew to the end of his opening speech:

". . . Gentlemen, I think it is material now just to state to you, that though no steps were taken to arrest these prisoners till Tuesday, the sixteenth of November, the period to which my narration has now led me, yet the government were not unapprised of their transactions . . ."

He talked on, but with not a word, Conor Macnamara thought, to say that of the seven on trial John was the only one arrested at a later date and not at the Arms. Nor any mention that the only evidence the prosecution has against him will be no more than the doubtful testimony of those who have turned King's Evidence in order to save their own miserable skins. But surely the defence counsel was bound to draw attention to this damaging flaw in the prosecution's case . . . ?

In addition to Guardsman Windsor, three other soldiers and a watchmaker had been persuaded to turn King's Evidence. One of these, a soldier named William Francis, volunteered information for which the prosecution had not asked:

"I asked him [Despard] what was to be done that day. He said, 'There was nothing to be done, for he expected some money and news from France'."

This astounding statement, although it caused a loud whisper of conversation from the public gallery, was not pursued by the prosecution, who hurried on to the next question.

Only a few other minor witnesses were called to conclude the prosecution's case . . .

Best was then called forward to present his defence . . .

A buzz of excitement went around the courtroom, and then a shocked silence.

No defence to be offered!

Conor Macnamara went cold . . .

No defence! The anger rose up inside him . . .

Collusion! It was the only explanation! Complicity between defence and the Crown. The trial had been cut and dried beforehand! With no defence there was only one verdict the jury could give. They had no choice but to find the prisoners guilty. Despard, John and the others were nothing but scapegoats. Pawns in the machinations of English politics. Blood sacrifices to discourage others . . .

Such then was the English concept of justice.

No! Not justice – but *injustice*; unchanged over the centuries. If this results in John's death someone will pay!

An eye for an eye . . . and a life for a life!

Call Lord Nelson! . . . Call Lord Nelson!

The cry came from the floor of the courtroom.

Macnamara looked up to see England's naval hero, dressed in dark, well-cut, civilian clothes, his hair almost white, climb up into the witness stand and take the oath. He listened as Nelson stated, under questioning, that he had become acquainted with Despard in the Spanish Main in the year 1779 and that during the period spent together, "No man could have shown more zealous attachment to his sovereign and his country than Colonel Despard did."

The prosecution asked, "But as to his loyalty for the last twenty-three years of his life, Your Lordship knows nothing?"

"Nothing," Nelson agreed.

The jury took hardly any time to reach their verdict of guilty.

But wait! The foreman of the jury was continuing, to add: "My Lord, we do most earnestly recommend the prisoners to mercy . . ."

Macnamara breathed an inward sigh of relief. This then was the judgment of the people. Mercy would surely mean a prison sentence, not the death penalty.

The seven prisoners stood to hear Lord Ellenborough pronounce sentence upon them:

"It remains for me to pronounce the sad and painful sentence of the law upon the crime of which you are convicted. And that sentence is, and this court doth adjudge – that you the several prisoners at the bar be severally taken from hence to the place from whence you came and from thence be severally drawn on an hurdle to a place of execution, and there be severally hanged by the neck, but not until you are dead, but that you be severally taken down again and that whilst you are yet alive, your bowels be taken out and burned before your faces and that afterwards your heads be severed from your bodies and your bodies be divided into four quarters and your heads and your quarters be at the King's disposal. And may God Almighty have mercy on your souls."

An appalled silence fell over the courtroom.

Hanged, drawn and quartered!

At the front of the gallery a woman began to wail. Soon her cry was taken up by others, including a number of men, their voices raised unashamedly in grief.

Conor Macnamara turned away, his eyes blind with tears. He forced his way through the crowded gallery.

Behind him he heard his brother's voice declare loudly from the dock:

"I am now under sentence of death. I declare before God this moment, and may God never receive me if I ever spoke a word to Windsor since I was born . . ."

Macnamara wished to hear no more. He stumbled through the door like a drunken man. Half running, half falling, he distanced himself from the courtroom, and headed towards the city.

As he ran his mind kept pounding the words.

Vengeance . . . I will repay!

SUNDAY, 20 FEBRUARY 1803: LONDON

Five o'clock on a cold and cloudy morning and the bell of St George's Parish Church, Newington, began to toll. The people left their houses and began to move towards Horse-monger Lane and the Surrey county gaol. Soon the area in front of the square, three-storeyed prison was crowded. They filled the street, occupied the windows of the dwellings opposite, climbed up on to the roofs and even spread on to Mr Edwards's tenter ground on the east side of the Lane.

At six o'clock large contingents of Life Guards and Scots Greys arrived. The soldiers were deployed to man all roads leading from the prison, and also to guard the area around the prison entrance-lodge. On its flat roof a large scaffold had been erected in view of the crowd, now rumoured amongst themselves to number at least 20,000.

On the edge of the crowd, below the scaffolding, a man in dark clothes stood silently, waiting to look for the last time on the face of his brother. He listened to the people's whisperings, and to the other, more serious rumours being bandied about.

He heard them tell of how France was suspected of being involved in Despard's plot – in point of fact had not one of the trial witnesses hinted at this very fact? But it was understood that despite intense interrogation each of the condemned men had refused to talk. The well informed amongst the crowd even knew Colonel's Despard's final words on the matter. "Me?" he was reported to have said to one of the prison officers on being returned to his cell. "They shall receive no information from me, no, not for all the gifts, the gold, and the jewels in the possession of the Crown."

Another rumour concerned Lord Nelson. The crowd had it on good authority that Despard had written from prison to his old friend, reminding him of the jury's recommendation for mercy and enclosing a petition for pardon. Apparently Nelson had passed it on – without personal comment or advocation – to the Prime Minister, Henry Addington, and the only outcome of the plea had not been the remission which Despard had hoped for, but only a change of sentence. The seven condemned men would no longer be hanged, drawn and quartered, instead they would be hanged until dead and then their heads cut off and displayed to the people as being those of traitors.

Suddenly the special guests invited to witness the execution – about 100 of them in all, officials of the courts, dignitaries – filed on to the roof of the entrance-lodge. This was a sure sign that the ceremony was about to commence, and the people swayed forward. Moments later seven empty coffins were brought up, together with the wooden block which would be used when they cut off the prisoners' heads. The multitude fell silent, waiting for the prisoners to appear.

The first was John! His face was white. He was taken to the scaffold; the executioner placed the noose around his neck, at which John called out in a loud voice, "Lord Jesus, have mercy upon me. O, Lord, look down with pity upon me."

The people murmured their sympathy. Women began to weep.

Within a short time Graham, Wratten, Broughton, Francis and Wood – the last two dressed in their soldiers' redcoats – were similarly noosed. Then Despard appeared. He showed no emotion as the noose was placed around his neck, himself adjusting the knot behind his left ear in the hope of instant death.

The dignitaries on the platform now stood to recite the Lord's Prayer and silence descended over the crowd as, to a man, they removed their hats and bowed their uncovered heads.

Hoods were pulled down over the prisoners' faces, and at seven minutes before nine the signal was given. The bars securing the trap doors were pulled back.

Conor Macnamara stood there, dry-eyed. He had no more tears to give. Sorrow and grief had been expended in the days immediately after the trial; now his heart was filled with a cold determination for vengeance.

The bodies hung there for half an hour in full view of the subdued crowd, then they were cut down and taken to the back of the scaffold.

A moment later the executioner stepped to the front of the flat roof. Holding a bleeding head by the hair, he lifted it high before the crowd and said loudly, "Behold, the head of a traitor, Edward Marcus Despard."

Minutes later the executioner held up another head. "Behold, the head of a traitor, John Macnamara."

John's sightless eyes stared at Conor, demanding retribution.

How to avenge himself against them? The ruling classes, not the people. He had no quarrel with the English people themselves; he had come to realise that they were just as oppressed by their aristocratic hierarchy as were the Irish people . . . and the Scots, and the Welsh; the people of India, the West Indies, and even the Americans – until they rebelled. Everywhere their ships could sail, the English presumed the divine right to rule!

Everywhere their ships could sail!

Conor Macnamara's thoughts went back to that summer's day in Swansea when he stood at the window of the Blue Boar Inn, watching Lord Nelson riding past, sitting proud in his carriage, glorying in his reputation; and the poor people, misled by the fables attached to the man's name, according him the adulation he so much craved!

He remembered Nelson's brief involvement in the trial when he had been called to witness to the character of Despard. The question put to him had been: "But as to his loyalty for the last twenty-three years, your Lordship knows nothing?" And his Lordship had replied staunchly: "Nothing!"

He remembered how Despard had written to Nelson begging him to intercede. But despite his power to influence, the friend who could have done so much had chosen to do: nothing!

Thereby condemning Despard to be executed.

And John with him.

By his very indifference Nelson bore the responsibility of his class, the Prime Minister, the Cabinet, the prosecutor

164

and the judges, all who had conspired to secure John's death.

Then *he* must pay the price.

It was Biblical justice.

An eye for an eye.

A tooth for a tooth.

And a life for a life.

By evening only drink could blot out the memory of John's severed head, the streams of blood, and the sightless eyes staring down into his.

Macnamara found a dark corner in the gin-parlour across the street from the lodging-house and began to drink . . . one gin after another . . . until the vision of John's head was shrouded in a fog. But it still wouldn't go away.

He made to his feet and found his way to the door. The cold air hit him. He staggered across the street . . . into the path of a horse-drawn wagon. The animal shied up in its traces, then descended, giving Macnamara's right leg a glancing blow from one of its hooves.

Macnamara fell back against the wall. He looked down at his shin. He could even *see* that it was broken, and yet he felt no pain . . . until some moments later when a blinding, searing agony reached up into his mind and brought him the oblivion he had been seeking.

CHAPTER 21

By 18 May 1803 the political chess-game was over; the French trade consuls had been expelled back to France, and the two countries were at war again.

Napoleon publicly claimed that Britain had deliberately manoeuvred to break the peace. His words were placed on record. "The English want war," he declared. "They are the first to draw the sword. I shall be the last to sheathe it."

Thus it was that, on 20 May, Vice-Admiral Lord Nelson sailed from Portsmouth on board his flagship, *Victory*, to rejoin the fleet.

Macnamara picked up his copy of *The Times* announcing the departure, and slowly tore it into small pieces. His leg had been slow to heal, and now with Nelson at sea and beyond his reach, there was only one way left to strike a blow against England. That was to offer his services to France.

Which meant journeying to Paris, and renewing contact with the only person he knew there in authority – Desmarest, Head of France's Sûreté Générale.

MONDAY, 17 OCTOBER 1803: PARIS

Macnamara arrived in Paris early in the morning. He found a lodging-house in a back street of the Faubourg St-Germain, then walked the short distance to the Hôtel Juigne. Inside he was searched for hidden weapons, and then asked to wait. Two hours went by before he was eventually conducted into the presence of Monsieur Pâques, Desmarest's assistant. On the man's desk was a file with his name, "Macnamara – Conor", printed on the front cover. Pâques made brief mention of having met Macnamara before, then asked his reason for being in Paris.

Macnamara replied, "To offer myself into the service of France."

"In what capacity?" Pâques asked.

"In any capacity," said Macnamara venomously. "Whatever will cause England the greatest harm."

Pâques looked at him silently for a moment, then picked up the file and left the room. Minutes later Macnamara found himself once more in the presence of Monsieur Desmarest.

At Desmarest's request they first discussed the failure of Despard's uprising. Having laid emphasis on his own success with the arms distribution from Culver Hall, Macnamara then explained how the revolution had been betrayed by a member of Despard's Revolutionary Committee.

The Head of the Sûreté listened silently to the brief narrative. Only when Macnamara had concluded did he say, "My assistant tells me that your hatred of the English is in no way diminished?"

"I have no quarrel with the people," Macnamara replied. "But as to the government and the aristocracy, the so-called ruling classes and all that they represent . . . their arrogance . . . the way they have repressed my own country . . . the word 'hatred' is no longer adequate to describe how I feel."

"Something has happened since last we met?" probed the Head of the Sûreté.

For a brief instant Macnamara saw again his brother's severed head. And then the vision was gone. He looked at Desmarest and explained.

The Irishman's obsession with vengeance was obvious in his every word. Long before he finished Pierre-Marie Desmarest had made up his mind.

"Your offer of service could be of interest," he said. "But I must first give the matter some thought. Tell me where you are lodging and someone will contact you there within the next few days."

Conor left and Desmarest called Pâques to his room.

Without looking up from his desk he closed Macnamara's folder and handed it to his assistant.

"Place this with the dead files," he instructed. "The Sûreté is unlikely to require it again."

It was past midnight, yet sleep eluded him. Macnamara sat on the edge of the bed.

There was a sudden knock on his door.

His pistol was on the table alongside the solitary candle. Macnamara picked the gun up, crossed the room, and positioned himself on the side of the door nearest the latch, his back flat against the wall.

In a low voice he asked, "Who's there?"

The answer came in an equally subdued tone, although it was unexpectedly melodramatic. "A friend of liberty, equality and fraternity."

Macnamara stretched his left hand to the wooden bolt, slid it back, and pushed the door open.

In the light of the candle the man's face appeared to be dark, and his features were most commanding. It was a face not easily forgotten, and it cast Macnamara's mind back to the evening he had spent with Despard in the Café des Bains Chinois in Montmartre.

The man said to Macnamara, "We have met before. My name is Philippe-Michele Buonarroti. May I enter?"

They were in discussion for almost three hours.

"We will provide you with an Illuminati contact in London," Buonarroti explained, "a member of our worldwide brotherhood. And an alibi which will allow you to move about the country openly, with no fear of arrest. Apparently the invasion will not take place for at least two years. Use the time well. The revolution must be nationwide, and orchestrated to take place at exactly the right moment—"

"It will require some form of signal," said Macnamara.

The Italian revolutionary waited.

"The Colonel's plan," Macnamara continued, "was first to

take over London, and then stop the stagecoaches, but as this failed, there is only one alternative: an assassination."

"Perfect," said Buonarroti, "but it must be someone so well known that news of it will spread around the country like wildfire."

"The King?" Macnamara suggested. "Or the Prime Minister . . . ?"

"The Prime Minister." Buonarroti's reaction was immediate. "Always the head of government, much more effective. Then it is agreed, Addington will be your target."

"Pitt," Macnamara interjected. "Addington has not much longer in office. Pitt will be the next Prime Minister."

"What does the name matter?" Buonarroti shrugged. "That will be the signal. The method will be yours to plan nearer the time of invasion." The revolutionary sounded well satisfied. "As for the King of England and Napoleon Bonaparte," he continued, "they can be publicly executed on the same day, one in London, the other in Paris, as a sign to the people that the social system which has long oppressed all of Europe has finally come to an end . . . to be replaced by a new order of government."

SUNDAY, 22 MAY 1803: ERMENONVILLE
In the Black Room the initiation ceremony drew to a close.

Together, as though by a hidden signal, the Areopagus – all seven hooded and cloaked – stepped out of the seven white circles inlaid into the black floor. They crossed the room until they reached the spot where Macnamara stood, naked and alone, before a black marble altar, built some six feet away from the wall. In his left hand Macnamara held an empty black bowl, in his right hand a long black-handled knife.

On the altar itself stood a seven-branched black candelabrum, the light from its black candles shining on to the cover of a book which rested alongside it. It was a large book, bound in black leather; on its front cover, inscribed in gold, were the words, "Le Grand Livre de la Vie et de la Mort".

At the sides of the main altar were two lesser altars of similar marble. The one on the left held a number of objects carefully

169

arranged: a linen cloth, water, salt, a wooden cross, slivers of metal, sticks prepared for a fire, two small axes, a length of rounded wood, a miniature spade, a ball of thread, a miniature ladder and a crown of white thorns.

The spokesman of the Areopagus and the two men who flanked him continued past Macnamara and took up their places on the other side of the altars, facing him. The remaining four men formed themselves into a half circle behind him.

The man who stood by the left-hand altar picked up an object, the small cross, and handed it, inverted, to the spokesman. In the same manner, inverted, the latter received the cross and made over it the sign of the triangle, intoning as he did so:

In the name of the only trinity, Liberty, Equality, Fraternity, these are the *true* meanings of the symbols.

The *cross* is to crucify the tyrants who persecute us . . . The *crown of thorns* is to penetrate their heads . . . The *thread* is the cord to lead them to the gallows . . . The *ladder* will help them climb them . . . The *slivers* are nails to pierce their hands and feet . . . The *pickaxe* will bite into their breasts and shed their impure blood . . . The *axe* will sever their heads like the head of the wolf who disturbs man's labours . . . The *salt* will preserve the head, a reminder of the eternal infamy of tyrants . . . The *pole* will display their heads . . . The *furnace* will burn their bodies . . . The *spade* will scatter their ashes to the four winds . . . The *fountain* will purify us from the vile blood which we shall have to shed . . . The *linen* will wipe away our stains, making us clean and pure.

Macnamara stepped forward. He placed the empty bowl upon the main altar and then held his hands aloft over it, presenting the dagger, point upwards, in the form of an inverted cross:

In the name of the Illuminati, I swear to sever all bonds which unite me with mother, brothers, sisters, wife, relatives, friends, or anyone to whom I have promised faith, service or obedience.

I shall not fall into temptation to betray what I hear in the Illuminati, for lightning will not strike as rapidly as the dagger which will reach me should I betray this oath.

This I pledge by the shedding of my blood.

He turned the knife inwards against his palms, grasping the blade tightly and his blood flowed into the open bowl on the main altar.

From the darkness behind the altar Buonarroti stepped forward to pick up the bowl and then presented it to the spokesman of the Supreme Council. The man raised the bowl to his lips, then passed it to the other members of the Areopagus, until each in turn had re-enacted the ceremony.

Together they repeated the closing words:

Together we stand.
Ourselves Alone.

The last two words Macnamara repeated in his own Gaelic tongue: *Sinn Fein.*

In the name of the Illuminati and to the fulfilment of their Cause.

Weishaupt stepped forward and opened the Illuminati's Book of Life and of Death. He began to write inside:

William Pitt.
Napoleon Bonaparte.
George III, King of England.

He passed the quill to Macnamara.

The Irishman, with the Areopagus's earlier blessing, added a name of his own choosing:

Lord Nelson.

On a grey morning in November the merchantman *Johannes*, out of Hamburg, crept slowly up the Thames.

As it passed Woolwich those passengers who were up on deck were presented with a close view of the prison hulk *Justitia*. Various chain-gangs could be seen labouring about it, each group supervised by a number of guards with drawn cutlasses. Some of them were employed on the embankment emptying lighters of ballast, others were wheeling the ballast in barrows to where their fellow prisoners were spreading it along the shore. Nearer the river a small group of convicts was making holes for large wooden piles, presumably to secure the embankment from being washed away.

The dark-suited man who stood in the bow of the *Johannes* gave them little more than a glance. Now the representative of the largest wine merchants in Hamburg, Conor Macnamara had other matters to occupy his mind. In particular there was the forthcoming meeting with his Illuminati contact in London – the same man who less than a year ago had supplied details of the run-down of the British Navy to the French Trade Consul in London – in order to plan his itinerary for the two years leading up to the invasion.

As the merchantman slipped by, Machen glanced up at it. Every vessel that passed was a source of encouragement to him, a symbol of that freedom which, one day, would be his again to enjoy.

He sensed the guard's eyes on him, and returned wearily to his pile-driving, gritting his teeth against the pain, a dull, nagging ache which even in sleep never seemed to leave his body.

One hellish year gone. Two more to go. And when it was over: no more of this damned country! Wash its dust off his feet! It was America for him and the start of a new life.

PART FOUR

Freedom is more than a word, more than the base coinage of statesmen, the tyrant's dishonoured cheque, or the dreamer's mad inflated currency . . .
"The Nabara" from *Overtures to Death* by Cecil Day Lewis

CHAPTER 22

1804–1805

In May 1804 Napoleon Bonaparte proclaimed himself Emperor of France.

By the end of that year his invasion army totalled some 165,000, most of them war-hardened veterans of the Egyptian and Italian campaigns. They were now openly garrisoned in great camps spread along France's northern coastline, with only a very narrow stretch of sea separating them from southern England.

Since Spain was now in the war, on the side of France, the combined strength of their two navies made an impressive force. Napoleon's plan was for them to gain control of the Channel as soon as possible so that the invasion of Britain, so long delayed, could begin.

In the midst of his final preparations the Emperor received news that Britain had sent two military expeditions abroad, one under Sir James Craig to Malta, and a similar force to India under Sir Eyre Coote. Bonaparte wrote to Arch-Chancellor Cambacares that in the case of both expeditions "they are neither militia nor volunteers they have sent, they are their best troops. If then our flotilla receives the signal and is favoured by six hours of fair wind, of fog and of night, the English will be surprised, having stripped themselves of their best troops".

The order was given to Admiral Villeneuve and the eleven ships of the line under his command waiting inside Toulon harbour.

Napoleon's more detailed plan was for Villeneuve and his

175

fleet first to sail to the West Indies, from where so much British wealth was derived, and once there to ravage the islands. That task completed, he was to head back again and join forces with the other ships waiting for him in French and Spanish harbours. The combined fleet, a veritable armada of sixty-six ships of the line, would then sail towards a demoralised England, smash the Royal Navy off Ushant – the pivotal point of Britain's maritime defence – and sail up the Channel to cover the invasion.

Villeneuve's fleet in Toulon was being blockaded by Vice-Admiral Nelson and his ships.

On 30 March 1805 Villeneuve escaped the blockade during a storm, broke through the Straits of Gibraltar and linked with seven ships escaped from Cadiz under the command of the Spanish Admiral Federico Carlos de Gravina. Two more ships escaped from Rochefort. The total force numbered twenty ships of the line, eight frigates and smaller vessels. They sailed for the West Indies.

Thus began phase one of Napoleon's plan.

It was 11 May before Nelson was sufficiently certain of their destination to enable him to give chase. He reached the West Indies in only twenty-four days. But ill-luck in the form of false intelligence – both innocent and deliberate – kept his weary ships dodging about the Caribbean Islands, searching for the combined Franco-Spanish fleet, without once setting eyes on them.

Then, on 13 June, Nelson was informed that the enemy were on their way back to Europe. Which meant that the second phase of Napoleon's plan was already well under way.

Nelson gave chase but when he reached home waters he found that the enemy fleet had again disappeared. Leaving his ships under the temporary command of Admiral Cornwallis, off Ushant, Nelson set sail for England to obtain further orders from the Admiralty.

At one o'clock on the morning of Sunday, 18 August 1805, *Victory* anchored off Spithead.

After two years and two months confined aboard his

176

flagship, Lord Nelson was concerned that his abortive attempt to find Villeneuve and the enemy fleet might have alienated the affections of the British public. However, on the evening of Monday 19 August, as his barge was pulled to shore, all his fears were alleviated. Despite the heavy showers every place that could command a view into Portsmouth harbour was crowded; hats waved, and the reassuring cheers carried across the waters.

At nine o'clock on that rain-dripping night he set off in a hired post-chaise for Merton, a village one hour out of London, where he and Emma Hamilton shared house.

There followed three weeks of meetings with both Lord Barham, the recently appointed First Lord of the Admiralty, and William Pitt, who had replaced Henry Addington as Prime Minister twelve months previously. The main topic of the meetings was the threat of invasion and the whereabouts of the enemy fleet.

"They will have made for either Toulon or Cadiz," Nelson told Pitt. "By now they will have collected some sixty to seventy sail-of-the-line and there will be difficulty in overcoming them."

"How many can we muster?" Pitt asked. The Prime Minister appeared worn out by the ceaseless responsibilities of his twenty-five years in politics. White-haired, dressed in a black tailcoat, waistcoat and breeches, he was pale and emaciated and looked much older than his forty-six years.

Knowing his own fleet to total no more than twenty-five ships of the line, Nelson answered, "I do not count our ships."

The uncertainty was settled early in September when the frigate *Euryalus* hove-to off the Needles with the news that Villeneuve was in Cadiz harbour, reprovisioning after the journey across the Atlantic.

Once again Nelson was called to Downing Street. He informed the Prime Minister that Cadiz could not long maintain so many ships and men. The enemy fleet must soon leave harbour. Battle was imminent.

Pitt asked, "Will you be ready to sail in three days' time?"

"I am ready now," replied Nelson.

The Prime Minister called his Secretary to the study. Within minutes, sealed orders were on their way to the Admiralty instructing Lord Barham to send a shutter-telegraph message to Portsmouth for the *Victory* to be made ready for departure.

Pitt returned to his conversation with Nelson.

"We must have one final meeting before you depart," he declared.

"I am in Downing Street on Friday," Nelson replied. "At Number 12. I have a meeting with Castlereagh at one o'clock."

Pitt consulted his diary:

"On that day the Cabinet is to meet at twelve o'clock. Then shall we say . . ." he looked up at Lord Nelson ". . . about three?"

Nelson inclined his head in agreement.

"Good," said the Prime Minister, making a note in his diary, "that's agreed. Friday 13 September."

CHAPTER 23

It was six o'clock in the evening when Machen's release papers were finally authorised, and then it took some time before his old uniform was returned from the hold, mildewed and even more unkempt after three years wrapped up in tarpaulin. Three long, miserable years of appalling conditions, filth, and hours of crushing, back-breaking labour which had made the minutes seem like days, days seem like weeks, and weeks, months. It had all threatened to send him mad, especially during the long, cold months of winter when his spirits had been at their lowest; yet, it had never succeeded . . .

He changed into the uniform, to find it was loose-fitting as a result of the weight he had lost. Then he was rowed ashore and set free on the south bank at Woolwich. It was a most wonderful feeling, the lack of fetters and chains around his ankles, the clean free air, the thought of what America had to offer as soon as he had cleared his name.

On his long walk to Clapham – he guessed it to be about fifteen miles – through the dark streets and country lanes of Greenwich, Lewisham and Lambeth, he tried to focus his mind on the words he would use to persuade Sir Robert Noble to help him. Instead, the nearer he approached Clapham, the more his thoughts had become filled with the memory of Jane Ashford: her face, her hair, and the remembrance of her deep, brown eyes had not diminished throughout his three years of captivity. And this in spite of the fact that Jane and he had been together for only three days, days so fraught and full of tension that there had been no time for any expression of affection to pass between them, no words other than those relating to the urgency of their mission, no moments of unspoken understanding, except ... and Machen recalled the long coach journey, when Jane's head had fallen on to his right shoulder, and she had slept, her hands clutched around the upper part of his arm, as though drawing on his strength. For hours he had not dared move until, as dawn approached, Jane had stirred, and, thinking her to be uncomfortable, he had gently moved his shoulder, glancing down at her as he did so, only to find her looking up at him with a strange, steadfast expression in her deep, brown eyes, a look of tenderness – no, more than that – almost of ...

Machen forced the memory away. That was three long years ago and though it was hard to accept that Jane had been dead that length of time, there was no purpose in brooding.

It was very late by the time he reached Clapham, and midnight before he found Glebe House. Heavy clouds filled the sky, blotting out the moon. Machen paused in the gateway; expecting the household to be well asleep by now, he had intended to find shelter in one of the outbuildings and seek Sir Robert's advice in the morning, but instead a solitary light gleamed out from a main downstairs window.

Perhaps Sir Robert had not retired? Machen started down the drive towards the house.

From behind came the sound of horses being ridden across the common. They came nearer and nearer, until they reached the gateway of Glebe House, and stopped.

Machen paused and listened. For a while there was nothing but silence ... and then he heard the gentle thudding of hooves approaching across the lawn.

Quickly he hid behind a near-by bush. The hoofbeats came closer, and then passed only a few feet away, five dim shadows on horseback, making towards the house.

For over three hours Jane had lain awake in her bed, determined not to sleep. For a week Sir Robert had been acting mysteriously and tonight she intended to find out why.

Every evening after returning from the Admiralty, as soon as dinner was over he had asked to be excused, and locked himself away in the library. Left to herself Jane had taken to retiring to her bed with a book to read and falling early to sleep, only to have her slumber regularly disturbed around midnight by the sound of voices rising up from the room below. Each morning at breakfast she had tried to question Sir Robert, only to be told that it was Admiralty business to do with the impending sea-battle.

Jane did not believe him.

Now, to keep herself awake she turned on to her side and, looking through the window at the dark, overcast sky, she allowed her mind to dwell on the last three years.

She was one month short of her twenty-fifth birthday and the end of her uncle's guardianship. Since her terrible experiences at Culver Hall, Noble had made an effort to be kinder, but his few acquaintances were men without families, probably fellow freemasons, and she had therefore made no new friends to replace those of her own age who had married and left the district. Sir Robert had once spoken of engaging a duenna and sending Jane to Bath for a season, but she had not shown any great enthusiasm for the scheme and it had been forgotten. In fact she had deliberately let the matter drop; what with the constant talk of war – the articles in *The Times* spoke of nothing else – she was happiest within her own world. Ensuring that the household ran smoothly, coping with the occasional visits of her dear aunts – cousins of her father – from Yorkshire, entertaining her few remaining friends to afternoon tea, always with their mothers in tow, her daily rides across the common – how she enjoyed them – her reading, especially the latest novels; all these and other routines kept her mind busy and occupied. With one exception. Her tapestry work allowed her mind to wander, to think about Richard, and as that was folly she had put it aside some time ago.

What *had* happened to Richard? His disappearance was a complete mystery. She realised it was impossible to get to know all there was to know about someone in only three days, yet she would have staked her life that it was completely out of character for him to have deliberately walked out of her life without a word. She remembered the coach journey to London when she had rested her head on Richard's shoulder and pretended to be asleep. After a while she had felt Richard look down at her and she had lifted her face up to his, and in his eyes she was sure she had seen . . .

She heard a horse whinny.

Throwing back the bedclothes, she ran to the window and looked out over the garden.

The moon broke through the clouds to reveal five horsemen approaching the house. She drew back hurriedly, and peering around the curtains she watched them draw to a halt at the edge of the lawns. One of the men dismounted and walked across the gravelled driveway to the main door. Meanwhile the other riders continued round the corner of the building, presumably heading for the stables at the rear of the house.

The man reached the top of the steps, then turned to his right, away from the door, and walked across the terrace towards the library. She could see the faint light filtering out of the window and on to the flagstones below, signifying that Sir Robert was still in the room.

As he passed beneath her window, the man looked up at the house. Jane stepped back in sudden fear.

Machen watched the man approach the lighted window and knock. It was a long double-doored casement which reached down to the floor. There was a short pause, then the window was pushed open from inside. The man passed through, the windows were closed, and the dimly made out figure of Sir Robert Noble pulled the curtains to. But not completely, for a thin sliver of light showed between them.

Machen ran across the grass, up the steps, along the terrace and peered through the window.

Surely not!

Machen stood there confused with shock. Macnamara! And with Noble! Were his eyes deceiving him? But no, they were not! Then his original suppositions could have been wrong. David Gregor may not have been the traitor after all! It could have been Noble who had tried to warn Despard.

But why? And how had he known?

And how had Gregor come to be killed?

Think! Calmly and logically. What could have happened on that night, three years ago, but making an assumption which until a few moments ago was unthinkable, that a man in Noble's position had been in league with a revolutionary like Despard?

In which case Noble must have known from the very beginning that Macnamara was in possession of Culver Hall, and that, by running away to Gower, Jane had placed herself in the Irishman's hands. This explained why Noble had not chased after her to bring her back. Consequently when Machen had arrived at the Admiralty, with one week still to go before the planned revolution, and had informed Noble that Jane was at the Golden Cross, the latter must have realised that something was wrong. But before Noble could question him, David Gregor had entered the room. Noble immediately rushed to the Golden Cross and solicited the story from Jane. As soon as he heard it, Noble would have concluded that the revolution was over before it had begun . . . and in that event? Machen's heart leapt at the sudden possibility! Perhaps, perhaps Jane was *not* dead after all! . . . Was this what was meant by Despard's remark that Jane had been taken care of? . . . Could it be that Noble, thinking the revolution had been thwarted, had instructed Jane to hire a chaise and driver to take her home, while he returned to the Admiralty to complete his duties for the day? But then, on his way down Whitehall, Noble must have met Gregor, the latter being on his way to Bow Street to inform the police. Then, assuming the two men to have conversed, however briefly, Gregor could have told Noble of Machen's plan to hide outside the Oakley Arms, while he, Gregor, went for the police . . .

In that moment Noble had found himself suddenly presented with an opportunity to save the situation. Outside the movement itself, only three people knew of the impending revolution.

First, there was Jane (*if* his hypothesis was correct, and Jane was alive after all!), by then on her way back to Glebe House and returned once again to Noble's guardianship. That would

183

have given Noble the confidence to assume that he could prevent her from talking to anyone during the next seven days leading up to the revolution. The second was Gregor, standing there in front of him on a dark November evening, in the shadows of the warehouses of Great Scotland Yard ... Machen remembered the cane stick which Noble carried. If it hid a blade then it would have taken only a few moments for Noble to kill the unsuspecting Gregor and hide his body. Which left only one other person in the know – himself, hiding outside the Oakley Arms. Within minutes of disposing of Gregor, Noble could have been calmly walking down Whitehall, across Westminster Bridge, and making for Lambeth to warn Despard ...

It was probably not until the following morning, when he arrived at the Admiralty, that Noble discovered his attempts had been in vain; that some time after he had warned Despard and then left, the police – informed by Guardsman Windsor – had descended in force on the Oakley and arrested everyone there. From that moment Noble had no doubt returned to playing the part of the innocent, attending to his Admiralty duties and his position as Jane's guardian ...

Machen thought, and thought again – the hypothesis was surely too incredible – but how else to account for Macnamara's presence at Glebe House? Yes, it was certainly possible; wild as it seemed, unbelievable as it seemed, Sir Robert Noble *must* have been responsible for David Gregor's death.

And Jane? Was it possible that she was alive? Here in this house? The sudden hope filled him with renewed strength and the bitterness of three years' imprisonment vanished in an instant.

Donning her dressing gown Jane sped down the stairs. Entering the drawing room she crossed to the connecting door to the library. She heard the window being closed, the curtains drawn, and then the familiar voice. It sent a cold shiver down her spine:

"There are rumours in the city that Nelson is about to sail. Are they true?"

"Yes, he has been given command of the Western Squadron. He leaves tomorrow, at ten in the evening to be precise. He will be driven through the night to Portsmouth. There, four ships of the line await him: the *Victory*, *Royal Sovereign*, *Defiance*, and the *Agamemnon*. They sail on Sunday, on the first tide."

"Then the time is arrived!"

"Yes."

"When is the next Cabinet meeting?"

"At midday tomorrow."

"Perfect! The underground movements are ready. Two days from now – just as soon as they receive the signal – the whole country will be in turmoil. And if Nelson does not sail until Sunday, then the revolution will be in time to prevent him. His failure to return will not help the Fleet's morale, especially if the rumours that the French outnumber them two to one are true?"

"Nelson thinks it probable."

Again there was a pause in the conversation and then, "Did you obtain the plans . . ."

"It has proved impossible. But I can sketch the layout."

"Just show me how to reach the Cabinet Room, and where the guards are placed."

Jane heard the two men cross the room.

Noble asked, "Have you decided which plan?"

"Yes. I will use the Lambeth squad. As soon as I send word they will cross Westminster Bridge and make a diversionary attack on the front of Number 10. While they draw the guards, I will lead my four men – all handpicked from the United Irishmen and willing to give their lives – into the back of the building . . ."

"This will give you access to the kitchen area," said Noble. "Number 10 is built on a slope. The Cabinet Room is on the floor above, overlooking the gardens, and on the same level as the front entrance into Downing Street . . ."

"Where are the guards positioned?"

"Two on the door to the Cabinet Room. Another two outside the front entrance."

"None at the rear?"

"No."

"The whole thing is almost too easy." Macnamara sounded contemptuous. "We can be in and out of the building in less than ten minutes."

"It's a pity that Nelson's meeting is not at the same time."

"What meeting?"

"With Castlereagh, the Secretary of War. One hour later, at one o'clock, in Number 12."

When the reply came, Macnamara's voice was so low that Jane could hardly hear the words. But there was no doubt of the underlying tone of menace.

"The Cabinet meeting is bound to take longer than an hour. If we delay our attack . . ."

"Put the thought out of your mind!" It was the first time that Noble had exercised any firmness. "Your objective is the Prime Minister. Even the decision to include the Cabinet is of your own choosing . . ."

"But think of the catastrophic effect of *Nelson's* death! The British fleet would be so demoralised that a French victory would be assured."

"The Supreme Council gave you specific instructions. You have already extended them without their authority. Do not think to go any further." There came the sound of a drawer being unlocked and opened, and then the rustle of paper. "Now, as to the inside of Number 10 . . ."

As he watched from outside, Machen continued to ponder the question. Why was someone like Sir Robert Noble involved with revolutionaries, first Colonel Despard, and now Macnamara?

What sort of organisation was it that could bind together an embittered, ex-army colonel, an Irish nationalist, and an Admiralty official with an aristocratic upbringing? What kind of a movement could it be?

Jane moved slowly away from the door, hardly daring to breathe, her mind in turmoil.

Sir Robert in league with Macnamara! The spectre of revolution was again looming over Britain, a terrible reality if they succeeded in their plan. Furthermore, if she understood

Macnamara's inferences, the revolution was somehow intended to affect the impending naval battle between Lord Nelson and the Franco-Spanish fleet, but exactly how and why was a mystery to her.

But why was Sir Robert involved with such men? What could he possibly have in common with them? What *could* he hope to gain?

She heard a chair scrape across the floor, signifying that one of the two men had moved away from the desk.

"Finally—" Noble started to say.

"Take your time," Macnamara interrupted. "We do not leave until morning. I have instructed my men to stable their horses. We will bed down in the straw."

"But the servants will see you," Noble objected.

"What if they do? You can say we were five horsemen who sought shelter for the night. In any event what does it matter? By this time tomorrow the Prime Minister and his Cabinet will be dead and our plans already in motion . . ."

Jane stepped back in horror. She knocked against a small table on which stood a china figure.

The ornament fell to the floor and splintered.

Through the window Machen saw Macnamara spin around, and half run across the library floor, out of Machen's vision.

A few moments later he reappeared, pulling Jane behind him, his right hand clamped firmly around her left wrist. She was struggling and kicking to force Macnamara to release her.

Machen could scarcely restrain himself from crying out her name. Jane! She was alive! God be praised!

He watched as Macnamara dragged her into the centre of the room, in front of Noble, and then let her go.

"Traitor!" Jane cried fiercely.

Behind her Macnamara said, "Then she obviously overheard."

Noble showed no emotion. "Jane, you do not understand . . ."

"Understand! I understand well enough that you are betraying your country!"

"Tomorrow I will have time to explain; but not tonight." Noble turned to Macnamara. "We'll take her to her room; tie her up."

Macnamara said, "Kill her. This is the second time she has interfered in our plans."

"No!" Noble's voice rose. "That I cannot allow. She will be safe in her room. I will ensure that no one speaks to her in the next two days. By then it will be too late for her to cause us any harm."

Jane could feel Macnamara's cold eyes on her back, and the terrible silence as he decided whether or not to comply.

Machen saw Macnamara take a step towards Jane. He stood back to kick the windows apart when the main door to the library opened and two men walked into the room. Machen watched as Macnamara turned and gave one of them instructions. The man nodded, took hold of Jane's left arm and propelled her from the room. The door closed behind them.

Noble's lack of reaction reassured Machen that Jane was under no immediate threat of harm, and he turned away from the window, calculating the odds against him. At least four men in the house, with perhaps the other two staying in the stables.

In that case there was only one sensible place to start. Machen headed for the stables.

Jane's captor forced her to a chair in the corner of her room. She watched him tear her bedsheets into strips. There was little point in resisting or calling for help: the three live-in servants slept in a separate wing, above the kitchen quarters, which could only be reached by a separate flight of stairs.

The man gagged her and tied her arms behind the back of the chair. Then he knelt down and bound her ankles separately to the front chair-legs, in such a way that she was thrust into a half-lying position with her legs forced apart. The man looked up at her and leered. Jane felt a sudden fear.

"I'll be back," he promised.

Jane pulled frantically at her bonds, ignoring the terrible burning sensation across her wrists.

The moon retreated behind the black clouds. Treading carefully, Machen made his way in a half circle to come up behind the stables.

He stumbled against a stone wall.

He paused to ponder on how best to create a diversion, then crept along the wall until he reached the corner of the stable block.

Someone shuffled his feet.

Machen stayed absolutely still. The sound had come from the front of the stable. At least that determined the position of one of the two men. He listened for any indication of the second man, but there was nothing. Machen narrowed his eyes, trying to penetrate the darkness, searching for the man who had shuffled his feet, but it was like looking at a black wall.

Then he must make the man come to him.

In the wall alongside him there was a door. Machen felt for the wooden latch, lifted it slowly, opened the door a matter of inches, then pulled it back, to thud against the surrounding frame. He repeated the action again a few seconds later, creating the sound of an unfastened door swinging to and fro in the strengthening wind.

He heard the man approach.

Machen flattened himself against the stable wall.

The man turned the corner of the building. Machen saw the glow of a lighted pipe. It gave him a target. He took a step forward and brought his clenched fist around in a savage blow to the side of the guard's head. The man fell senseless to the floor.

Machen waited for the shout which would declare that the second man had overheard, but again there was only silence. He made to step over the unconscious figure, but then paused, knelt down and with his hands searched the earth floor. They touched the still warm pipe. He picked it up, the tobacco glowing red inside the clay bowl. Machen turned the man over on to his back and felt through his pockets until he found the pieces of touch paper he was looking for.

He also found a pistol and a knife.

He stood up, crept across the yard to the barn and continued into the building until he could hear straw rustling under his feet. Again he knelt down, drew on the pipe and applied the touch paper to the hot tobacco. The paper flared. Machen cupped his hands around it and brought it down to the straw; within seconds there was a small fire, small tongues of flame licking their way towards the main stack.

Machen left the barn and recrossed the yard to the main door of the stable block, and passed inside. At first the horses moved about restlessly but soon they quietened down.

Leaving the door slightly ajar he waited.

Before long the glow of the fire could be seen through every crack in the wooden door-frame, illuminating the yard and buildings in a dancing red glow. Soon the barn was completely ablaze, and wisps of burning straw thrown up by the flames were being whirled across the yard on to the roof of the house. Already the thatch was well ablaze in three places; the flames were taking hold and spreading rapidly.

Suddenly three men appeared shouting in the rear doorway of the house. Feverishly they began to attack the fire with pieces of sacking.

Behind Machen the eight horses were becoming agitated as they smelled the fire.

Hearing the noise, one of the men broke away from the fire and ran to the stables. As he burst in Machen brought the pistol barrel down on to the back of his head and he collapsed. Dragging the unconscious figure to the centre of the floor, he returned to the stable door and cried out as if in pain.

The nearest of the two other men spun around and came running across the yard, saw his companion lying unconscious in the stables and ran over to him. Machen stepped from behind the door and seconds later the man was sprawled out alongside his companion.

Machen dragged the two men into a corner and turned his attention to the horses. Smoke from the fire was creeping into

190

the stable, increasing their panic. Machen took the knife out of his belt, and cut through the restraining ropes. In a matter of moments he had released all eight horses; eyes rolling with fear, they galloped madly out of the stables.

He crossed to the stable door and looked out.

The one remaining man had given up the fight. He stood motionless staring from the barn to the now burning house, his back to the stable, and did not even hear as Machen ran across the yard. He swung the pistol, the barrel thudded against the nape of the man's neck, and he dropped to the floor.

Machen turned and ran to the back of the house.

The door was wide open. He entered the empty kitchens. Above him he could hear the frightened screams of the servants, and then the hurried clump of footsteps descending the back stairs. Machen ran across the kitchens, through another door, and down a long passageway into the main hall of the house. High above him the ceiling under the roof was already ablaze, with small pieces of burning wood hurtling down to the floor of the hall.

From above, a woman screamed.

Machen tore up the staircase.

The scream was repeated from behind a closed door on his right. Machen hurled the door open. Jane was still tied to the chair but she had somehow worked her gag loose. Some feet in front of her a burning timber from the ceiling was blocking the floor from the wall to the bed. The four-poster was itself on fire; the draw curtains around it a mass of flames.

On the other side of the room was Macnamara, the pistol in his right hand trained on Jane.

Macnamara spun around as the door crashed open. His eyes showed shocked fury as he saw Machen. He turned and fired. Machen felt a searing pain through his shoulder; it spun him around and across the landing.

Through the open doorway he saw Macnamara hurl open the window, climb on to the sill, and jump out.

Machen glanced at his bleeding left shoulder. The ball had passed through his jacket, but it was only a surface wound and he could still move his arm.

He sped back into the room, kicked aside the blazing timber, and threw himself down at Jane's side. Feverishly he cut at the cords binding her wrists and ankles to the chair and picked her up. She threw her arms tightly around his neck, burying her face in his shoulder.

He carried her out of the burning room and to the stairs. Half way down, he heard a shout behind him. Machen turned his head. There was a brief glimpse of Noble's enraged face, and then the man was upon him.

Machen tried desperately to keep his balance, but Noble's impetus was too strong. Together the three of them fell down the remaining steps and landed on the floor of the hall.

Machen was the first to recover.

Jane lay still.

Noble was on his knees, attempting to rise. Machen brought his clenched fist down savagely on to the back of the man's neck; he collapsed on to the floor, and remained there.

Above him Machen heard the creaking of timbers. He bent to pick Jane up, and burst into the library. On the desk were the plans that Noble had drawn up for Macnamara. Machen carried the unconscious Jane through the long window, laid her on the terrace, then hurried back into the library, stuffing the papers inside his shirt. From the hall came a roar as the ceiling collapsed. Machen sped back to Jane, gathered her up in his arms, and as he ran down the terrace steps the roof of the house caved in.

From the lane, Conor Macnamara witnessed the collapse. Within minutes the whole house was engulfed in flames, a fitting pyre for the shot, meddlesome lieutenant and the interfering Englishwoman, still tied to her chair.

He turned and walked down the lane. He looked at his watch in the light of the fire. Almost three o'clock. Nine hours in which to reach Downing Street in time for the Cabinet meeting.

There was plenty of time.

Guided by the three night-attired servants, Machen carried Jane to a vicarage a short distance down the lane.

The vicar was a grey-haired, genial, elderly man.

He literally pulled Machen into the house, and called for his wife.

Soon the good lady had put Jane to bed, bound up Machen's wounded shoulder, and left him in the study before a freshly lit fire with apologies that they could only offer him a chair to sleep in.

The vicar's wife woke him up to a breakfast of two eggs and a rasher of bacon.

Jane, she explained, was still in bed. "Let her sleep on," she suggested to Machen. "It will do her the power of good."

After breakfast he put on his dried clothes and walked back up the lane to Glebe House. There were a number of curiosity-seekers walking the gardens, but the house and outbuildings were nothing but black-charred ruins. Machen slowly made his way back to the vicarage, wondering how he could begin to explain to Jane that her home was completely destroyed.

The vicar was awaiting his return. He invited Machen to join him in the study.

Moments later Jane walked in. She was very pale and the vicar, having bade her good morning and asked if she had slept well, discreetly left the room.

"Richard, what time is it?"

"Ten minutes to twelve," he said, looking at the vicar's mantelpiece clock.

Jane's hands flew to her face in dismay. He crossed over to her and placed his hands firmly around her shoulders.

"What is it?" he asked.

"The British Cabinet meets in Downing Street at twelve. Macnamara plans to assassinate them."

Unconsciously Machen tightened his grip on her shoulders. "But surely he will no longer go through with it?"

Jane remembered the hatred in Macnamara's voice.

"Richard, I believe he will."

CHAPTER 24

Macnamara stood on the grass in St James's Park, behind Downing Street.

He looked at his pocket watch: five minutes to twelve. Time to move.

He had reconnoitred the area some weeks ago. As a result he knew that behind Numbers 10, 11 and 12 Downing Street, there was one long garden, surrounded by a high wall. In this wall, directly behind Number 10, stood a solid, wooden door which opened up on to Horse Guards Parade.

It was kept locked. But hours ago, while it was still dark and there was no one about, Macnamara had forced the lock with an iron bar. The door was now closed only on the latch. He felt the musket tight against his body, under his long cloak, and walked casually across the Parade and up to the door, opening the gate with the authority of one used to attending Downing Street on business. The people walked past, giving him hardly a glance. He passed through into the garden of Number 10 and closed the door behind him.

In front of him was a rambling, densely foliaged shrubbery. Macnamara looked up at the buildings. No outraged face appeared in any of the windows. He dropped to his knees behind the nearest bush and began to prepare his next move.

In the Cabinet Room, Prime Minister Pitt called the meeting to order.

Gathered around the long oblong table were: the Prime

Minister himself; Viscount Castlereagh, the Secretary of State for War and the Colonies; the Earl of Camden, President of the Council; Lord Eldon, the Lord High Chancellor; the Earl of Westmorland, Lord Privy Seal; Lord Hawkesbury, Secretary of State for Home Affairs; Lord Mulgrave, Secretary of State for Foreign Affairs; the Earl of Chatham, Master General of the Ordnance; the Earl of Buckinghamshire, Chancellor of the Duchy of Lancaster; the Duke of Montreal, President of the Board of Trade; the Duke of Portland and Lord Harrowby (Ministers without Portfolio); and Lord Barham, First Lord of the Admiralty.

This last Cabinet member had been over eighty years old when, as Admiral Sir Charles Middleton, he was asked by Pitt to become the First Lord of the Admiralty, with the title Lord Barham. In office only since 30 April, he was a brilliant tactician who already, in four and a half short but hectic months, had done much to improve the efficiency of the British Navy and to making its tactics as close to an exact science as its nature would allow.

The first matter on the Prime Minister's agenda was to explain Nelson's controversial battle plan. Lord Barham, as First Lord of the Admiralty, had been privy to the plan when Nelson had first explained it, and was therefore cognisant of the unorthodox tactics the admiral intended to use. But it was bound to cause protest from the more conservative elements of the Cabinet.

Pitt cleared his throat and began.

Macnamara was certain he had made the right decision.

During the early hours of that morning he had walked up and down St James's Park, his eyes half closed, deliberating. Finally, he had decided to revert to the Illuminati's original plan to assassinate the Prime Minister; and that would be more easily accomplished by one man, working on his own.

He had two plans.

The first hinged on the fact that the Cabinet Room overlooked the garden. Sometime during the course of the meeting the Prime Minister was bound to come in sight of the window.

When he did there would be one carefully aimed musket shot; William Pitt would be dead, and Macnamara already through the gate and making his escape.

The alternative plan was more dangerous. But he had taken the Illuminati oath to accomplish his mission, even at the cost of his own life. Should the Prime Minister not appear at the window, Macnamara would enter the kitchens and take one of the kitchen staff – preferably a woman – as a hostage, and lead her up the stairs to the ground floor at musket point. On pain of the hostage's death the two guardsmen outside the Cabinet Room would be forced to drop their arms and precede him into the Cabinet Room. One swift, fatal shot at the Prime Minister, then a knife held to the hostage's throat, and using her as a shield, he could retreat the way he had entered, and into St James's Park. Admittedly it was risky but he had the element of surprise on his side.

By two minutes to one the Cabinet meeting had become heated, being equally divided between those who favoured Nelson's plan and those who thought it strategical suicide.

Pitt, who was on Nelson's side, walked away from the table and crossed to the window. He stood there, looking down at the garden, summoning up the right words with which to sway the objectors.

Macnamara's eyes closed to slits as he focused on the figure at the window.

There was no doubt. It was William Pitt. The Prime Minister stood still, looking down into the garden. A perfect target!

Macnamara closed his left eye and squinted along the barrel of his musket. He aimed at the centre of the Prime Minister's breast, feeling the trigger tight against the first finger of his right hand; but then, as suddenly as he had appeared, Pitt moved away from the window. Macnamara lowered his musket. It was time to attempt his second plan.

A clock struck one.

Macnamara looked at Number 10 Downing Street then across at Number 12.

Within the latter's walls at this very moment, unprotected, was Lord Nelson, hero of the people and commander of the English battle fleet!

Unprotected, that was the important factor; whereas Pitt had two guards. What if one of them put the life of the Prime Minister before that of the hostage, and fired his musket? The assassination having failed, there would be no signal, and the revolution would be lost.

During Macnamara's weeks in Paris, Buonarroti, the Italian revolutionary, had schooled him well in his theories of military strategy. Philippe would certainly agree that in these circumstances the better military tactic would be to assassinate the commander of the battle fleet rather than the Prime Minister. The emotional blow which the British fleet would suffer when they heard of Nelson's death could well tip the scales between success and defeat. And Nelson's assassination would still act as a signal for the revolution to commence.

But even more than this he was haunted by the ever-recurring nightmare of the execution and the awful memory of John's severed head looking down at him, his eyes, even in death, demanding vengeance.

No, John, I have not forgotten my vow.

An eye for an eye!

And Nelson's life for your life!

In the Cabinet Room Pitt turned from the window to see Viscount Castlereagh slowly withdraw his watch from his pocket. The gesture was not lost on the Prime Minister. He faced the Secretary of War.

"Castlereagh, I am well aware of the time, and of your meeting with Lord Nelson. If we can but bring this overlong discussion to a conclusion . . ."

But Pitt's sigh evidenced that he was not too optimistic.

In the small waiting room on the right of the hall in Number 12, Lord Nelson pulled out his watch: one o'clock. It seemed that

Castlereagh intended to keep him waiting; or the Cabinet meeting was running late.

Machen pulled his horse to a halt, dismounted, tethered the labouring animal to a hitching post alongside the wall at the rear of Downing Street, from where, according to Jane, Macnamara intended to make his assassination attempt.

A clock struck one.

If Jane was right and Macnamara had continued with his threat, then whatever Fate had decided must have happened now. But the people on the streets gave no sign that anything unusual had taken place. Surely if Downing Street had been attacked and Pitt assassinated, the city would by now be in uproar?

It was then he saw the forced lock. He hurled the gate open and Macnamara was revealed in the far corner of the garden, but making for the end house, and not for Number 10!

Machen shouted a warning, and began to run, through the flowers and bushes.

Macnamara turned. His right arm came out of his cloak; in his hand he held a musket.

Machen stopped running.

Exasperated at hearing the same arguments repeated over and over Pitt was pacing the Cabinet Room. Suddenly he heard a shout. It sounded as if it came from the garden below.

The Prime Minister hurried to the window and saw two men facing each other across the lawn, one well dressed and holding a musket, the other in old naval clothes, faded and torn.

Pitt turned to his Cabinet. "Two men in the garden, one of them with a musket!"

The entire Cabinet rose as one from the table, scraping their chairs on the floor in their anxiety to observe this dramatic event. They hurried to Pitt's side. Lord Barham, being the eldest and therefore slower on his feet than the others, was the last to arrive.

Camden pointed at Macnamara. "Dressed like a gentleman. The other looks a ruffian."

Eldon: "Probably some footpad."

Pitt: "But how did they get into the garden?"

Eldon: "Someone must have left the gate open. No doubt the attack took place on the other side of the wall. The victim saw the gap and ran into the garden to find refuge."

Hawkesbury: "Why doesn't he use his gun?"

Eldon: "Damned footpad's not staying still! Keeps bobbing about, making a difficult target."

Camden disagreed. He pointed to the way the gentleman was circling himself around to get to the garden wall, all the time forcing the footpad back against Number 10. "He's trying to take the man alive. See how he's manoeuvring the man around, blocking his escape."

Pitt agreed. He called out, and one of the two guardsmen on duty outside the Cabinet Chamber rushed into the room.

The Prime Minister gave him instructions.

Neither man was ready to take the initiative.

Machen thought: If I rush him, he will shoot, and probably hit me; but while I keep moving about he cannot take the chance. By now, someone in Number 10 must have seen us and help will be on the way.

Behind him he heard a door open, and then the thud of running footsteps. Machen saw fear and hesitation appear in Macnamara's eyes.

The footsteps halted, and suddenly, for some inexplicable reason, Macnamara smiled.

A voice said, "Don't move," and Machen felt the barrel of a firearm against the small of his back.

Macnamara turned and ran for the gate, his musket clutched in his right hand to discourage pursuit.

Machen spun around, to face a young guardsman: "Your rifle! Quickly!"

The soldier stood still, unsure what to do: the Prime Minister had given him no instructions to shoot.

199

Machen hit him full on the chin. As the man staggered back, Machen grabbed at the rifle and wrenched it from his grasp. He turned; Macnamara had already reached the gate. There was no time to aim. In one movement he brought the rifle to his shoulder, pointed it, and fired. Splinters of wood flew from the gatepost above Macnamara's head. In the next moment the Irishman was through the gateway and into the lane.

Machen dropped the firearm and made after him, and as he ran he could see Macnamara through the opening in the wall, trying desperately to free the waiting horse from the hitching post.

Machen was not half way to the gate when the Irishman succeeded, leapt on to the animal's back, and galloped away across Horse Guards Parade and into St James's Park.

Machen turned and looked up at Number 10 Downing Street. A sea of startled faces returned his gaze from a large window on the first floor.

In the meantime the guardsman had recovered, picked up his rifle, and was advancing on Machen with bayonet fixed.

On the first floor Pitt opened a window and called down: "Guardsman! Put that man under arrest!"

Machen looked up at the Prime Minister, declared his naval rank and name, and demanded to speak to someone on a matter vital to the security of the nation.

Machen was conducted under armed escort into the Prime Minister's study where he found William Pitt and Lord Barham waiting. Machen handed over Noble's papers and the sketch-plan of Number 10, and then began his explanation, but within minutes the Prime Minister suspended further discussion until the guardsman was out of the study. Noble's papers were then handed over and Machen asked to continue. From two leather chairs on opposite sides of the hearth Mr Pitt and Lord Barham listened to his story very intently.

At last Pitt said, "Mr Machen, I must confess that, for the life of me, there is one thing which I am completely unable to fathom."

"Sir?"

"You say this Macnamara's plan was to assassinate myself and the Cabinet?"

"Yes, Prime Minister; according to all that Miss Ashford overheard."

"And yet, when you entered the garden, the man was making for Number 12?"

Machen nodded.

Pitt suddenly leaned forward in his chair.

"At one o'clock Lord Nelson had a meeting in that building," he said quickly. "Noble would have been aware of this and could have communicated it to Macnamara. Is it possible that Nelson was also a target? Before Nelson's meeting with Castlereagh is over there must be an escort of marine guards posted outside Number 12. They are to accompany Lord Nelson back to Merton and then remain with him until he rejoins the *Victory*. I have a meeting with Nelson at three, when I will personally explain to him the reason for these precautions; in the meantime could you, Barham, arrange the escort?"

Nodding his agreement Lord Barham rose slowly from his chair but before he left the room the Prime Minister extended his right hand to Machen:

"Mr Machen, mere words will never be able to express our indebtedness. By your courage and perseverance you have prevented the most heinous of crimes. As of this moment you have my word that all false charges and convictions against your name will be obliterated; you might even receive some pecuniary compensation, but certainly your naval rank will be fully restored." Pitt turned to the First Lord of the Admiralty, "Barham, if I could make one further proposal?"

The First Lord paused by the door.

"Lieutenant Machen is the only man who knows what this Irishman looks like. I think he should accompany the escort, with instructions to stay close to Lord Nelson in the event that Macnamara makes such an attempt. Heaven knows there will be plenty of opportunity, especially in Portsmouth, the damn place is sure to be crowded with people come to watch *Victory* sail away."

Lord Barham agreed and left the room. The Prime Minister turned to Richard:

"Mr Machen . . ."

"Sir?"

Machen's thoughts whirled around inside his head. He was being asked to risk his life – and his happiness – again! With the arrogance of those born to lead, the Prime Minister had assumed Machen's compliance.

"That being agreed, as soon as Lord Nelson has safely left Portsmouth you are to return to Downing Street."

Yet Machen's conflict was suddenly resolved. Britain was at war, Lord Nelson must be protected. This time when Machen answered his voice no longer reflected doubt.

"Sir, it would be appreciated if word could be sent to Miss Ashford telling her of my whereabouts for the next few days."

"Rest content, Mr Machen, she will be informed. In return I would ask that you devote your attention to ensuring your Admiral is returned safely to the *Victory*. If the French have indeed been successful in gathering a fleet of some sixty ships," the Prime Minister looked straight at Machen, "then the outcome of the impending conflict could well be decided by Lord Nelson's battle plan."

At Merton, the noise of wheels on the gravelled drive signified that the moment for Nelson's departure had finally arrived.

Nelson went upstairs to take one last look at his love-child, Horatia. The little four-year-old lay fast asleep, and Nelson knelt down beside her bed. He remained some ten minutes in the room, offering up silent prayers and gazing tenderly at her. Then he returned downstairs to take his leave of Emma. They embraced, both too full of emotion to speak, before Nelson suddenly tore himself free, walked out of the house, and climbed into the post-chaise.

Machen, in a hastily found new uniform, and the mounted escort fell in around the carriage, protecting from all sides the man charged with the fate of the very nation.

They journeyed through the night and arrived at the

George, in Portsmouth High Street, at six o'clock the following morning.

At the dockyard, Nelson was informed by the captains of the *Royal Sovereign*, *Defiance* and the *Agamemnon*, whose ships were to have sailed with the *Victory*, that they required more time to prepare. Nelson instructed them to follow after with the greatest possible speed, then he returned to the George.

Everywhere the throngs followed him, shouting out their huzzas, calling his name, stretching out their hands to touch him.

With Machen and his escort surrounding him, the admiral left the George by the back entrance. Portsmouth was thronged with people come to see his departure and Nelson was almost immediately recognised, and by the time they reached the outer beach an immense crowd had gathered, pushing against the protective lines of soldiers in their scarlet coats.

As Nelson approached the stone steps many of the people dropped to their knees, uncovered their heads, and called for God's blessing upon the small figure, who looked too frail to undertake the great responsibility being placed upon him.

Five paces in front of Nelson, Machen gazed anxiously over the faces of the crowd, searching for Macnamara. Thankfully, he saw no sign of the man.

The admiral's barge from the *Victory* was waiting, riding the swell of the waters, her crew sitting upright, oars raised, caps off. With them was Flag-Captain Hardy, anxious to welcome his commander back aboard.

To the cheers of the crowd swelling up to a mighty roar, the oars dipped, and the barge pulled away. At eight o'clock on the following morning, Sunday, 15 September, His Majesty's Ship *Victory* put to sea.

But by then Machen was back in London, as instructed by Pitt.

CHAPTER 25

SUNDAY, 15 SEPTEMBER 1805: LONDON
William Pitt drew the heavy dark-blue curtains across the window, shutting out the dark night. On the polished wooden cabinet across the study stood a silver candle-holder, the flames from its six lighted, waxen tapers mingling with those from the fire to cast a warm glow over the room.

The Prime Minister walked back to his leather chair on the left of the hearth and sat down, placing a half-empty glass of port down on a small side-table beside his chair. Then he leaned forward and picked two logs out of a large metal scuttle and threw them on to the fire, sending a shower of sparks dancing and crackling up the chimney.

Finally Pitt sat back in his chair, and looking across at Jane and Richard, he resumed his conversation.

"It will be necessary for you both to swear and sign oaths of secrecy," he instructed. "You will find the offices of the Depot of Military Knowledge on the top floor of the Commander-in-Chief's headquarters in Whitehall."

Pitt stretched out a hand and drained the remainder of the port.

"The Depot," he continued, "has four branches. The first – which is the department you will be assisting – collects information from agents, working internally both within our own shores and overseas. The second department collates details of troop movements. The third is building up a library which can be used for studying past and current military operations in every country on the globe; and the fourth is devoted to the collection, preparation and copying of maps. Only our most intelligent officers are employed by the Depot. One of them, a lieutenant-colonel, has already been delegated to question you."

"He will receive our fullest co-operation, Prime Minister," Machen confirmed.

Pitt poured himself another glass of port. He seemed reflective.

"That a certain revolutionary mood exists I accept." The Prime Minister cleared his throat. "I would be the first to admit that some of the legislation we have been forced to introduce over the past years – the Combination Acts for example – could perhaps be interpreted as repressive by the minority radical element." The Prime Minister toyed with his goblet. "Neither does this Macnamara's involvement come as any great surprise. Wherever there is trouble, turn over the nearest stone, and underneath it you can depend upon finding a United Irishman . . .

"But for the life of me I cannot understand why a man of the standing and position of Sir Robert Noble should have become embroiled in revolutionary intrigue. What on earth could he have hoped to gain? Furthermore, the fact that Noble *was* involved must inevitably lead one to ask whether he was an isolated example?' The Prime Minister leaned forward in his chair. "Or does it mean that there may be others like him, men of equal position and standing, also involved?"

Pitt turned his face and looked reflectively into the fire. Then suddenly his mood changed; he returned his empty glass to the table and stood to his feet, the meeting at an end.

"Still, this is for the Depot of Military Knowledge to ascertain. In the meantime it behoves the rest of us to bend the knee and pray to Almighty God that Lord Nelson be granted the victory which will keep Britain safe from Napoleon's grasping hand."

SATURDAY, 28 SEPTEMBER 1805: LONDON
The fortnight had passed all too quickly. The meetings with military intelligence were over.

Jane closed the door to her hotel room and leaned against it, her legs trembling. It took a moment to steady herself, then she crossed to the bed and pulled her nightdress out from under the sheets.

She climbed into bed and pulling the blankets over her she lay there watching the weird shadows created by the sputtering flame of the wax nightlight. Her body tingled with strange sensations. She turned on her side to face the window and looked up at the star-studded night sky.

Tomorrow she and Richard would part. Earlier that evening, as they sat down to their last meal together, she had seen the unspoken love in his eyes, and felt his almost startled reaction when their hands accidentally touched. But dinner had passed by, they had climbed the stairs, and said their good nights on the landing without Richard giving the slightest spoken hint of his feelings.

She knew why. It was nothing to do with the burning down of Glebe House. That particular burden she had removed from his shoulders some ten days before when she thanked him for rescuing her and reassured him that material possessions could always be rebuilt: though she knew her tone reflected great regret. But the barrier which Richard imagined existed between them was much deeper than this. And Jane had sensed what it was. To his stubborn, male way of thinking he was a man of no means, while she was a young woman of untold wealth, increased even more – since they had met three years ago – by her inheritance of the estates and enterprises of her uncle, John Lucas. Richard Machen, one could almost hear him say, was no fortune hunter. And that was the barrier. His obstinate pride. Somehow she must make him realise that love could remove all obstacles.

The question was how?

It was a moment for decision. Tomorrow would be too late, and this strange emotion which possessed her, her mind, her whole body, might be lost to her unless she could find the courage to act now. She thought of Richard and more than anything she wanted this night as a time to set apart from all that had gone before, to break his resistance, and to whisper about the joys that a new tomorrow could bring. It was a night that could belong to them; the moon which shone through the window might have been specially created, the majestic sweep of the sky and the muffled sounds of the city, the fire that warmed the room and the flames which made her body glow were things they should be sharing together at this very moment, in a world of their own making where nothing would matter but what they would find in each other's arms, oblivious to all else but themselves. Her feelings, her wants, her desires, she knew were against all of society's accepted conventions; nevertheless . . .

There was a knock on the door. Jane rose from her bed, put on her dressing gown and crossed the room. "Yes?" she asked in a low voice.

The answer came: "It's Richard," and she hastened to open the door.

He stood framed in the doorway, in white shirt and breeches, his jacket removed. He looked down at her and she saw by his eyes that the wanting, the desiring was not hers alone. He entered the room, bolted the door and came and stood close up to her, but as yet their bodies had not touched.

"Richard?" She could hear her voice tremble.

"I love you," he said simply, his voice husky with emotion and longing.

Her reply was given in a whisper, "And I love you."

He gathered her up in his arms and carried her over to the bed.

And love was as she knew it should be.

CHAPTER 26

SUNDAY, 13 OCTOBER 1805: BAY OF TRAFALGAR

Off the south-west coast of Spain, the *Agamemnon* ploughed on through the grey rollers, the spray bursting beneath her weathered figurehead.

Richard Machen stood near the foremast, the white sails stretching and billowing above his head. He listened to the wind whistle through the rigging, keen and fresh, and its salt-water smell mingled with the ship's odours of tar and rope to create an excitement within him.

Despite the gravity of the Prime Minister's fears, and his own heartfelt longing for Jane – so little time had they been given together – it was good to be back on board a fighting ship again.

Already, on the horizon, Machen could see the sails of eighteen ships of the line. He looked steadfastly towards them, praying that Nelson was safe and that Pitt's fears, and his own, would prove groundless.

Fourteen days earlier, a message had arrived at his hotel, summoning him to Downing Street immediately. There he was shown directly to Pitt's study. Lord Barham was also present.

The previous evening the Prime Minister had received the first preliminary report from the Depot of Military Knowledge. This brought three facts to Pitt's attention:

First: that Macnamara, in his assassination attempt, had

been making *away* from Number 10, where the Prime Minister and the Cabinet were in conference, and was headed *towards* Number 12 – and Lord Nelson.

Second: that under the expert probing of the lieutenant-colonel, Jane had remembered most of the conversation she had overheard between Macnamara and Noble. In particular that Macnamara's opening question had been about Nelson; and furthermore, that during the discussion Macnamara had suggested delaying the assassination plan by one hour . . . so that he could make an attempt on Nelson's life.

Third: that a link, admittedly tenuous, had been established between Macnamara and Nelson in that when the Irishman's brother was executed for treason some two and a half years ago, along with Colonel Despard, Lord Nelson had been called as a witness to Despard's character. In addition Nelson had received a letter from Despard pleading for him to intercede for clemency. There was little doubt that if Nelson had possessed the power to secure Despard a remission of sentence then John Macnamara would also have been reprieved. Taking these facts into consideration, the report suggested that Conor Macnamara was holding Lord Nelson responsible for the death of his brother.

It seemed unlikely, but there had to be the chance that Macnamara could have volunteered to join either the *Defiance* or the *Royal Sovereign*, both due to leave Portsmouth with the *Victory*, but unable to do so on time, not least because they were short-handed. And Lord Barham had conceded that, when he reached the fleet, it *would* be possible for Macnamara to transfer himself on board the *Victory*. With the fleet keeping watch on Cadiz harbour, at night-time most of the ships would be hove-to, with little distance between them. If the Irishman was a strong swimmer he could wait for a calm, dark night on which to cross to the *Victory*. Once he had reached it he could climb up the hawser, catch at the martingale at about the dolphin striker, swarm up to the bowsprit and then on to the fo'c'sle head. From there he would drop down on to the main deck and make his way to Nelson's cabin . . .

Pitt concluded: ". . . And now you understand my reason for recalling you to duty, Mr Machen. For I am unable to rid myself of this strange fear that even now Macnamara could be heading for the battle fleet and, although Lord Barham does not himself subscribe to it, he has had the grace to show me the possibilities."

Machen stood and awaited his new instructions.

"The *Agamemnon*, the last of the three ships instructed to sail after Lord Nelson, is now almost ready for departure. Lord Barham will send a telegraphic message to Portsmouth informing her captain, Sir Edward Berry, that you will be sailing with him under sealed orders. The first of these is for Captain Berry himself, instructing him to make all haste to reach the fleet, the second is to be handed to Captain Hardy, of the *Victory*; it will be your authorisation to be granted an audience with Lord Nelson. The third and last of the sealed orders is for the Admiral's eyes alone. It will contain my personal message, explaining the reason for my concern and requesting Lord Nelson to take whatever steps he deems necessary to protect his person."

Lord Barham said, "William, I think you will find your fears to be unfounded and that Mr Machen will find Lord Nelson hale and hearty—"

"Prime Minister, Lord Barham, if I might be allowed an opinion?"

"Please, Mr Machen," consented Pitt.

"Gentlemen," said Machen, "with respect to you both, if Macnamara is so intent on assassinating Lord Nelson that he is willing to sacrifice his own life, then he would not have sailed on board either the *Defiance* or the *Royal Sovereign* . . ."

"But these are the only two ships—" the Prime Minister began.

"No, sir!" Machen lowered his voice. "There is the *Victory* itself to consider. Macnamara could have volunteered aboard Lord Nelson's flagship."

The Prime Minister objected, "But damn it, the *Victory* left Portsmouth less than forty-eight hours after the Downing Street affair!"

"Sir, if Lord Nelson was indeed Macnamara's target, then within hours of that plan failing he could have been on his way to Portsmouth, and aboard the *Victory* before Lord Nelson had even left Merton!"

"Then as we sit here and talk, Nelson could already be dead!"

"Only if we follow this ridiculous line of reasoning . . ." Lord Barham allowed.

"True, Barham," William Pitt admitted. "But follow it we must. The consequences of Nelson's assassination, the demoralising effect on the fleet, is a thought too appalling to contemplate."

That Sunday evening Richard and Jane attended service at St Paul's Cathedral. As it was already dark the torches were lit along the towering stone walls, the glow of their flames shining over the sea of heads filling the long, western nave.

The text of the sermon, from Revelation 22, God's final victory over evil, was related to the present evil threatening Britain, and culminated in a request to God that He grant Lord Nelson and his fleet victory over the French.

Then came the last anthem of the service; the strains lifted into the dark void of the enormous dome that rose above the centre of the cathedral:

"I know . . . I know that my Redeemer liveth . . ."

With no time to arrange an official wedding before Richard left for Portsmouth the cathedral provided a perfect setting for their promises to each other.

Richard took Jane's hand in his. He bent his head down and whispered. "Before God, I, Richard Machen, take thee, Jane Ashford, to be my wife . . . until death do us part."

Jane's eyes looked back into Richard's as she returned the promise. "Before God, I, Jane Ashford, take thee, Richard Machen, to be my husband . . . until death do us part."

That night as they lay with their arms around each other in the refuge of their bed, the last words of their vows came back to Jane . . . until death do us part . . . and she was glad that they had ignored convention; in her heart and mind and soul she was married to Richard; her arms clasped tighter around him.

"What if Macnamara is not with the fleet?" she whispered.

"I must remain," he replied in a low voice.

"Then you will take part in the battle?"

Machen could find no words.

"How long before you must leave?" her words were whispered, and so full of both love and despair, that he almost could not bear to listen.

"The chaise will be here at seven," he replied.

"Oh, Richard!" she sobbed, clinging to him all the more, "unless you return to me, I cannot live . . . !"

That night their love was a union in which tenderness, desperation and passion all seemed to dominate at the same time. The need for each other became overwhelming . . . and yet, at first, they moved slowly, gently, in unison, their bodies pressed so tightly together that not a space existed between them . . . the desire became stronger . . . and stronger, until it possessed them both. A sudden, sublime ecstasy. And then, as dawn broke, they held on to each other as though they would never, never let go.

All that was fourteen days ago. Fourteen days since he boarded the *Agamemnon* and gave Pitt's sealed instructions to her captain, Sir Edward Berry, the man known in naval circles as "the stormy petrel of the sea". Berry had known seven general actions, including the Battle of the Nile, when he had been captain of Nelson's flagship.

Since then the *Agamemnon* had made excellent progress to reach the British fleet in only eleven days.

Four hours after sighting the first sails, the *Agamemnon* hove-to and signalled to the *Victory* that she had joined the fleet.

An hour later, the ship's boat taking her captain, Sir Edward Berry, to a meeting with Lord Nelson left *Agamemnon's* side. Richard Machen was also on board.

CHAPTER 27

Although he carried sealed orders from the Prime Minister, Machen had to wait while Nelson first conferred with Sir Edward Berry. But he could feel how the atmosphere of an impending battle dominated *Victory*.

Nelson sat at his working desk. The great stern-windows behind him extended the whole width of the *Victory*, affording Machen a panoramic view of other British ships sailing close to the flagship. Like a pack of wolves, he thought, gathered around their leader, waiting for the prey to appear.

The admiral immediately recognised Machen as the officer in charge of his escort from London to Portsmouth, briefly welcomed him on board, and accepted Mr Pitt's letter. After reading in silence, he looked up and fixed his solitary eye on Machen.

"It would appear, Mr Machen," he said with a wry smile, "that our Prime Minister has no conception of life aboard a fighting ship preparing for battle."

"No, my lord. Nevertheless he is deeply concerned for your safety."

"And I much appreciate that concern. But having already failed in Downing Street, if this . . ." Nelson looked down at the letter ". . . if this Macnamara had intended a second attempt he would surely have made it in Portsmouth where there was ample opportunity. To suggest he might have volunteered on board the *Victory* is, frankly, quite preposterous."

Machen decided to stay discreetly silent.

"However," said Nelson, "in deference to the Prime Minister's wishes I am prepared to compromise."

"My Lord?"

"I will allow you to stay on board *Victory*, but *not* to search the ship or interfere with our routine as Mr Pitt requests. You are a gunnery officer, Mr Machen?"

"Yes, my lord."

"What action have you seen?"

"I was with Your Lordship at the Nile."

"Were you indeed? With which ship?"

"*Audacious.*"

"Indeed! Under Davidge Gould." Nelson unhesitatingly recalled Machen's captain. "*De Conquerant* surrendered to you, despite your fore and main mast being severely damaged.

"Well, now you are on board, Mr Machen, you will serve *Victory* as an additional gunnery officer. My plan dictates that at the commencement of battle my flagship must inevitably draw much of the enemy's fire, with the consequent possibility of heavy loss of life. If any of my gunnery officers falls, you will be required to fill the breach. But come," Nelson indicated towards a larger table which stood near the door, "let me explain my plan of action to you."

Taking Machen by the arm Nelson crossed the floor of the cabin in his stockinged feet, further proof of that common touch which had made him so beloved of all who sailed under him.

The admiral pointed to the plan laid out on the table-top. It showed, he explained, in small ship-by-ship outline, the anticipated positions of the two fleets just before battle. The strength of the ships of the line under Nelson's command had increased to thirty-three while the enemy fleet, it was anticipated, would be reduced to thirty-five.

Once the enemy fleet had cleared Cadiz harbour it would form into one long line of two or perhaps three ships abreast, all presenting their sides to the British. In other words, the conventional formation for sea-battle. Nelson, however, intended to form his fleet into three separate columns with at least half a mile between them, *Victory* at the head of one column, Vice-Admiral Collingwood in the *Royal Sovereign* leading the second, and Rear-Admiral Thomas Louis in the *Canopus* (sent to Gibraltar eleven days earlier, with four other ships, for revictualling, but expected back any day now) at the head of the third. The three British columns, the ships being strung out one behind the other, would then sail in line like arrows towards the Franco–Spanish fleet, piercing through their ranks in three separate places and bringing utter confusion to an enemy unprepared for such unorthodox tactics.

Machen was full of admiration. It was a bold plan, a radical departure from the traditional naval strategy of fighting sea-battles, but one which would necessarily incur considerable risk. He could see now why Lord Nelson had warned that the *Victory* would draw heavy fire. It was inevitable. As it was for the *Royal Sovereign* and the *Canopus*. During the approach they would be the three leading British ships, out alone at the advance of their divisions, subject to the most terrible enemy broadsides, with no opportunity to return fire until they reached the enemy lines.

Aware of these hazards, Nelson emphasised his contempt of French and Spanish gunnery, which would enable the British ships to reach the enemy fleet relatively unscathed. Then his tactics would reap their reward, spreading havoc amongst the enemy and ensuring that the British fleet would win the day.

"Nevertheless, you will now appreciate why I have need of your services, Mr Machen; for it is certain that on the run-in, the *Victory* will sustain a high loss of life."

"Yes, My Lord."

"In the meantime, I have no objection to you making your own searches between duties, as the Prime Minister wishes, but only provided they do not interfere with the good running of the ship."

"Yes, My Lord."

And with this concession Machen was instructed to report to Captain Hardy.

That evening Machen attended the purser's berth, on the orlop-deck, below the water-line, in order to examine the muster book.

If Macnamara had volunteered on board the *Victory* it was the obvious place to start the search, for although Macnamara would certainly not have given his real name, this ledger recorded the physical characteristics of every man on board – the colour of hair and eyes, height, chest measurements, and any distinguishing features like scars and tattoo marks.

The *Victory*'s muster book listed some 819 persons, including officers, seamen, servants and Marines. According to the purser, Walter Burke, the flagship had sailed with 31 men under the full complement allowed, but as 26 of those aboard were supernumeraries, borne for victuals only, she was officially around 50 below fighting strength.

Over half of the ship's company were Englishmen. They, together with Irishmen, Scotsmen and Welshmen, made up most of the crew, but there were also nearly 100 men of other nationalities on board, including Frenchmen, Spaniards, Scandinavians, Indians, Germans, Italians, Portuguese, Swiss, Dutch, Kanakas and over twenty Americans.

Machen concentrated on the descriptions of the 200-odd volunteers, an unusually high number for a ship of the line going into battle. Most of these would have chosen the *Victory* in order to boast they had sailed with Lord Nelson.

From their descriptions there were at least forty men on board who resembled Macnamara. The majority of the volunteers had no previous sea experience, and would probably now be part of that largest, humblest division of the ship's company, the waisters. These, stationed in the waist of the ship, were men who did all the ship's dirty work – the scavengers, swabbers, pumpers, pigsty keepers, sewer men; or they could be holders, living in the perpetual semi-darkness of the stinking hold, creeping about among the casks.

It was late evening by now, and Machen knew how difficult it would be to search the lower gun deck where most of the men slept, their hammocks slung from the beams overhead, with no space between them. This principal deck of the ship, 180 feet long by 50 feet wide, was shared by some 600 of the crew, squeezed between two long batteries of 32-pounder guns in their blood-red carriages – thirty in all – which formed the *Victory*'s main armament.

The heavy rope cables also stretched along this deck, in midships nearly as far aft as the main mast. Right forward in midships, across the bows, was the manger, which served as a sheep-pen, pigsty and cattle byre. This part of the ship was only some four feet above the waterline and consequently for most of the time the port-lids had to be shut tight – lashed and caulked – to prevent the sea pouring through. As a result the dimly lit lower gun deck always was a dark and noisome place, and impossible to search at night.

Machen decided to delay his search until the morrow, in between his new duties.

The following day a signal from the frigates watching Cadiz harbour reported that the enemy ships were at the harbour mouth. It could mean only one thing . . . that the enemy fleet would come out at the first favourable wind.

From *Victory* the order went out to the ships of the British fleet for exercises to be redoubled; perfect gunnery and timing could well mean the difference between victory and defeat.

The increased activity on board ship gave Machen no time to search.

There followed three days of waiting, of continual exercises.

Then at six o'clock on the morning of Saturday, 19 October, the frigate *Sirius*, signalled from Cadiz harbour: ENEMY HAVE TOPSAIL YARDS HOISTED. One hour later came a second signal: ENEMY SHIPS ARE COMING OUT OF PORT.

From *Sirius* the message passed to *Euryalus*, from *Euryalus* to *Phoebe*, from *Phoebe* to *Mars*, and at half-past nine on that Saturday morning, it was received on board *Victory*, then some fifty miles from Cadiz.

Without a moment's hesitation Nelson signalled to the British fleet: GENERAL CHASE, SOUTH-EAST.

It was not until between two and three o'clock in the afternoon that the whole of the enemy fleet cleared harbour. At last their fighting strength was known: thirty-three ships of the line; two ships must be remaining in Cadiz.

Forming five sailing columns, they steered westward, in a wind which had now shifted to west-north-west.

Daylight on Sunday, 20 October found the British fleet close to the Straits of Gibraltar. It was raining heavily and the weather was cold and overcast.

The towering cliffs of Cape Trafalgar could just be seen upon the eastern horizon, through heavy sea mist.

But there was no sign of the enemy fleet.

Nelson therefore made sail to the north-west, and presently hove-to for Admiral Collingwood to come on board for a meeting. Admiral Louis in *Canopus*, together with *Queen*, *Spencer*, *Tigre* and *Zealous*, had not yet returned from Gibraltar. Nor had the *Donegal*, which had been despatched to fetch them three days before, when the enemy fleet was first sighted at the harbour mouth.

This left the British fleet reduced to twenty-seven ships. Furthermore, Admiral Louis had been the man chosen to lead the third arrow formation.

Nelson's bold plan might well have to be discarded and more conventional tactics adopted.

The meeting lasted an hour, after which Collingwood returned to the *Royal Sovereign* and the British fleet resumed its course.

During the course of that Sunday morning the weather cleared, the wind shifted, but the day passed with no sight of the enemy.

At eight o'clock the British fleet turned away from the wind and stood to the south-west.

And at midnight, Lord Nelson sent for Machen.

His head bent to the fluttering glow of a small oil-lamp, Nelson sat writing at the desk. Behind him the panes of glass in the stern-windows shone black against the night sky.

"Mr Machen," he began, his face calm and composed, "at first light we shall at last face the enemy." He paused.

"At this very moment, no more than twelve miles away, our frigates lie within sight of the lamps in their stern-windows.

Tomorrow there will be such a battle that Villeneuve will regret he ever left Cadiz."

Machen was suddenly aware of the lines of weariness, and the pain etched into Nelson's face.

"Mr Machen," Nelson said, "I have been reading Mr Pitt's report. If one assumed the possibility that this Macnamara could be on board *Victory*, how important is it for him to be apprehended?"

Machen remembered the Prime Minister's concern about the growing unrest in Britain's industrial cities, and the disquieting thought that others of the standing of Sir Robert Noble might have involved themselves in revolution. His reply was uncompromising: "My Lord, Mr Pitt is so anxious for Macnamara to be interrogated that I am under specific instructions to find him wherever he may be. He is desperate, resolute, and most dangerous."

Nelson closed his one eye as though in prayer. Then opening it he looked steadily up at Machen.

"Then my mind is made up," he said in a quiet voice.

"My Lord?"

"A month ago, Mr Machen, while you were waiting to escort me from Merton, I went upstairs and knelt by the bedside of my little daughter, Horatia. She lay there, but four years of age, fast asleep, so innocent, so unknowing of the true world around her, that I was called to pray to God that her life might be a long and happy one . . ."

Nelson was silent for a moment as he recollected the scene. Machen had the discretion not to interrupt.

"Following a family tradition, my father was a rector at Burnham village in Norfolk," the admiral continued. "Although, like King David before me, I have strayed much over the years, my father's teaching has never left me. I am convinced that God has chosen to answer my prayers for Horatia in His own special way. I believe that tomorrow the Almighty has called me to win not one battle, but two."

"Two, My Lord?"

"Yes, Mr Machen. The first against Napoleon, the second against these subversive elements constantly seeking to wreck our society and its future."

"With respect, My Lord, how . . . ?"

Nelson stood to his feet and crossed to another chair. On it there lay a naval-blue coat. He picked it up and brought it over to Machen.

It was an old undress coat, its skirts lined with white shalloon, and on its left breast, embroidered in light silver silk, the stars of Lord Nelson's four Orders of Knighthood. They stood out boldly against the blue cloth.

"Mr Machen, I am countermanding your previous instructions. Tomorrow morning, in the hours before battle commences, I will stand on the quarter deck, wearing this coat. Being the only man on board who knows what this Macnamara looks like, you will stand near to me. If the man is on board, he will realise that he cannot reach me other than by using a musket. These stars will act as a target and draw the man out into the open. You must therefore be ever-vigilant, Mr Machen."

"But, My Lord," Machen protested, "surely these Orders will act as a target not only for Macnamara, but also for the sharpshooters in the French riggings?"

For the first time in their conversation Lord Nelson smiled. "Mr Machen, I would not be so foolish as to wear this coat into battle. If Macnamara has not made his attempt by the time the first broadside is fired, I think we can assume he is not on board. I will then change back into less conspicuous apparel. Nevertheless, Mr Machen, do not forget that in this I am entrusting my life into God's hands. Therefore, whatever happens tomorrow will be in accordance with His will."

With these words Lord Nelson escorted Machen to the door.

Machen turned away, leaving the Marine guard standing to attention outside the cabin.

In the murky light from the lanterns on the lower gun deck the men were mostly silent. Tonight there would be no boisterous singing or loud talking, as each man contemplated the impending battle.

Macnamara lay in his hammock thinking of how he would kill Nelson . . .

Already, when the admiral had been making tours of inspection, there had been two occasions on which he could have accomplished his goal, but the moment had not been right. To achieve his plan, timing was of the essence.

Now, at last, the perfect moment had almost arrived.

Tomorrow morning, on sighting the French fleet, the drummer of Marines would beat to quarters. The roll would be short, quick and determined, and directly it ceased each one of the hundreds of men on the gun deck would spring to his allotted task and clear the ship ready for action.

Much of this activity would be on the upper decks: helping the carpenter and his mates to remove the wooden bulkheads and carry them down into the hold; clearing Nelson's and Hardy's cabins of furniture; taking the hammocks from the nettings and lashing them to the lower rigging, to protect the men engaged on the open gangways; hanging strong rope netting under the masts, to catch any broken timbers or men shot down from the topmasts; filling buckets of water to be sent aloft should the sails be set on fire.

Among the countless other tasks to be performed, there was one, just one, that would give him the freedom to pass up through the decks and past the Marine guards posted at the hatches.

Unfortunately he had not been allotted to this task. However, the crew of the *Victory*, like any other British ship of the line, included many quota men – criminals, poachers, gypsies, and convicted felons – who had chosen to go to sea rather than to prison. Very few of the seamen were not susceptible to a bribe.

Conor Macnamara had chosen his man carefully, and tomorrow they would exchange duties.

Then, when the moment was right, England's hero would die.

With Nelson's death, a signal would have to be made to the *Royal Sovereign* for Vice-Admiral Collingwood to take command. Every ship would see the signal. Nelson is dead! The Admiral is dead!

Despair would spread like wildfire through the fleet, regardless of rank, ensuring Britain's defeat by the numerically superior Franco-Spanish ships.

Macnamara accepted that, if caught, he would pay with his life; it was a sacrifice he was prepared to make to advance the Illuminati's cause.

He had sworn this on oath before the Supreme Council.

And John would be avenged.

CHAPTER 28

Machen was on the quarter deck before dawn. As the *Victory*
ploughed through the sea he could feel the whole ship vibrate
beneath his feet, its timbers creaking and groaning.

He had not slept. All night the fleet had kept up a barrage of
signal guns, rockets and Bengal fires, both to confuse the
enemy and to emphasise the British presence threatening them
from beyond the horizon.

There was a light, westerly wind, sometimes almost
calm; but an ominous, slow swell on the waters indicated
that somewhere in the Atlantic a westerly gale was blowing
up.

Machen estimated the British fleet to be some twenty miles
off Cape Trafalgar. A small peninsula less than 100 feet high, it
had dangerous rocky ridges and a tidal race about half a mile
wide, making it not only a bad place to be caught in any storm,
but even worse after battle, Machen thought, for any ship with
its sails or masts gone, or the steering shot away.

Through the gloom he saw Lord Nelson emerge on to the
quarter deck. He was wearing his old undress uniform; the
silver stars of his Orders stood out boldly against the naval-
blue cloth.

"Good morning, Mr Machen."

"Good morning, My Lord."

"I fear there is a storm brewing."

"Yes, My Lord."

"But thankfully, not for some hours yet. It will at least hold

223

off until I have given the enemy such a drubbing as they never had before."

Nelson crossed to the side of the ship, and stood there motionless, gazing across the slow-moving sea towards the hazy horizon.

Within the next few minutes the other officers were also gathered on the *Victory*'s quarter deck, among them Captain Hardy; John Scott, Nelson's secretary; Alexander Scott, the ship's chaplain; William Beatty, the surgeon; and Thomas Whipple, Captain Hardy's clerk.

In the background Machen overheard their whispered conversation. The enemy, he heard them say, were believed to have Tyrolean riflemen dispersed amongst their ships and would certainly have sharpshooters in their tops. The stars on Lord Nelson's uniform would act as the most inviting of targets for them. He must be asked – diplomatically – to consider changing his coat.

Too late!

The haze lifted, and there was the enemy fleet, like a flock of giant white birds sailing on the water, half way between the British fleet and Cape Trafalgar, at a distance of only ten miles, and sailing in a two-column formation stretched along some four miles of the sea.

"Mr Pasco!" Nelson called for his Signal-Lieutenant.

"My Lord."

"With this wind it could be midday before we reach the enemy, nevertheless it is time to prepare."

The first signal Mr Pasco was instructed to make to the fleet was Number 72: FORM THE ORDER OF SAILING IN TWO COLUMNS.

Then despite the absence of Admiral Louis and his six ships, Machen thought, Nelson means to go ahead with his original battle plan.

The British fleet began to form itself, with Collingwood leading the southern division, a total of 15 ships of the line, and Nelson spearheading the northern column. This should have given him 12 ships, but during the night, the 64-gun *Africa* had lost touch with the fleet, with the result that she was now so far away to larboard of Nelson's column it meant he had only 11 ships: 26 ships against the enemy's 33 ships. And a controversial, untried battle plan.

The second signal was raised. Number 76: BEAR UP AND SAIL LARGE ON THE COURSE SIGNALLED. Then came Number 13: PREPARE FOR BATTLE!

Immediately the open decks became a bustle of highly efficient activity: the topmen slung their lower-yards with chain and prepared their muskets, swivel-guns, pistols and hand-grenades; strong rope netting was hung under the masts; Marines fell in on the poop deck and fo'c'sle, muskets and sidearms at the ready for when the enemy's topmen and musketeers came into sight. Wet sand was sprinkled over the decks both as a fire precaution and to prevent the men from slipping in the blood soon to be shed.

The gun crews also went about their well-rehearsed routine preparations, the gun captains hurrying to the gunner's storeroom to obtain the square leather cases, filled with powder tubes for insertion into the touch-holes, and also the flinted gun-locks to fire them; the men casting the standing guns loose from their lashings, striking their port-holes open, clearing away the side tackles, the preventer tackles, the breechings, taking out the tampions, casting off the leaden aprons, making ready the crows and handspikes and laying the sponges for use. All around them scampered the powder-boys, bringing up boxes full of cartridges ready for the first broadsides.

Machen was impressed by the speed at which the *Victory* prepared itself; the officers, and indeed the men, had done their work well. He also knew that similar preparations would be keeping apace below decks, while down in the cockpit of the *Victory* Dr Beatty and his assistants would be setting out the tables and instruments to tend the wounded, preparing tourniquets and plugs for those not requiring amputation.

Most of these tourniquets would be distributed about the gun decks by the men told off for cockpit duty, their harrowing task to succour the stricken, plugging their wounds, carrying the seriously wounded down to the cockpit, and heaving the dead and dying overboard, through the open gun ports.

Victory was now ready. Together with Captain Hardy and the four frigate captains – Blackwood, Dundas, Capel and

Prowse – who had come on board earlier that morning to receive the admiral's instructions, Nelson began Commander-in-Chief's Inspection.

Machen followed. If Macnamara was on board then this, surely, would provide the opportunity for him to make his move.

But the inspection passed off without incident. The party visited each gunnery deck, Nelson praised the men for the manner in which the hawse holes had been barricaded, and reminded the gun crews not to waste shot.

Machen, watchful as ever, concluded that Macnamara was not after all on board.

The day wore on.

At the speed at which the two fleets were drifting towards each other in the lifeless breeze, it would be another hour before battle commenced.

The sweating gun crews had stripped to the waist, and most had black silk handkerchiefs tied around their heads and over their ears to deaden the roar of the guns.

Veterans of battle sat silently polishing their cutlasses, occasionally lifting their heads to size up the nearing enemy fleet.

"I am to my cabin, Mr Machen," Nelson suddenly declared. "Will you attend me?"

And he made for the main hatchway which led down to the upper gun deck.

Macnamara had come up from the surgeon's cockpit to his station on the upper gun deck, near to the route that Nelson must take to reach his cabin.

In his hands he held a pile of tourniquets from the cockpit. Under the tourniquets was a long bladed knife.

From the veteran sailors aboard *Victory* Macnamara had learned of Nelson's habit of retiring to his cabin at least an hour before battle commenced, in order to pray.

An hour before battle was the perfect time in which to spread confusion about the fleet, by assassinating its linchpin, the admiral with the charmed life.

But time was running out . . .

At that moment he heard the sound of footsteps at the top of the hatchway.

Macnamara took hold of his knife. Through the open tread stairway he first saw the back of a pair of white-breeched calves and then the officer's body came into view. The man was too big to be Nelson!

Instinctively Macnamara stood back. Then, as the man turned, Macnamara saw his face.

Machen! Of all the men on earth!

Macnamara walked slowly away towards the port-side guns, his mind in turmoil. Desperately he tried to think: How the hell had *that* man got on board? *Why* was he here? He took a deep breath; no matter, *Nelson* was the target. Macnamara took hold of the knife and turned.

But Nelson had already descended the steps and reached the cabin, screened by Machen who had opened the door for the admiral to precede him.

Then it will have to be when Nelson makes his way back to the quarter deck, Macnamara thought. Another ten minutes or so will make little difference.

Nelson's quarters were scarcely recognisable. With the exception of his desk, all furniture had been removed into the hold.

Nelson's pocket book lay open upon the desk. The admiral bent down and began to write in the diary, finishing aloud as he wrote:

"For myself, I commit my life to Him who made me, and may His blessing light upon my endeavours for serving my country faithfully. To Him I resign myself and the just cause which is entrusted to me to defend."

Lord Nelson then closed his eyes, and whispered: "Amen! Amen! Amen!"

The door of the cabin opened. Machen spun around, but it was Mr Pasco, the Signal-Lieutenant.

"My Lord, the *Royal Sovereign* is nearing the enemy fleet. What are your further signal instructions?"

Nelson got to his feet. "Lead the way back on deck, Mr Machen," he said. "Mr Pasco and I will follow."

"Your coat, My Lord," said Machen. "Should you not change it?"

"There is no time, Mr Machen," Nelson replied.

Macnamara watched the three men cross the deck towards the main hatchway, Machen first, with Nelson and Pasco walking behind, side by side.

If only he had a pistol! But firearms were not issued to the stretcher parties, and until this moment he had thought the knife should have sufficed.

But there could still be a moment! When Machen ascended the steps first and Nelson was preparing to follow.

Macnamara prepared himself.

Then Machen stood aside to allow Nelson to climb through the hatchway before him.

When the three men returned up on to the quarter deck it was an imposing panorama that presented itself to them.

The sky was cloudless, the sea richly blue. The combined enemy fleet had shaken itself out into a vast arc, a concave bow at which the two British columns were thrusting themselves. The sides of some of the enemy ships, like those of the British fleet, were painted with double yellow streaks, others in red, and a small number of the vessels were all black. The huge man-of-war *Santissima Trinidad*, with all of 130 guns, had four distinct lines of red with white between them, her head splendidly ornamented with a colossal group of white-painted figures.

The enemy was port-side-on to the two approaching arrow formations, its broadsides directed towards the British fleet, waiting for its ships to get within gun range.

The rate of approach was now only about one and a half knots. And the ominous swell from the west had increased.

"My Lord?"

The signal-lieutenant was given his instructions, and signal Number 63 was hoisted as a warning of the approaching storm: ANCHOR AS SOON AS CONVENIENT.

"Mr Pasco!"

"My lord?"

"Signal to the fleet, 'ENGLAND CONFIDES THAT EVERY MAN WILL DO HIS DUTY', but you must be quick, for I have one more message to send."

"It will be quicker if Your Lordship will permit me to substitute 'expects' for 'confides', because the word 'expects' is in the vocabulary, and 'confides' must be spelt."

"That will do, Pasco." The gap between the fleets was narrowing. "Make it directly."

The signal was hoisted and acknowledged by the other ships.

"And now, Mr Pasco . . ."

Signal Number 16 was hoisted at the top-gallant mast-head: CLOSE ACTION.

The distance between the two British columns had so narrowed that they now appeared to be formed together in a wedge formation, aiming at almost the same point in the enemy fleet. But Collingwood's *Royal Sovereign*, her planks lined with copper below the water to increase her sailing speed, was in the forefront, and it was obvious to all that she would be first to come under fire.

Nelson struck his thigh as he watched.

"See how that noble fellow Collingwood carries his ship into action," he cried.

And as he spoke the guns roared as the French ship *Fougueux* opened up at the *Royal Sovereign*.

Every ship in the British fleet immediately hoisted a White Ensign and a Union Jack.

At last battle had begun.

Machen watched as *Royal Sovereign* now came under the direct fire from the 112-gun *Santa Ana* and four or five other ships, as well as the *Fougueux*.

With so little breeze it seemed an eternity before *Royal Sovereign* cut through the enemy lines and Collingwood at last was able to reply in kind. As his ship, her sails in tatters and much of her rigging gone, passed under the stern of the Spanish *Santa Ana*, the British gunners poured a full, double-shotted ripple broadside into her from close range, and such was their speed of reloading that they followed this with a further burst only a minute later.

Even from *Victory*'s quarter deck it was obvious that Collingwood had delivered *Santa Ana* a crippling blow. Dark smoke poured from the battle scene, and Pasco, watching through his looking glass, cried, "Top-gallant gone."

Nelson turned sharply. "Whose? Is it *Royal Sovereign*?"

Pasco kept the glass to his eyes. "No, My Lord, an enemy's."

"Collingwood is doing well," said Nelson and turned to view the approach of his own column.

Victory's own targets lay before her, a group of four ships, sailing together in a diamond formation, among them the *Bucentaure*, the flagship of Villeneuve himself.

Bucentaure, being the nearest of the four, was the first to fire a broadside at *Victory*.

It fell short.

A second shot fell alongside.

The third passed over her.

Victory was now in range of the French ships. There followed a hail of shots, the last of which went through *Victory*'s main top-gallant sail. On board *Victory* the men exchanged worried glances, as they knew full well the French gunners now had the *Victory*'s distance! In the light breeze *Victory* drifted slowly nearer, still not broadsides towards the French and therefore unable to return their fire.

A round shot flying across the quarter deck tore the man talking to Captain Hardy in two. Captain Adair of the Marines had the two parts immediately thrown overboard.

Nelson called out, "Is that poor Scott?"

Adair confirmed that it was, indeed, Nelson's secretary.

Mr Whipple, Hardy's clerk, was called up to replace Scott. Minutes later, he too was mortally wounded.

On the poop deck, one double-headed shot killed eight of

the assembled Marines. Nelson called Captain Adair over and ordered him to disperse his men around the ship, and along the open gangways between the quarter deck and the fo'c'sle.

And now *Victory*'s steering wheel was blown to pieces. Instructions were shouted for the tiller to be urgently manned. From this moment the flagship would be physically steered from the gun-room by ropes.

Captain Hardy came up to stand alongside Nelson. A shot hit the forebrace bitts on the quarter deck, and a splinter took away the buckle of Hardy's left shoe.

Nelson smiled grimly. "This is too warm work to last long, Hardy!"

"Yes, My Lord," Hardy replied. "If I might be permitted to draw Your Lordship's attention to the coat you are wearing. The decorations could well draw an enemy sharpshooter's attention."

"It is too late to be shifting a coat," Lord Nelson replied. He turned and called Machen over.

"Stay near to me, Mr Machen! Even though it appears that Macnamara is not aboard, nevertheless you will remain my watchdog. I have no time to concern myself with assassins; I must concentrate on teaching these French dogs such a lesson as they will never forget."

"Yes, My Lord," and Machen withdrew into the background, his eyes continually scanning the faces of the men crouching around him on the open decks.

From the time of that first shot *Victory* had been under attack for some forty minutes, unable to reply. Her mizzen topmast was shot away two-thirds up, her sails riddled with holes.

But at last she was almost on to the enemy ships.

"Port to helm!" Nelson now ordered Hardy to steer for the *Bucentaure*, the flagship of Admiral Villeneuve.

"I fear, Sir," Hardy warned, "that if we hold this course, we are bound to run on board one of the enemy ships."

"I cannot help it," Lord Nelson replied. "It does not signify which we run aboard of. Go on board which you please. Take your choice."

Victory passed under the enemy ship's stern, the signal to

231

open fire was given, and a 68-pound cannonade containing one round shot and a keg filled with 500 musket balls, was fired into the stern-cabin windows of the *Bucentaure*. A cloud of black dust and a shower of splinters fell on to *Victory*'s quarter deck; so close had she passed under the *Bucentaure* that the French ensign nearly hung over *Victory*'s side.

Victory now gave the *Bucentaure* the whole of her larboard broadside, each gun, as it bore, double and some treble-shotted. It was obvious to all on board the British flagship that the *Bucentaure* could take no further part in the action, while hundreds of her sailors must have been either killed or seriously injured.

The French 74-gun *Redoutable* now ranged up on *Victory*, and as Captain Hardy had predicted he was unable to avoid her. The two ships collided, *Victory*'s yardarm caught in the *Redoutable*'s rigging and the two ships stayed locked together, while *Victory*'s starboard guns continued to smash into the *Redoutable*'s side. The French captain retaliated with a deluge of musket balls and hand grenades, obviously intending to board *Victory*.

From the starboard side of the poop, the quarter deck, the gangways and the fo'c'sle, the British Marines returned the French gunfire, but the lurching of both ships in the heavy swell made it almost impossible to achieve accurate aim.

Victory's three gun decks were still in action, the cannons thundering, recoiling, flashing fire, starboard guns aimed at the *Redoutable*, with the larboard still firing at the *Bucentaure*. Below decks the blinding black smoke from the guns blew back through the open port-holes, billowing across the decks and up the hatches.

Throughout the deafening confusion the stretcher parties were busy on deck, carrying the wounded down to the cockpit for the surgeon's attention.

On the upper gun deck, Macnamara carried a wounded Marine across his shoulders. Pausing by a gun port he tore off the Marine's distinctive red jacket and ammunition pouches before pushing the man overboard. Then he picked up the man's musket and made his way to the fore-hatch, which led up to the fo'c'sle.

Donning the red jacket, he made for the port-side gangway, away from the French ship *Redoutable*, and took his place alongside the Marines directing their fire towards the more distant *Bucentaure*. As he alternately fired and reloaded the musket, Macnamara moved down the gangway, until he eventually reached the foot of the quarter deck. Stretching upwards above him was the main rigging.

Macnamara turned and climbed up into it, as if seeking a better vantage point, until he was above the quarter deck, close to where *Victory*'s steering wheel had once stood.

Machen found himself unable to stand by during the battle.

Picking up a musket and ammunition pouch lying beside a dead Marine, Machen joined the Marines who were firing up at the sharpshooters in the *Redoubtable*'s rigging.

Behind them Nelson and Hardy were pacing up and down the quarter deck. Not far from Nelson, Macnamara could see Machen's back as he fired up at the Frenchman's rigging. His turn would come. But first His *Lordship*!

Macnamara coiled his arm around the rigging to steady his aim against the ship's movement. He looked down the barrel at the small, slight figure pacing the quarter deck below. It was too late for Nelson's death to affect the outcome of the battle. But this would be for John!

Nelson turned. The silver emblems on the man's coat presented a wonderful target.

Macnamara fired.

Behind him Machen heard a cry of pain.

He turned, and saw Nelson on his knees on the floor of the quarter deck.

Machen made to run forward, but Sergeant-Major Secker and two near-by seamen got there before him, and Hardy turned and ran back to bend over the prostrate figure.

Machen looked up at the rigging of the *Redoutable*. By now there were only two sharpshooters left in the mizzen top. He took aim at them and fired. By his side, Midshipman Pollard

233

and Captain Adair and two of the Marines who had all witnessed Nelson fall were also firing back.

One of the French sharpshooters was hit. He slumped against the rigging. Machen reloaded and looked up to see Mr Pollard take aim at the remaining French marksman; the midshipman fired and the man fell out of the shrouds on to the *Redoutable*'s poop deck.

As Machen moved across to congratulate Mr Pollard a musket ball smashed into the deck just where he had been standing.

But it came from behind!

Machen spun around. Above him, in *Victory*'s port-side rigging, he saw Macnamara, and knew who had fired the fatal shot at Lord Nelson.

A sudden anger possessed him. He forgot about the need to capture Macnamara alive.

He raised his musket, took aim, and fired.

Macnamara flung up his arms, and fell in an arc from the rigging, out over *Victory's* side and into the waters below.

Machen rushed to the side of the ship. As Macnamara's body rose slowly to the surface, he saw it carried, face down, past *Victory*'s stern, to be lost in the gun smoke and the flotsam.

He turned to see Nelson's body being carried down below to the surgeon's cockpit. Someone had placed a large handkerchief over his face.

Machen stood rooted to the deck of the *Victory*, overwhelmed by guilt. He had failed on both counts, failed to protect Nelson and failed in his mission to bring Macnamara back alive for the Depot of Military Knowledge to interrogate. Because of his rash anger the Irishman was dead and the secret, underground revolutionary movement to which he belonged could continue to grow, perhaps to erupt again some time in the future.

Lord Nelson's sacrifice had been all in vain . . .

Machen suddenly thought: Macnamara's canvas bag! All sea-men were allowed to keep such a bag, holding their personal possessions, as part of a pile stored around the mess-table! If only he could find Macnamara's, it might contain something, anything, which might provide a clue for the officers in military intelligence.

His thoughts returned to the battle still raging on all sides, as far as the eye could see. Time to go below and search when the battle was won.

The battle continued for another four hours, but Machen remembered little of subsequent events.

At half-past five the battle was all over and the British fleet had triumphed.

A thick fog of lavender gunsmoke drifted slowly towards the Spanish mainland. The heavy scent of battle burdened the air.

Suddenly the French ship *Achille*, belching black smoke and flames from her hull, blew up in a series of reverberating explosions. And with this violent conclusion to the conflict a terrible silence descended over the heaving waters.

The promised storm was not far away.

Time only to patch and mend the broken ships, and pick up survivors; time only for Machen, searching desperately through the canvas bags piled about the mess-table area, opening one after another, hurling them aside, to suddenly rise triumphant with a bag which contained a page from *The Times*, dated Monday, 21 February 1803, describing the execution of Colonel Despard and his six co-conspirators, folded inside a small book bound in black leather. Machen was immediately transferred on board Admiral Collingwood's *Royal Sovereign*. Shortly after, the tempest struck.

Within hours the storm was at gale force and, with its steering wheel gone, *Victory*, with the body of Nelson aboard, was forced to make for the safety of Gibraltar.

The storm lasted four days. It was not until 26 October, when the wind showed some signs of abating, that Collingwood instructed Lieutenant Lapentoire, in command of the schooner *Pickle*, to carry his despatches back to the Admiralty. Machen sailed with him.

The official despatches would convey these cold statistics, calculated before the storm had taken its toll of the prizes:

Of the 33 enemy ships involved in the battle 1 had blown up,

17 had been captured, 4 had escaped and 11 had returned, battered, to Cadiz. Some 4,500 enemy sailors were dead, and 9,500 men taken prisoner.

In spite of the storm, not a single British ship had been lost. Some 450 men were dead – one-tenth of the enemy losses – and 1,200 wounded.

Right to the end, Nelson had continued his policy of annihilation. Because of it the British Navy was still undisputed master of the seas, and there was no longer any fear that Napoleon could ever invade England.

On the great day of the Battle of Trafalgar, Nelson had won one of his battles.

But the second?

Machen stood alone on the rain-lashed deck of the *Pickle* fervently praying that the coded book he had found in Macnamara's canvas bag would prove the instrument to Nelson's prayers.

TUESDAY, 5 NOVEMBER 1805: LONDON

The fog was the thickest that London had experienced for many a year. It descended in a pall on the city, reducing visibility to only a few feet. The muddy streets and alleys rang out with ghost-like echoes as pedestrians and coach drivers alike shouted their warning halloos like fog-horns on a silent sea. By midnight the streets were totally deserted.

Soon after midnight a post-chaise crawled in from the west. Over Westminster Bridge it crept, cocooned in mist, and into Parliament Street. Here Machen got out, took his leave of his travelling companion and disappeared into the fog. Lieutenant Lapentoire continued in the carriage along Parliament Street, up Whitehall and in through the gates of the Admiralty.

Lord Barham, the First Lord of the Admiralty, was woken up to be told of Lapentoire's arrival. Having read the despatches, he sat with his staff composing messages to His Majesty the King, the various government Ministers, and then worded a statement to be published in a Gazette Extraordinary later that day.

At ten minutes to five Lord Barham left the Admiralty,

crossed its now empty forecourt, and set off down Whitehall. He moved slowly, taking care to keep his balance on the wet, uneven pavement, with his coat collar wrapped high against the cold, a cocked hat firmly clamped down on his head.

Reaching Number 10, he was instantly recognised by the guard and conducted to the Prime Minister's study. A large fire already burned in the ornate fireplace.

He crossed the room. William Pitt and Richard Machen rose to greet him. Pitt clasped the old man around the shoulder. It was a gesture of compassion and friendship and Richard Machen stood back respectfully. There was a long silence before Barham was able to bring himself to ask the question:

"Well, Mr Machen? Was Nelson shot in battle, or . . ." he hesitated, ". . . was it Macnamara . . . ?"

Machen concluded his report.

The fire had almost gone out. The Prime Minister picked a large log up from the hearth, and threw it on to the red-glowing embers. He sat back and looked at Barham:

"My friend, what can one say at a time like this? Words are inadequate. And doubly so when emotions are so mixed." Pitt hesitated then added gruffly. "I ask myself, which should come first, the joy of victory, or the grief of Nelson's death?"

"Assuredly it must be the victory, Prime Minister," Lord Barham replied heavily. "Nelson would have wished it so."

Pitt relaxed back into his chair. "That much is true, My Lord. This signal victory has rid us of the threat of invasion for many years to come. Yet," and Pitt stopped, his hand before his eyes, "tomorrow, when the news is proclaimed, I am sure that my emotions at this moment will be repeated in the hearts of every English man and woman. Their sorrow, I know full well, will be greater than their joy in the victory."

Pitt stood up and crossed to the far wall. He drew open the heavy ceiling-to-floor curtains. The fog had lifted, and the light of early morning streamed in through the windows, bringing with it the muffled roar of a city already awoken to a new day, not yet aware of the mixed news it would bring.

William Pitt turned to the candelabrum and snuffed out the

candles. He sat down again. "And now," he said, stretching across and taking the black leather-bound book from Machen's grasp, "to dig out these revolutionary moles."

"Moles, Sir?"

"This is how I view them, Mr Machen. Despard, Noble and Macnamara: political vermin working underground like moles, hidden from our sight, yet we know them to be there, busy working to undermine the fabric of our society. Therefore, like moles, the only way to find them is to dig them out. Believe me, no stone will be left unturned."

Lord Barham spoke up from the depths of his chair. "It is a great pity, Mr Machen, that you were not able to take this Macnamara alive."

"Yes, My Lord."

Barham turned to Pitt. "Will you inform the Depot of Military Knowledge of the truth of Lord Nelson's death?"

The Prime Minister considered carefully before replying. "It would be of no benefit to them," he said finally. "The fewer people who know the truth, the better."

"Sir!"

"Yes, Mr Machen?"

"With respect, Sir, we do not know the truth."

"In what way do you mean, Mr Machen?"

"Until the *Victory* returns we cannot be absolutely certain that Macnamara succeeded. The fatal shot may well have come from one of the French marksmen on the *Redoutable*."

"And of this certainty, Mr Machen, we must remain mercifully ignorant—"

"I'm afraid not, Sir!"

"How so, Mr Machen?"

"Prime Minister, the British musket ball is unfortunately of a different shape from the French, being round, rather than slightly oval. Because of the storm the *Victory* was forced to make for Gibraltar. By now, Doctor Beatty may already have conducted the autopsy. If he discovers the musket ball to be British he will immediately realise—"

"That the fatal shot came from the *Victory*," concluded the Prime Minister and lapsed into silence as he considered the repercussions of such news.

It was Lord Barham who spoke:

"Such an autopsy report would create a public furore, with questions both in the House and in the newspapers . . ."

The Prime Minister turned:

"Mr Machen!"

Richard waited.

"I regret that before allowing your request to retire from the Service and return home to Gower I have one final duty for you to perform."

"Sir!"

"Yes, Mr Machen?"

"With your permission, I should first like to get married."

"When?"

"As soon as possible, Sir!"

"Tomorrow, Mr Machen! Then immediately after, report back to me."

THURSDAY, 5 DECEMBER 1805: PORTSMOUTH

Early in the morning there was warning of the approach of a large ship of the line under low jury masts.

The news was brought up to Machen's lodging-room. He rapidly completed his tenth – or was it his eleventh? – letter to Jane, packed his few possessions, including the diary he had completed but two days before, and hurriedly made his way down to the port.

He watched as the *Victory*, with Nelson's flag at half mast, sailed slowly in on mirror-flat water, to anchor at Spithead, the hushed crowd which had quickly gathered even speaking in whispers as they gazed at her.

Machen was one of the first on board. He conveyed to Captain Hardy the Admiralty's instructions to sail the *Victory* on to Sheerness; whence Lord Nelson's body would be taken straight on board the Chatham barge and conveyed to Greenwich. There it would lie in state in Wren's magnificent Painted Hall until Wednesday, 8 January. The state funeral would be on the following day.

Taking his leave of Hardy, Machen searched out Doctor Beatty.

He found him in the surgeon's cockpit on the orlop deck as usual, and learned that the post-mortem had not yet been performed.

Beatty explained that because of the storm after the battle Nelson's body had been preserved in rum in the largest cask on board ship. Later, in Gibraltar, the rum was substituted by spirits of wine, the best preservative the base had been able to provide. The *Victory* had then sailed for Portsmouth to await Admiralty instructions.

"When am I to proceed with the autopsy?" asked Beatty.

"As soon as we set sail," Machen replied, handing him the Prime Minister's sealed orders.

WEDNESDAY, 18 DECEMBER 1805: LONDON
Number 10, Downing Street.

The Prime Minister sat behind his desk and gazed at the report before him:

> H.M. Ship, *Victory*. 15th December
>
> About the middle of the action with the combined fleets, on the 21st of October last, the late illustrious Commander in Chief, Lord Nelson, was mortally wounded in the left breast by a musket ball supposed to be fired from the mizen-top of the *Redoutable* . . .

William Pitt looked up at Machen. "I would have preferred that Beatty had chosen a stronger word than *supposed*," he commented drily.

"To quote Dr Beatty, Sir, he refused to . . . perjure himself," Machen·explained somewhat apologetically. "He insisted that he be allowed to thus qualify the report."

"Then it must suffice, Mr Machen."

The Prime Minister continued his reading:

> . . . supposed to be fired from the mizen-top of the *Redoutable*, French ship of the line, which the Victory fell on board of early in the battle. His Lordship was in the act of turning on the quarter deck, with his face towards the enemy, when he received his wound; he instantly fell, and was carried towards the cockpit, where he lay about two hours . . .

Pitt read through to the end, carefully absorbing Beatty's description of how Nelson died, and then the medical summary detailing the course and final position of the musket ball discovered as a result of the autopsy.

Pitt raised his head. "I will have the report delivered to the Admiralty later today. In the meantime, where is the musket ball?"

"Dr Beatty promised to dispose of it," Machen replied.

"Oh did he?" was Pitt's response. "Let us hope he keeps his promise!"

A short while later Machen left Number 10 Downing Street for the last time, the Prime Minister's parting words ringing hollowly in his ears: "I only wish there were some way the country could acknowledge your services Mr Machen, some special honour or reward, but unfortunately, in view of the very peculiar circumstances . . . I know you will understand . . . ?"

As he walked away, Machen did not look back. He felt like a politician's puppet. It made it no easier that, in fact, he did understand. But to him justice would always be spelt *Justitia*.

GOWER

It was the last day of the year 1805. Outside the cottage swirling gusts of wind whipped particles of sand against the small glass windowpanes. To Machen, the mounting passion of the flurries heralded a day of gales which soon would rise from the white-crested waters that rolled, then crashed, against the rocks surrounding the building.

Inside the cottage all was snug, its strong walls a safe refuge from both the elements and the harsh world outside. He and Jane sat nestled together on the wooden settle. In front of them the fire roared in the wide, open hearth. Machen was reading aloud from his diary and as Jane listened she leant forward to pick up a log and threw it on to the crackling blaze. Sitting back she moved closer to her husband, her head moving down to rest lightly on his shoulders.

Richard reached the last page. With an air of finality he closed the book and turned to look down at Jane.

"Was that how it was?" he asked gently and his eyes caressed her pale, beautiful face.

"Exactly how it was," she replied and in her voice there was a faint huskiness.

"I have left nothing out?"

"Nothing."

Machen stood up and held out his arms, Jane rose swiftly and moved into them. He drew her close to him, holding her safe. Together the two stood before the fire, silent in a long embrace. Outside the wind had risen to storm force, the sea was in ferment, its angry breakers lashing the shore.

"You hear it?" he asked. "Nature has its storms. But after the storm comes the calm. Our calm, Jane, lies before us. It is for us to take it and make of it what we will."

EPILOGUE

Buonarroti, Réal and Desmarest – the Illuminati's Military Council – sat around the table in the former's garret apartment. It was bitterly cold, the temperature inside the room only slightly above that outside, with a hailstorm beating down on the roof as though threatening to break through the ceiling, driven by a freezing easterly wind which whistled into the room through gaps in the cracked panes and the ill-fitting window frames.

But for Buonarroti the bitterest chill came from Desmarest's words:

"It is over, Philippe. Fouché knows of the Illuminati's existence. He has been granted a special audience with Napoleon later today. Within hours a contingent of the Palace Guards will be making for Ermenonville. If the Council is captured alive and just one made to talk, then we three will find ourselves facing the guillotine."

"But how did Fouché . . . ?"

"A week ago a man was washed up, half drowned and almost frozen to death, on a beach near Calais." The familiar coldness had gone from Desmarest's voice, to be replaced by raw anxiety: "He was, it seems, a prominent member of the English House of Commons, and one of the leaders of our movement on that side of the Channel. As we already know, from the sudden purges taking place over there, the British Illuminati have somehow been discovered. Fearing arrest this man apparently panicked, fled to Dover and tried to reach France, only to have his yacht wrecked by a storm less than 100 yards from shore."

"How much did he reveal?"

"Too much," Réal interjected. "Although he died within an hour of being discovered, he was first interrogated by the officer commanding the garrison at Calais, a zealous man," Réal added with spite, "who thought the Englishman to be a military spy. A copy of his report, detailing the prisoner's feverish ramblings about the Illuminati and Ermenonville, eventually reached the Minister's desk, and although everyone before had dismissed it as but the wild imaginings of a dying man, Fouché did not. Six hours from now the search party will be on its way and all will be lost."

Buonarroti crossed to the window and looked out at the wintry scene, a low, leaden sky, and the clustered rooftops of Montmartre almost obscured by the driving hail. He shivered, pulled the collar of his greatcoat up about his ears, then turned to face Réal and Desmarest:

"If I start now, I will reach Ermenonville long before the Guards."

Réal and Desmarest stood to their feet, relief showing in their faces.

"Warn them to escape," Réal agreed.

"Leaving no evidence behind," Desmarest added.

"By the time the soldiers arrive," Buonarroti assured them, "there will be nothing left to find."

Nothing left to find!

Buonarroti rode away from the château. Behind him, across the floor of the Black Room, lay the seven members of the Supreme Council, killed by the bloodied sword now back in its scabbard at Buonarroti's side, in accordance with their own vows:

> They shall not fall into temptation to betray the cause, for lightning could not strike as rapidly as the blade which reached them lest they betrayed their oath!

Temptation ... or forced out of them by torture ...
whichever, the danger had been removed! As for the aims of
the Illuminati, they could be safely left in his hands, the
revolutionary with the vision, the man with the determination
to ensure that this world would one day achieve its true state:
one vast, people's republic that would encompass the globe!

Buonarroti set his face towards Geneva where lived other
men of like vision, free from the persecution of tyrants like
Bonaparte; free to gather together and form a Supreme Council, with himself as the spokesman, to translate that aim into a
reality.

HISTORICAL NOTE

The ruins of Richard Machen's cottage are still to be seen, half-buried in sand, at the edge of Port Eynon Head; and rumours of a tunnel which connected it to Culver Hall are so strong on Gower that it is mentioned in most of the books written about the area.

It was while I was researching into the life of the first John Lucas, the pirate who once sailed for King Henry VIII – I was intending to write an adventure novel of smugglers based on his exploits – that I was led to the house built by Richard and Jane Machen some miles along the coast from Culver Hall. Its present owners, a retired couple, were only too happy to let me search through the hundreds of old books filling their attic. Among them I found a diary. Although yellow and brittle with age, Richard Machen's writing was still decipherable.

The story it told led to my making detailed researches at various libraries, museums and records offices in both London and Paris. They in turn led me to the archives of the Depot of Military Knowledge (Britain's first permanent military intelligence organisation and the embryo of the current-day Secret Services).

Here I found an old file, tattered and almost unreadable after nearly two centuries of storage. Inside it was Conor Macnamara's coded book, and the various reports – including the final one – of the lieutenant-colonel placed in charge of the investigation by Pitt.

The title written in copperplate scroll on the cover of the file, so faded that it could barely be seen, was . . . "The Illuminati Conspiracy". But first:

Doctor Beatty, after conducting his autopsy on the body of Lord Nelson, did *not* dispose of the musket ball, but kept it as a souvenir.

It is now on display at Windsor Castle. To the ordinary eye it appears round, the shape of a leaden pellet fired from a British musket, rather than oval.

The original autopsy report written in Doctor Beatty's longhand is held by the Wellcome Institute of the History of Medicine in London. (A photostat copy is shown in Appendix I.) The word "*supposed*" to which Pitt objected is at the end of the third line.

William Pitt died on 23 January 1806, fourteen days after Nelson's state funeral.

Nelson's prayers that his daughter, Horatia, be granted a long and happy life, were answered. After her mother's death she went to live with Mrs Matcham, Nelson's favourite sister, and, in 1822, married the Reverend Philip Ward. As the wife of a clergyman and the mother of many sons, she lived her life out in the quiet of the Kent countryside, and died at the age of eighty-one.

Napoleon died on the island of St Helena, on 5 May 1821. The post-mortem examination was conducted by Dr Antommarchi, Napoleon's doctor at St Helena. He was assisted by Walter Henry, a British army surgeon, who in his medical report to the Governor of St Helena, wrote the following words.

There was scarcely any hair on the body, and that of the head was fine and silky. The pubis much resembled the mons

247

veneris in women. The muscles of the chest were small and the hips wide. The penis and testicles were very small and the whole genital system seemed to exhibit a physical cause for the absence of sexual desire and the chastity which had been stated to have characterised the deceased.

Joseph Fouché was, in fact, dismissed by Napoleon on 14 September 1802, just two months before Colonel Despard's revolution was due to take place. Having come to the conclusion that Fouché's position as Minister of Police gave him too much power, Napoleon knew that he had to pacify the man. He called him to the Tuileries, where he thanked him for his loyalty in glowing terms.

However, Fouché had guessed at the reason for his call to the Palace, and his reply was therefore already prepared.

"May I remind you, Monsieur," he said, "that in the secret police funds I have amassed the sum of 2,400,000 francs."

"Keep half of it?" Napoleon suggested.

Fouché accepted and vacated his apartments at the Hôtel de Juigne that same day. His outside business interests had grown to such an extent over recent years that they now brought him in ten times as much as when he was first appointed Minister of Police.

But his successor, Claude-Ambroise Regnier, was unable to cope with the demands of the Police Ministry. Napoleon was forced to dismiss him.

On 18 July 1804 it was announced in the *Moniteur*:

"Senator Fouché is appointed Minister of Police ... The Ministry of Police is re-established".

Fouché was subsequently made Duke of Otranto.

After Napoleon's downfall he again changed colours and served the incoming royalist government of Louis XVIII; he retired, a millionaire, and died a natural death in 1820.

In the archives of the Depot of Military Knowledge is the tattered file entitled 'The Illuminati Conspiracy'.

According to the file, the code used by Macnamara –

presumably given to him by the Illuminati – was one invented by a French nobleman, one Blaise de Vignere, in the sixteenth century. (An example is included in Appendix II.) It was Vignere's claim that without the code word it was indecipherable, but in the few hundred years since Vignere's death methods of breaking codes had improved. It took less than a week for the Depot to establish that the key to Macnamara's book was the Gaelic for "Ourselves Alone" – "Sinn Fein".

This immediately gave them innumerable names and addresses throughout Britain, and ideas on how and why men like Philippe-Michele Buonarroti and Sir Robert Noble, products of respectable family backgrounds, became involved in revolution. The Illuminati movement in Britain was quietly but systematically purged.

Meanwhile in France the discovery of the seven bodies at Ermenonville brought Fouchés enquiry to a halt. But the fear of revolution caused Napoleon to tighten his grip on that country and most of the leading members of the French Illuminati slowly lost their zeal.

Pierre-François Réal continued as Administrator of Police, became a Councillor of State, and in the year 1808 was rewarded by being made Comte de l'Empire. His apostasy from the cause was completed in the year 1812, when he declared, "The common people have never been properly put in their place."

Pierre-Marie Desmarest continued as Head of the Sûreté. He became a Chevalier de l'Empire in 1811 and remained at the ministry until Napoleon's abdication in 1814. He retired to Compiègne to spend the rest of his life quietly, and mainly engaged in studying botany.

But one Illuminati member, Philippe-Michele Buonarroti, never lost his revolutionary zeal.

From 1806 he lived openly in Geneva (the surrogate prisoner who had replaced him on the Isle of Oléron was himself released from his new prison at Sospello in the same year, on the authority of Joseph Fouché – Fouché's reasons for this are far from clear, and one can only assume that a sum of money must have changed hands). Buonarroti remained true to his convictions and his radical enthusiasm never waned. He claimed that the Illuminati's political ambitions would always continue, calling the movement The Massoneria Illuminata and describing it as a vast family which extended all over the world.

Buonarroti even established his own secret society, known as the Sublimes Maîtres Parfaits, for the purpose of teaching his revolutionary doctrines to others.

Among these much influenced by Buonarroti was one Auguste Blanqui, leader of a secret society known as the Blanquists. In 1881, the year of Blanqui's death, they joined forces with another society known as the Marxists, to found the Comité Révolutionnaire Central (the Central Revolutionary Committee).

Eight years later, in 1898, this body became known as the Revolutionary Socialist Party. And the revolutionary theories of Buonarroti, extended by Blanqui, were thus put into practice by one Vladimir Ilyich Ulyanov, also known as Lenin.

APPENDIX I: DR BEATTY'S LONGHAND REPORT ON THE DEATH OF LORD NELSON

MS 5141

H: M: Ship. Victory 15th December

"About the middle of the Action with the Combined Fleets on the 21st October last, the late illustrious Commander in Chief Lord Nelson, was mortally wounded in the left breast by a Musquet ball, supposed to be fired from the Mizen top of La Redoutable French ship of the line, which the Victory fell on board of early in the battle; his Lordship was in the Act of turning on the Quarter Deck with his face towards the enemy, when he received his wound, he instantly fell, and was carried to the Cockpit where he lived about two Hours. —

"On his being brought below, he complained of Acute pain about the sixth or seventh Dorsal Vertebra, of privation of sense and motion of the body and inferior extremities: his Respiration short and difficult, Pulse weak small and irregular, he frequently declared his back was shot through; that he felt every instant a gush of blood within his breast; and that he had sensations which indicated to him the approach of death: in the course of an hour his Pulse became indistinct and was gradually lost in the Arm, his extremities and forehead became soon afterwards cold: he retained his wonted energy of mind, and exercise of his faculties until the latest moment of his existence; and when Victory as signals as decisive was announced to him he expressed his pious acknowledgements thereof and heartfelt satisfaction at the Glorious event in the most emphatic language, he then delivered his last orders with his usual precision, and in a few Minutes after expired without a struggle

[Course and Site of the Ball ascertained since Death]

The Ball struck the forepart of his Lordships Epaulette, and entered the left shoulder immediately before the Processus Acromion Scapulæ which it slightly fractured, it then descended obliquely into the Thorax, fracturing the

251

APPENDIX II: THE CODE USED BY THE ILLUMINATI

Messages were coded in the following way:

a Original message to be sent: The I l l u m i n a t i

b Apply code word to message: S i n n F e i n S i n n F
Keep repeating code word throughout message.

c To Code: On the alphabetical chart opposite, look along top line for the message letter T, and along vertical line for code letter S. Where they intersect is the coded message letter, in this case Z. Similarly H and I give B, and so on.

d Coded message therefore reads: ZBJFUTOBKVNUX

e Alphabetical chart:

	A	B	C	D	E	F	G	H	I	J	K	L	M	N	O	P	Q	R	S	T	U	V	W	X	Y	Z
A	A	Z	Y	X	W	V	U	T	S	R	Q	P	O	N	M	L	K	J	I	H	G	F	E	D	C	B
B	B	A	Z	Y	X	W	V	U	T	S	R	Q	P	O	N	M	L	K	J	I	H	G	F	E	D	C
C	C	B	A	Z	Y	X	W	V	U	T	S	R	Q	P	O	N	M	L	K	J	I	H	G	F	E	D
D	D	C	B	A	Z	Y	X	W	V	U	T	S	R	Q	P	O	N	M	L	K	J	I	H	G	F	E
E	E	D	C	B	A	Z	Y	X	W	V	U	T	S	R	Q	P	O	N	M	L	K	J	I	H	G	F
F	F	E	D	C	B	A	Z	Y	X	W	V	U	T	S	R	Q	P	O	N	M	L	K	J	I	H	G
G	G	F	E	D	C	B	A	Z	Y	X	W	V	U	T	S	R	Q	P	O	N	M	L	K	J	I	H
H	H	G	F	E	D	C	B	A	Z	Y	X	W	V	U	T	S	R	Q	P	O	N	M	L	K	J	I
I	I	H	G	F	E	D	C	B	A	Z	Y	X	W	V	U	T	S	R	Q	P	O	N	M	L	K	J
J	J	I	H	G	F	E	D	C	B	A	Z	Y	X	W	V	U	T	S	R	Q	P	O	N	M	L	K
K	K	J	I	H	G	F	E	D	C	B	A	Z	Y	X	W	V	U	T	S	R	Q	P	O	N	M	L
L	L	K	J	I	H	G	F	E	D	C	B	A	Z	Y	X	W	V	U	T	S	R	Q	P	O	N	M
M	M	L	K	J	I	H	G	F	E	D	C	B	A	Z	Y	X	W	V	U	T	S	R	Q	P	O	N
N	N	M	L	K	J	I	H	G	F	E	D	C	B	A	Z	Y	X	W	V	U	T	S	R	Q	P	O
O	O	N	M	L	K	J	I	H	G	F	E	D	C	B	A	Z	Y	X	W	V	U	T	S	R	Q	P
P	P	O	N	M	L	K	J	I	H	G	F	E	D	C	B	A	Z	Y	X	W	V	U	T	S	R	Q
Q	Q	P	O	N	M	L	K	J	I	H	G	F	E	D	C	B	A	Z	Y	X	W	V	U	T	S	R
R	R	Q	P	O	N	M	L	K	J	I	H	G	F	E	D	C	B	A	Z	Y	X	W	V	U	T	S
S	S	R	Q	P	O	N	M	L	K	J	I	H	G	F	E	D	C	B	A	Z	Y	X	W	V	U	T
T	T	S	R	Q	P	O	N	M	L	K	J	I	H	G	F	E	D	C	B	A	Z	Y	X	W	V	U
U	U	T	S	R	Q	P	O	N	M	L	K	J	I	H	G	F	E	D	C	B	A	Z	Y	X	W	V
V	V	U	T	S	R	Q	P	O	N	M	L	K	J	I	H	G	F	E	D	C	B	A	Z	Y	X	W
W	W	V	U	T	S	R	Q	P	O	N	M	L	K	J	I	H	G	F	E	D	C	B	A	Z	Y	X
X	X	W	V	U	T	S	R	Q	P	O	N	M	L	K	J	I	H	G	F	E	D	C	B	A	Z	Y
Y	Y	X	W	V	U	T	S	R	Q	P	O	N	M	L	K	J	I	H	G	F	E	D	C	B	A	Z
Z	Z	Y	X	W	V	U	T	S	R	Q	P	O	N	M	L	K	J	I	H	G	F	E	D	C	B	A